# Summer
## IN THE INVISIBLE
# City

DIAL BOOKS
An imprint of Penguin Random House LLC
375 Hudson Street
New York, NY 10014

Copyright © 2016 by Juliana Romano

Library of Congress Cataloging-in-Publication Data

Names: Romano, Juliana, author.
Title: Summer in the invisible city / Juliana Romano.
Description: New York, NY : Dial Books, [2016] | Summary: "Sadie has always idealized her absentee dad and the popular girls in her school, but as she grows her photography skills and develops a crush on a guarded boy, she starts to see things as they really are"— Provided by publisher.
Identifiers: LCCN 2015034393 | ISBN 9780525429173 (hardback)
Subjects: | CYAC: Coming of age"—Fiction. | Love"—Fiction. | Fathers and daughters"—Fiction. | Photography"—Fiction. | BISAC: JUVENILE FICTION / Family / Marriage & Divorce. | JUVENILE FICTION / Art & Architecture. | JUVENILE FICTION / Social Issues / Friendship.
Classification: LCC PZ7.1.R668 Su 2016 | DDC [Fic]"—dc23 LC record available at http://lccn.loc.gov/2015034393

Printed in the United States of America
1 3 5 7 9 10 8 6 4 2

Design by Mina Chung • Text set in Kepler

*For my teachers*

# Summer
## IN THE INVISIBLE
# City

### juliana
#### romano

**DIAL BOOKS**

*Before*

# *Chapter 1*

Memories are like plants: if you care for them, they grow. I've relived this one night so many times that what was once just a sapling has now become a tree, its roots twisting deep into the dirt.

I was standing on the roof at a New Year's Eve party during winter break of tenth grade. It was below freezing, but we stayed outside anyway because up there we could be reckless and loud. And sometimes the cold feels good, the way it holds your heart in its claws.

Below me, the city spread out in all directions. Sparkling lights lined up in the neat rows of Manhattan, and the bridges to Queens and Brooklyn draped like beaded necklaces across the glassy East River. Looking at New York from above at night is like looking at a galaxy full of stars.

"This is the best."

I turned and Noah Bearman was standing next to me. A lock of dark hair fell helplessly across his face, grazing the top of his sharp cheekbone and covering one of his dark eyes. He was wearing a sweatshirt that looked nowhere near warm enough. His hands were shoved into his pockets and his shoulders were hiked up to his ears, like maybe his muscles were cramping from the cold.

"What is?" I asked, trying to act like it was normal that he would be talking to me.

"This," he said, looking at the view. His breath froze when he spoke, making icy, geometric shapes in the night air.

I pulled a cigarette out of my pack and lit it. I hate smoking, but I thought it made me look cool. If Willa were there, she would have made me put it out. I sucked hard, hoping I seemed experienced.

He watched as I took a drag and then asked, "Can I get one of those?"

"Sure," I said. I held the pack out to him.

He paused before taking a cigarette, and I willed myself not to stare at him. Still, I couldn't help notice the way the winter air had made his full lips even redder, and how it had turned his nose adorably pink.

"Which one do I want?" he murmured.

"What do you mean? They're all the same," I replied, confused.

He looked at me and his eyes twinkled. "Are they?"

Noah kept his eyes glued to mine as he reached into the pack and pulled out all the cigarettes. Then, he stuffed them all in his mouth so that they stuck out in every direction like crazy teeth. The whole time he kept looking at me.

I said, "Those are my cigarettes. They're expensive. Don't waste them."

Noah didn't answer me. He couldn't speak anyway, with

his mouth full of cigarettes. He held out his hand for my lighter and I gave it to him. He flicked it on and wiped the flame across the tips of the cigarettes, torching them all. They lit up at once.

I was aware that Noah was doing something so strange and twisted that it verged on being mean. But he was trying to tell me something. And anything Noah Bearman wanted to tell me, I wanted to know.

"What are you doing?" I asked, my voice tiny now.

He reached up and took the cigarettes out of his mouth, grabbing them with his full fist. Then he dropped them on the ground and stomped on them.

"I just did you a favor," he said. "Don't be mad."

"I am mad." I pouted. But I wasn't.

"I'm Noah," he said, as if I didn't know who he was.

"I'm Sadie," I told him.

"So the girl with the red jacket has a name."

Noah Bearman wondered about my name?

An icy wind howled, licking across the roof and whipping against us so hard that I had to turn my back on it and cower.

"You're shivering," he said, tapping my elbow with his own.

Even with the fabric of his sweatshirt and the thick wool of my coat between us, and even though it was just his elbow knocking against mine, Noah's touch made the cold night turn hot.

"Come on," he said. "Let's go inside."

So we did.

In some ways, it doesn't matter what happened next, or back at school, or in the year and a half since then. That night was perfect and I'll always have it. I'll hold on to the memory tight as I want, because it's mine.

June

# Chapter 2

Summer came suddenly this year. Last week, it was cold and rainy. But this morning, on the walk to school, the sky above the city was a bright, unblemished blue and the air felt bathwater warm on my skin. Around the edges of the asphalt basketball court, grass has been sprouting, winding its way through the chain-link fence that divides our school from the sidewalk.

I'm taking Photo 2 at my high school this summer, so I've spent every afternoon for the past two weeks in the photo lab: perfecting my technique, loading and unloading rolls of film, and soaking my prints in tubs of developer. These days, my hair smells like darkroom chemicals even after I shower.

"Sadie," my photo teacher, Benji, calls out. "I'm ready for you."

I hand Benji my photograph and watch as he inspects my latest print. He's made me reprint five times already, and from the expression on his face, I'm guessing he's about to make me do it again.

The old wall clock says it's only 10:30 a.m., which means Photo 2 is less than half over, but I'm already tired. I work harder in this class than I ever do during regular school.

"Hmmm. Okay," Benji says. He grabs his Sharpie and starts making dots next to areas I need to fix, and my heart sinks. Benji has X-ray vision for photographs. Compared to him, the rest of us are basically blind.

"Here . . . and here . . . and this. . . ."

Benji's punk-rock haircut, a long swatch of glossy hair, slips from side to side as he works. From far away, he looks like a teenager because he's so skinny and not even taller than me, but up close, you can see that he's older from the way his pale, thinning skin falls across his bones. Behind him, ribbons of long black negatives hang from a clothesline, gently twisting in the breeze of the ceiling fan.

Benji hands my picture back to me. "Try again. Lighten this area so you can find some more detail and texture in there. There's a shadow blocking this corner. Do you see what I mean?"

I strain my eyes to see what he's talking about.

The assignment was to take a picture of something no one had ever seen before, so I photographed the inside of one of my overstuffed drawers. It's a mess of things—an old set of photo booth pictures of me and Willa, some random markers and old gum wrappers, and an *ArtForum* with Allan on the cover. I like the drawer because everything is all mixed together—the things I saved on purpose and the things I saved by accident.

"Nice work, though," Benji says, after a minute. I look up at him and he smiles, revealing the crooked teeth of someone who never had braces. "It's interesting that you photographed such a small space. Very smart. Keep it up."

"Okay, thank you," I say, groping for the perfect words to show Benji how much I care about his class. "I'll try to fix that shadow. I think I get it now."

The photo classroom is divided in two rooms: the lab where Benji helps us with our pictures and where we meet as a group, and the darkroom where we print. The rumor is that when our school raises enough money, they'll get rid of the whole thing and put in a digital lab with a bunch of computers and printers. But I love this creaky, old-fashioned equipment. All my best memories from eleventh grade are of afternoons spent down here, watching my pictures emerge in the chemical baths like hallucinations.

I go back into the darkroom and linger by the door while my eyes adjust. For the kind of photo we are doing, all of our materials are light sensitive, which means that if the film or the paper gets exposed in the wrong way, the pictures will be ruined. The darkroom isn't pitch-black, though. There is a special amber-colored safelight that glows an eerie red and that doesn't damage photos or film. Everything looks flat and strange in here, just a mess of black shadows and crimson shapes. People look like cardboard cutouts instead of real humans, with heartbeats and insides and skin.

I go to my favorite enlarger in the corner. There are ten enlargers, one for each student, and they are basically big mechanical cameras that expand your picture from the size of film to the size of a photo. Next to the enlargers is a row of chemical baths that make the image stick to the paper. The chemicals reek of something sour, but now that I'm used to them, I kind of love the scent. They smell toxic and good at the same time, like gasoline or spray paint or nail polish remover.

I pull a piece of glossy photo paper out of my bag and set it carefully on the base of the enlarger. I crank the old, creaky lever to lower my negative down and watch the picture shrink on my page.

There are a lot of things about Benji's class that are more intense than in Photo 1. He's a stickler for technique, which means everything takes ten times as long as it normally would. But even harder is that Benji always comes up with open-ended assignments that you can solve a lot of ways. I always thought that kind of freedom would make things easier, but actually, it's the opposite. When there are no rules, you have to decide for yourself what's right and wrong.

"Psssst, Sadie Bell," Izzy whispers, snapping me out of my daze. Even in the murky safelight of the darkroom, I can see the bleached tips of her long curly hair.

"Why are we whispering?" I whisper back. Nobody whispers in here. The music and the vents are so loud you don't have to.

"It's more fun this way," Izzy replies. "So, listen, tomorrow is my half birthday and I'm gonna do something. Do you want to come?"

Izzy's words zap me to attention. I've always admired Izzy from afar, like the way her eclectic mix of gold bangles and friendship bracelets seem to glow against her dark skin. But she has never invited me to hang out with her and her friends before.

I'm so flattered it takes me a minute to realize she's waiting for me to reply.

"Yes. Definitely. I'd love to come to your half-birthday party," I gush.

"It's not really a party." Izzy rolls her eyes. "A bunch of us are just gonna go to the beach."

"That sounds really fun, I'll come, that sounds so great," I blather, practically drooling with excitement.

"Good. You've got to get some sun in," Izzy jokes, poking the bone-white skin of my forearm. "You're gonna be the palest person in the world from spending every stupid day in this dungeon."

I smile and nod, too stunned to be able to form normal, complete sentences.

"I gotta go finish printing before Benji bites my head off," she says. And then she turns and walks away, blending into the grainy red haze of the darkroom.

I turn back to my enlarger, but my mind is zinging too hard for me to think about photography. Izzy said a bunch of people were going to the beach. Does that mean Noah Bearman? They were friends before he graduated and he might be back for the summer, so it's possible. I know I shouldn't want to see Noah after everything that happened. I know the only thing I should try and do is not think about him. Willa tells me that all the time.

But Willa has never been left behind. She doesn't know it's impossible to make yourself forget about someone just because you want to. I know it sounds crazy, but sometimes it feels like the person who hurt you is also the only person who can heal you.

Another student pushes past me, and suddenly, I remember where I am and what I'm supposed to be doing. I adjust my paper and then flip the switch on my enlarger. The machine wheezes as the light grows bright for a fraction of a second before snapping back to black.

That night, Willa and I sprawl across her bed, doing this really stupid thing that we've been trying to perfect for years: painting each other's toenails simultaneously. Her bare feet are in my lap, and mine are in hers.

"Don't be mad if I mess up," Willa says. "This is a hard color."

I peer at my feet, which are stained purple.

"You're doing such a bad job! I'm doing a way, way better job than you." I laugh.

"That's because I'm staying so still, and you keep moving," Willa replies. "And because I have no manual dexterity."

"That's not true," I say. But we both know it's true. I sigh. "Willa. Seriously, is that the best you can do?"

Willa puts down the nail polish and makes a don't-be-mad-at-me puppy-dog face. "I'll pay for you to get a pedicure. Will that make you happy?"

"Typical," I tease. "Just throw money at the problem."

Willa's thick glasses are wedged onto her face, etching pink imprints on the sides of her nose. Willa could be pretty if she tried, but she insists on not trying. I think it's because she wants to be different from her older sister, Danielle, who is super social and gorgeous.

"How was lab? Did you cure Ebola yet?" I ask.

"Yes," Willa deadpans. She is taking AP Bio with all the other geniuses at a high school near her apartment so she doesn't have to take it during the school year.

My phone beeps and Willa grabs it before I do. She reads the screen and scowls at me.

"What's wrong?" I ask.

"Are you stalking your dad again?" she asks, hurling the phone at me.

I catch it and read the screen. It's a Google alert: *Kaplan and White announced today that Allan Bell will be doing a walk-through of his exhibit on July 14th. Tickets will go on sale the week prior.*

"Sadie," Willa whines. "I thought you'd stopped."

I put the phone down and concentrate on painting her teeny-tiny pinkie toenail. "I guess I forgot to turn off my Google alert," I lie. "It's not a big deal."

"Well, at least you've stopped stalking Noah," Willa says. "We're making progress."

It stings to hear Willa joke about him like that, but I push the feeling away.

"That reminds me," I say, wanting to change the subject, "I'm going to the beach tomorrow with Izzy Tobias for her half-birthday party."

"I'm sorry—did you say *half* birthday?" Willa scoffs.

"Yeah, because her birthday is so close to Christmas she

celebrates it now," I explain. "Anyway, I'm sure you can come if you want."

Willa doesn't say anything and I see a ripple of something roll across her face, but it's gone before I can decipher it. "I can't tomorrow."

"Why not?" I ask.

"I have to stay home and catch up on all the TV I missed." She play kicks me so that I almost drop the nail polish.

"Don't do that. I'm gonna mess up!" I squeal.

"I don't care about my toes." She laughs. Then she rolls away from me and stretches like a cat.

Willa's room could use a makeover. She still has the floral lavender wallpaper she picked out in third grade and a framed Dr. Seuss illustration on the wall. My mom and I have moved apartments every few years so my rooms have never had the chance to be really *mine*. I don't envy Willa's room, with its fading little girl decor, but sometimes I can't help wondering what it would feel like to have a room that was so completely your own.

"We hear the photography class you're taking is very competitive," Annette, Willa's mom, says over dinner. It's just me and Willa and her parents because her sister is in Spain for two weeks with her roommate from Yale.

"I mean, yeah, I think a lot of people wanted to take it," I say. "But that's just because everyone thinks it's an easy A."

"Don't downplay it," Willa says, kicking my shin under the table. "Sadie is the best artist in school."

"It's not really like that," I say. "There's no 'best artist.'"

"The fact that you're saying that proves that you're the best," Willa retorts.

"Is there more rice?" Willa's dad asks, his watery blue eyes scanning the table.

"No, Gene, you've had enough carbs," Annette snaps.

Gene is small and weak looking, and there's something about his shy, nervous demeanor that makes it seem like he's always dissolving.

"Gene's lost ten pounds. He looks great, right?" Annette asks me.

"Yeah, great," I reply automatically.

"He looks exactly the same," Willa groans. "His whole diet is totally fake."

For some reason, it's when Willa is mean to her dad that I feel the most jealous of their relationship.

Even though I've technically gone further than her, she is way less scared of boys than I am. She's really good friends with her downstairs neighbor, Miles, and she lets him see her in her pajamas and they eat gross food together, just like she and I would. Sure, Miles is a big nerd, but still, he's a *guy*. I was never friends with Noah. Not before everything happened. And not after, either.


I get home to an empty apartment. It's after eight, but the sun is still out, and the last strands of light that lie across our floor are threads of gold. I love this time of year. The way that sunlight stretches into the night, as if the day is yawning.

I get a glass of water from the kitchen and see that my mom left me a note on her *"Be Here Now"* stationery telling me she's teaching till late and not to wait up. Which I knew already because she told me that a million times earlier and texted it to me. My mom forgets everything.

In my room, the sounds of the city—sirens, people shouting, music spiking from cars—leak in through my cracked window. I open my laptop and flip through some Tumblrs and music videos and watch five minutes of a movie on Netflix. It's the same restless cycle I always fall into when I'm home alone, and it's boring. I wonder what Izzy is doing now. And Noah. I even wonder what some of the other random people from my photo class are doing. Are they finishing dinner with their families, or walking their dogs, or hanging out at a party that I don't know about? Or are they by themselves, at their computers, like me?

I close my computer, and in the moment that follows my room is flooded with its own emptiness. But then I see my camera, resting on top of my dresser. It's staring at me from across the room, its glossy lens like the eye of an animal, and I know I'm not alone.

# Chapter 3

I've basically memorized Allan's Wikipedia page. *"Allan Bell, (born 1960, Pittsburgh, PA), lives and works in Los Angeles. Bell is an interdisciplinary artist whose work has been identified with movements in performance, film, institutional critique, and photography. B.A., Harvard University."*

Allan's first big break was in the Whitney Biennial when he was twenty-five. He had already shown his work in galleries, but that show put him on the international art world map. For his project, he took over a room and built an installation that was composed entirely of labels from cans of food. The space appeared, at first glance, to be an average suburban living room.

After that, he stopped making big colorful installations and got into photography. From photography, he moved to film, and by the nineties he was mainly making videos and doing performances in which he would circulate around a gallery, pretending to be a visitor.

Ten years later, Allan was in the Whitney Biennial again. This time, he showed a film called *Love*. It was 135 minutes of scripted dialogue between two actors walking through a dreary office park in Denver.

The night of that Whitney opening, my mom's roommate, Karen, was supposed to go with her boyfriend. When Karen's boyfriend canceled at the last minute, Karen dragged my mom. She and Allan met that night. I was born a year later.

Now, I sit at my computer and reread the last e-mail he sent. Ever since he gave me my camera two years ago, we've started e-mailing. I'll send him articles I find that mention him, and he put me on his mailing list so I always receive notices about his lectures and upcoming shows. I love picturing Allan typing my name into the address bar of his e-mail. I wonder if he stares at my name and wonders about me, the way that I stare at his name and wonder about him.

The announcement says his show opens in two weeks, but he still hasn't reached out to see if I'm coming or if we can meet up while he's here. He must be really busy getting ready. So, I remind myself to be brave and do what I have to do.

From: Sadie Bell
To: Allan Bell
Subject: Visit to NY?
Dear Allan,

How are you? I see that you are having a show in the city that opens soon. I am here all summer so maybe we can see each other when you're here?

Yours, Sadie

*Chapter 4*

The next morning, I wait for Izzy to pick me up on the stoop outside of our apartment. The red bricks of the old brownstone next door are crumbling, as if the spongy summer air is somehow softening them. An old woman crosses the street diagonally, shading herself with a small parasol. The city smells and even sounds different in the summer, with fragrances that have been frozen all winter coming loose. A taxi rolls down the street with its windows open and music bounces out of the stereo inside.

When Izzy pulls up, I see that Phaedra Bishop is sitting in the passenger seat, sunglasses holding her blond hair off her face.

"Hey, you guys know each other, right?" Izzy asks as I climb into the back.

People always assume that just because you go to school with someone, you know them. The reality is that Phaedra and I have never spoken to each other.

"Hi," I say nervously.

Phaedra glances over her shoulder at me and gives me a quick, polite smile. Then she turns back to the road.

"Where did you learn to drive?" I say.

"My dad taught me in the country last summer," Izzy says. "He's such a bad teacher, I literally can't believe I learned at all. He was such a dork about it, too; he even made me watch a drivers' ed video."

"Do you drive?" I ask Phaedra.

She turns and looks at me and her eyes are blank, like I'm a stranger on the subway. Phaedra is so pretty that just looking at her feels like staring, even though I've gone through her Facebook pictures a million times. After a minute, she gives me another small smile and says, "No. Do you?"

"Nope," I say, feeling my face burn.

Phaedra Bishop is basically famous. Her family owns everything. The Bishop *B* is stamped on the packaging of half of the foods you see at the supermarket. Phaedra dropped out of a fancy New England boarding school in the middle of ninth grade to come to our public arts magnet in the city, which already made her more intriguing than everybody else. And then, a few months later, the *New York Times* published a story about her family in the Style Section. Next to the article, there was a picture of Phaedra in front of their brownstone. I remember staring at that picture, overwhelmed by all the millions of things I could be jealous of in that one small image. Not just what she looked like, but her flawless style, and her perfect family, and the way all of it came so easy because she was born into it. And I don't think I was the only person who felt that way. I bet everyone who saw that picture, even old people and little kids, felt jealous of her right that second, too.

I've never been to the Rockaways and as we get farther from Manhattan, the buildings get smaller and the spaces between them larger, until the city has transformed into an unrecognizable landscape. The sky seems to drop as we drive, as if the buildings in Manhattan actually keep it propped up high, like a tent.

"Who else is coming today?" I ask. All I really want to know is if Noah is coming, but I'm afraid to ask. If I told them what happened between me and him, I'm not sure what they'd think. It could make me seem older and experienced, and that would be good. But on the other hand, they might see through my story to the truth.

"Random people," Izzy says. "Justin Chang and some of his friends, I think."

"Who is Justin?" I ask.

"He's our friend from Xavier," Izzy says. "Who Phaedra is hooking up with."

"We're just friends," Phaedra insists.

"Shut up. You are *not*," Izzy teases.

"We are, too! Just like you and Roberto." Phaedra laughs. She says Roberto with a rolling *r* so it sounds super Italian.

I'm about to ask Izzy who Roberto is but then she jumps up in her seat, turns up the volume on the radio, and screams, "Yes!"

It's a Taylor Swift song that was really popular when we were in seventh grade. Everyone, even people who don't care about pop music, know all the words. If Willa were here, she'd cover her ears and moan about how it brings back too many bad memories of awkward middle school dances.

There's no traffic this far out and Izzy's car speeds along. I catch my reflection in the rear window. My hair is going wild, and I'm struck for a moment when I realize I look like I belong.

Izzy cranes her neck back toward me and says, "Did you know Phaedra met Taylor Swift? They hung out all night at some party."

"That's not true." Phaedra laughs. "We talked for a few minutes. She was really nice."

"Wow," I say. "What was that like?"

But Phaedra doesn't answer. She sinks into her seat and pulls her sunglasses down over her eyes. And just like that, she disappears back into the illusion of her, silent and beautiful and mysterious. Maybe she's just a mirage, just some imaginary thing that everyone wants to believe in.

Izzy looks for parking on a residential street near the beach. I can't see the ocean yet, but I can taste the briny salt in the air, and I can almost hear the water rushing on the shore.

We park in front of a sleepy-looking house with the lights off and an air conditioner sagging from the front window. We lug a cooler and a bag of towels and walk slowly, our bodies pressing against the wall of hot air. We're near the airport, and overhead planes circle the sky, flying so low that you can see the logos painted onto the bellies of their rusted metal shells.

The bright, crowded beach comes as a surprise after the quiet neighborhood. There are hundreds, maybe thousands, of people stretching out in every direction with their beach umbrellas and multicolored towels scattered around them like confetti.

"Our meeting spot is this way," Izzy says as we trudge through the sand past all the different camps of beach-goers.

"I see Justin," Phaedra announces. "They're over there."

I look where Phaedra is pointing and my heart sinks. There are eight or nine people sitting around a beach umbrella, but Noah isn't one of them. There's one girl I've seen around school, but other than that, none of them are NYSA students. I guess if you are popular enough at your own school, you get to be popular at all of them.

I hang back while Izzy and Phaedra greet the group. A handsome guy with dimples and shiny black hair reaches out for Phaedra, and she lets him hug her for a second before pulling away. That must be Justin.

"Is anyone else coming?" I ask Izzy as we crawl around on all fours, spreading out the beach blanket.

"I don't think so," she says. "It's hard to get here so people always say they are coming and then they don't show."

"Oh, okay," I say, trying not to sound disappointed as I smooth out the corner of fabric.

Izzy finishes and collapses onto her side. "I don't care who comes. I've accepted the fact that I'm destined to never have a really fun birthday celebration. That's what happens when you're born a week before Christmas."

I laugh. Suddenly I feel someone looking at me, and my eyes glance up. There's a boy on the other side of Izzy, in between the edge of her beach blanket and the others. Even though he's a few feet away, the afternoon sun is so bright I can see that his eyes are a see-through glass green. He has dark blond hair, and he's wearing a gray T-shirt that's soaked from ocean water.

"When is your birthday?" Izzy asks me.

"Hmm?" I say, my attention snapping back to her.

"Your birthday?" Izzy asks. "Or what, you don't have one? You totally wouldn't."

"What do you mean? Of course I have a birthday." I giggle, confused.

"No way," she says. "You're very, I don't know. I can't explain it. You're just the kind of person who wouldn't have a birthday. Go with it."

"Okay?" I say uncertainly.

"It's not a bad thing," Izzy says. Then she rolls away from me and crawls up to where Phaedra is sitting.

I check to see if the boy with the green eyes is still looking at me, but he's talking to someone else.

Unobserved, I take my camera out of my bag and walk down the beach by myself. I wander down the shore, catching snippets of conversations, arguments, and laughter. I stop far enough from the crowds that the only sound is water crashing. Then, I turn and face up the beach so I can take a big shot of all the umbrellas and the families. All these city people are clustered together, desperate for space.

I wish Noah could see me now, barefoot on the beach with the wind in my hair. I can practically feel him reaching up inside my denim skirt, the thick material keeping his hand close to my skin. It's funny: I didn't know how much I wanted him to be here today, how much I was counting on it, until I realized he wasn't coming.

When I get back to the group Izzy is looking up at me, using her hand as a visor.

"Hey, before you sit down, can you do something for me?" she asks, making a cute little puppy-dog face. "It's a gigantic enormous favor but if you do it, I'll love you forever."

"Okay," I say, intrigued.

"Can you take the cooler and go get us more water from the car? There's a bunch more bottles in the trunk," she begs, folding her hands together in a prayer position.

I look over my shoulder in the direction of the car. The hot sun burns down on the beach. It's at least a ten-minute walk to the car with no shade the whole way.

"You don't have to, never mind," Izzy says, waving her hand. "We'll be fine."

"I'll go with you," someone says.

Izzy and I both look up and the boy with the green eyes is standing a few feet away.

"Oh. Wait, what?" I say. "Really?"

"Yeah. You can't carry a cooler full of water alone," he shrugs. "I don't mind."

"Omigod, you guys are my saviors. I love you," Izzy sings. Then she closes her eyes and sinks back down onto her back. Without opening her eyes she says, "The keys are in my purse."

I pack my camera into my backpack, fish the keys out of Izzy's purse, and stand up.

Now that we are face-to-face I see that this guy is tall. He's wearing navy blue swim shorts and his calves are long and skinny.

"I'm Sam," he says.

Sam. I play the name over in my mind.

He runs his hand over his cropped blond hair and sand shakes out of it. I hate myself for thinking this because it's so cheesy, but it looks like gold dust in the sunlight.

"I'm Sadie," I say.

"Sa-die," he repeats. And the way he says it, so slowly, so gently, it seems to break apart, the syllables floating into the salty sea air.


Sam carries his sneakers in one hand, his finger hooked into the backs, and the empty cooler in his other as we walk toward the car.

Now that we are away from the group, our aloneness feels strange.

"So, you're a friend of Phaedra and Izzy?" I ask.

Sam shrugs. "Justin's a good friend of mine. And he and Phaedra hang out. So, yeah, I see them. You?"

"I go to school with them," I say. "Izzy and I are kind of new friends. I don't know Phaedra at all."

"Phaedra's okay." Sam shrugs. "She's just, you know, one of those city kids who thinks the world outside of New York City doesn't exist."

That surprises me, but I don't show it. Instead, I wrinkle my nose and say, "There's a world outside of New York?"

Sam looks at me, trying to tell if I'm joking. He doesn't

laugh, but I feel like I can see the smile pressed between his lips.

"Do you come here a lot?" I ask him after a minute.

Sam shakes his head. "Never been before. But I've only lived in the city for a year."

"Really? Where'd you live before?" I ask.

"New Hampshire," he says. "We moved here last summer. Moved in with my mom's boyfriend."

"Wow. New Hampshire. That must be so different," I say softly.

Something dark crisscrosses Sam's face. "It's different."

"I've never been there," I say. "I bet it's pretty."

"Pretty. Huh. Yeah, it's pretty," he mumbles.

"You say that like it's a bad thing," I say.

"Well, it's not, but . . ." Sam says. "It's hard living there."

"Hard how?" I ask.

Sam shrugs. "Everyone is unhappy."

And he says it in a way that I know not to ask any more questions.

When we get to the car, Sam puts the cooler down and I take out Izzy's key chain. I push one of the buttons on the car remote but nothing happens.

"Is this right?" I ask, trying again.

"Lemme see," Sam says.

He takes the key chain and flips it around. "This way."

He pushes a button and the car double beeps.

"Thank you," I say. "I don't know anything about cars."

"I don't either," he says. "I just know about remote controls."

I laugh. And for some reason, my laughter makes me blush, and my blushing makes me shy, so I try to stop laughing.

Sam pops the trunk open and I open the cooler and we start loading it up.

"I saw you taking pictures earlier," he says, handing me a bottle of water.

I expect him to follow up, but when he doesn't, I say, "Yeah, I'm taking a summer photo class."

"Pretty sweet-looking camera you have," he says.

"Oh, yeah, thank you," I stammer. "It's a Leica. It was a gift from my father. It used to belong to him."

"Catch," Sam says, tossing me a water bottle. I grab it and load it into the cooler.

"What are you into?" I ask.

"What do you mean?" he replies.

"You know. What do you like to do?" I ask.

Sam pauses, squints up at the sky, and then looks back at me.

"I like walking to cars to get bottled water with girls I just met," he replies.

"Be serious," I say, trying not to laugh.

"I am," he replies. He picks a bottle of water out of the trunk and throws it up in the air so it spins. He catches it with one hand. "I'm into water bottles."

"Impressive," I say. But I kind of wish he had answered for real.

We head back toward the beach with the heavy cooler. The wind has stopped and it makes the air feel a lot hotter. A plane coming in for landing at JFK tilts to the side and its wings reflect the sun for a second, flashing a white, blinding light.

"Do you mind if we stop for a minute? I'm starving," Sam says. We're right by an open parking lot where there are food trucks set up and picnic tables scattered around.

"Sure," I say. "Sounds good."

Sam gets food while I stake out a table. A minute later, he slips into the seat across from me and spreads out his burger and fries.

"Help yourself," he says.

I take a French fry.

"So are you doing anything this summer?" I ask. "Besides getting water bottles out of cars with girls?"

Sam smiles a little. "Not much. I went back to New Hampshire last weekend to see people. And I spent a week in Vermont with my dad."

"He lives there?" I ask.

Sam nods. "Yeah. He works on boats on a lake there in the summer. And then in the winter he works at a ski resort."

"So he likes outdoorsy things?" I ask.

Sam thinks and then says, drily, "He likes partying with rich people."

His honesty surprises me. I say, "That's . . . kind of harsh."

Sam takes a bite of his burger and shrugs. "He'd be the first to admit it. It's so weird, his whole business is basically selling nature to city people. It's this entire industry. Like being outside is this thing that people have to buy."

"That's a funny way of putting it," I say. "Maybe because you grew up somewhere rural, you just don't realize what a luxury it is to be outside on a boat or on a ski slope or whatever."

"A luxury," he repeats, frowning. "That's exactly what I mean. Nature isn't a luxury. That's so backward."

Sam finishes his burger, crumples up the paper, and tosses it in the trash can.

"Are you and your dad close?" I ask.

"Close?" Sam repeats, laughing a little. "Nah. But he's all right. He's fun to hang with. He's great at just hanging out and drinking."

"How can you be good at drinking?" I ask.

Sam looks at me for a second and his eyes latch onto mine. He smiles, but the sadness doesn't fade from his eyes. He says, "Easy."

And then I say something that I haven't said aloud to anyone, not even to Willa. I stare into Sam's eyes and say, "I'm gonna see my dad this summer, too."

*Chapter 5*

B y the time we head back to the sand, the sun has moved directly overhead and it seems to have grown hotter as it moved higher in the sky. After a few minutes, Sam stops walking, puts down the cooler, and wipes the back of his hand across his forehead. Sweat makes his hair stick up around his forehead like a little kid. Then, without warning, he pulls his T-shirt off over his head by the collar. I watch the bottom hem as it rises up, revealing his skinny stomach and the faint trail of hair disappearing into the top of his jeans. Without his shirt on, he's skinnier than I imagined.

He looks at me and I look away, embarrassed that he caught me staring.

"That feels much better," he says, draping his crumpled T-shirt around his neck. "You should try it."

"I don't know," I say, blushing.

Sam laughs a little. "Don't be shy. I mean, it's not like it's anything I haven't seen before."

"Oh really?" I tease. "You've seen a girl in a bathing suit before?"

Sam doesn't say anything, so I look up at him. Now it's his turn to blush. It looks like Sam's been outside a lot, because the tops of his shoulders and nose are sunburned and freckled, but he's still pale.

"Tell me more about your town," I say. There are a million things I want to know about him all of a sudden, and I'm just not sure what to ask.

"It's not a town. It's a city. There are forty thousand people."

"Forty thousand?" I repeat. "Is that a lot or a little?"

Sam rolls his eyes. "It's a city. You know. We have electricity and running water. We even have the Internet."

"Shut up." I laugh. "I just want to know . . . what's it like?"

"I can't explain it," Sam says. "It's just, home. You can't see where you're from. It's like looking at something too up close, you know? You can't see the big picture when you're in it."

"I don't agree with that," I object. "I can see New York perfectly."

"No way." Sam laughs and knocks his elbow lightly into mine. I glance up at him, watching his eyes sparkle with laughter. But then, slowly the humor fades, until he is back to how he was before, some hidden sadness lurking in his expression. And then he smiles a little and says, "Okay. Maybe you can."

Sam and I walk past people on bikes and Rollerblades, and old ladies walking under parasols for shade.

"So when are you going to see your dad?" Sam asks.

"He's coming to New York. He lives in California, but he's having an art show here," I tell him. "So, I'm gonna go see it. And see him."

"An artist. Like a painter?" he asks.

"He's more of a conceptual artist," I say.

"Conceptual? What does that mean?" he asks.

"So, he started out doing performance art and doing these weird interventions. Institutional critique. I don't really get it. But I think it's basically just a way of saying that you're questioning the system."

"That's sweet. Questioning the system is good," Sam says.

"Yeah," I agree. "It's pretty interesting how they go about doing it, like staging weird protests and stuff. He teaches at this really important art school. Which sucks 'cause I never get to see him."

"Seems like he taught you a lot about this stuff, though," Sam says.

And then I tell him another thing I never tell anyone. I say, "I barely know him. Everything I just told you, I know from the Internet."

The words are out and I can't believe it. They are so true and so private that I feel tears swelling up behind my eyes. I put down the cooler and wipe them away before they streak through my sunscreen.

Sam waits. He doesn't seem shocked by my confession or weirded out that I'm crying in front of him. He just reaches into the cooler, grabs a water, and hands it to me.

"I've never told anyone that," I say, after I take a sip of water. "Tell me something you've never told anyone. So that we're even."

"I already have," Sam says, not missing a beat.

"What part?" I ask, looking back up at him.

"All of it," he says.

I take a drink of the water bottle and steady my breath. When I'm certain I'm not going to cry again, I say, "Let's go. I'm ready."

But Sam doesn't move. He's only a foot away from me, and he's looking at me very seriously. His lips are parted, and I can see the uneven bottom edge of his teeth.

He's looking at me as if he's inside my mind, and I'm suddenly sure he's about to kiss me. I can imagine exactly how it would feel. It's so clear to me, it's as if it's already happened, like this is a play we've rehearsed a million times.

But then he says, "We should get back."

"Yeah," I say. I can't believe I thought he was about to kiss me. Maybe I'm going insane in the heat.

"If we take too long," Sam adds with a crooked smile, "your friend Izzy is going to give you a real institutional critique."

And that makes me laugh for real.


When we arrive at our setup, Phaedra and Izzy are both dripping wet from having been in the ocean. I lie on the blanket and let the sun melt away all my thoughts, the afternoon growing gooey and vague. Eventually, one of the girls who I don't know hands out cupcakes and we sing "Happy half birthday to Izzy" while Izzy buries her face in the sand and moans in fake embarrassment.

After cupcakes, Phaedra stands up, brushes sand off her body, and buttons up her sundress.

"Are you ready to go soon? I should get home," she says to Izzy.

I've noticed that Phaedra doesn't talk a lot, and when she does, she doesn't raise her voice. She must be used to people listening to everything she says.

"I'm ready," Izzy says, hoisting up the bag of towels. "Sadie? You good to go?"

I look around. Sam is playing Frisbee with Justin on the smooth, damp sand by the water. Light smashes on the breaking waves behind him. I want to say something to him but I'm not sure what.

"Come on, I'm dying," Izzy says. "This bag is so heavy and I'm so hot. Let's go."

So I leave without saying good-bye.

We stop for gas on the way back to Manhattan and I go inside to use the bathroom. There's a display of touristy key chains and postcards next to the cash register. I buy a postcard that shows a 1950s-style girl lying on a striped towel and that reads "Greetings from Rockaway Beach" across the top.

"You bought a postcard?" Izzy says, when I climb back into the backseat. "That's random."

"I collect them," I reply. And then, trying to sound as casual as possible, I say, "So, who's that guy Sam?"

"That guy?" Phaedra asks, from the front seat. "He's a friend of Justin's. He's from Maine."

"No, he's from Vermont," Izzy corrects.

"Same difference," Phaedra says, with a laugh. And then she adds, "He's from somewhere."

Then, Phaedra and Izzy start gossiping about Justin and

some other boys who were there today. But I don't listen. I stare out the window and watch the buildings thicken as we get closer to Manhattan.

*Sam-from-somewhere*, I think. But he isn't just from somewhere. He's from a real place and there are real people there, and schools and old friends and disappointing dads. I wonder if I will see Sam again. The city is so big it has a way of sucking people in and making them impossible to find, like a grain of sand hidden on the beach.

# Chapter 6

Here's what's supposed to happen: In fifth or sixth grade, you slow dance with a boy at someone's older brother's Bar Mitzvah or at a school dance. You never go out with him, but two years later, you kiss him at a game of spin the bottle and analyze it for months with your friends. Then, in eighth or ninth grade, you get a nice, clingy boyfriend. This boy should be sweet and maybe a little nerdy. With him, you get to practice making out. But after a couple months, you get bored and dump him. Then, junior year of high school you meet someone perfect. He's smart and nice and you become friends. And then, senior year, you realize you're in love with each other and you lose your virginities to each other. You're convinced you'll stay together forever.

Here's what happened to me: This guy Dwight was my first kiss on the last day of seventh grade. Our teacher told the two of us to go to the office and get more cups during a pizza party, and when we stepped into the hallway, Dwight kissed me. In the middle of the school in the middle of the day, with the hall monitor only a few feet away. It never happened again. I don't know if he kissed me because we were alone together, or if it was something he'd been planning for a while. Either way, it was more surprising than pleasurable. His tongue lurched into my mouth for a second and then it was over. Afterward, when we looked at each other, I felt embarrassed, as if I'd done something wrong—even though I knew I hadn't.

In ninth grade, I started at NYSA, the New York School of the Arts. Noah was a junior then. He had first period in the same room I had second period, so every morning we'd pass each other as I went in and he came out. We never spoke. But I liked how tall he was. I liked his dark hair. I liked the way he wore beat-up black boots and his eyes sparkled all the time like he'd just heard a joke, even when no one was talking.

Before the rooftop party, I thought Noah was cute, but I would never say I had a *crush* on him. But that New Year's Eve, as soon as he spoke to me, a crush blossomed in my heart. Or maybe that's not the way to put it. As soon as he paid attention to me, something crushed my insides. It felt more like a crushing than a blossoming.

I would have done anything to keep his attention.

Sitting in the backseat, listening to Izzy and Phaedra casually talk about hooking up with boys and who-dated-who, fear rises up around me, familiar and menacing. It's the fear I've lived with ever since that night with Noah a year and a half ago: I lost my virginity to someone I barely knew and then I basically never talked to him again. I messed up my order and now I might never get anything I want.

# Chapter 7

Back in my room, I pin up my new Rockaway Beach postcard, and then I sit back and admire my collection. I've been collecting postcards of New York City since I was eleven. I have over a hundred. A lot of the tourist stands sell the same ones, so I'm always excited when I find something new. I love the super-fake-looking postcards, where all the most famous buildings are inexplicably jammed together, or where the sunset has too many colors in it. My favorite is one I've had for years: it's a bird's-eye view of Manhattan so you can see all the buildings and Central Park, and even the edges of the island. But in the postcard, everything is organized and shiny, as if the world itself is a jewel that can be polished.

The sound of my mom closing the front door snaps me out of my daze. I get up to greet her.

"Hi, honey," she says, letting her purse slide down one of her ivory arms and drop onto the floor. "I'm so happy to see you. And to be home."

"Me too," I say. "Can we get Indian food? I'm so hungry."

"Perfect," she says. "Let's go. I'm starving, too."

She unpins her hair and it tumbles down over her shoulders. My mom is fifty-seven, but she's young looking enough to pass for someone in their forties. She was a professional ballet dancer when she was young, and now she's a Yoga teacher. Even though she hasn't danced for years, no amount of time can wring the dancer's body out of her.

We walk down the narrow plastic-smelling staircase of our small East Village apartment building. On our way out, we pass the newest tenant in the downstairs apartment, and he's exactly like the last one: a single graphic-designer type with graying hair and plastic glasses. This building is okay. My favorite building was the last one we lived in. It was in Morningside Heights, and it had wobbly floors and big windows that made light rush in like waterfalls, bleaching out all the colors of our furniture. Plus, there was a big family that lived downstairs and they had three dogs and a rabbit, and they let me come over and hold it whenever I wanted.

"Did you have fun at the beach?" my mom asks, when we sit down at our favorite restaurant.

"It was okay. Have you ever been to the Rockaways?" I ask her.

"Hmm . . . have I?" she muses. "Yes. I'm pretty sure."

"Did you like it?" I ask.

"Did I? I think so." She shrugs. And then she points to the eggplant. "Have you tried the bharta tonight? It's especially good. I don't know how they make it so good here."

"It's weird how much where you're from affects who you are," I say. "There was this guy at the beach from New Hampshire and it just made me think, wow, what would that be like, you know?"

My mom nods and reaches for the naan.

"Did you ever wish we lived in the country? So we could be outdoors more?" I ask.

"I feel like we're outdoors plenty," she replies. "You walk to school every day."

"I know but still. It's weird how nature is this commodity that people have to buy and sell," I say, thinking about what Sam said earlier.

My mom takes a bite of rice and smiles. "There is so much going on in that mind tonight, huh?"

After dinner, I go into the new FroyoWorld on our corner and get a huge vanilla and chocolate swirl. My mom waits outside because she's too disciplined to get one herself.

We walk back to our apartment up Avenue A, watching people flow in and out of the trendy bars in sloppy, drunken packs. A taxi pulls up in front of us and a gaggle of sorority-looking girls in high heels tumbles out.

"This neighborhood is always changing," my mom muses, after they've passed. "It's funny. When Allan lived in this neighborhood and we used to come down to see him, it was so much quieter. Now, it's so busy."

I'm so surprised to hear Allan's name I almost stop walking. My mom never talks about him. For the first time, I realize that she doesn't know he's coming to New York this summer. I have no idea how to tell her that I want to see him by myself.

"Let me have a bite of that," my mom says, eyeing my Froyo. "You're not even eating it and it's melting."

I hand her my spoon and she takes a huge bite and then another, avoiding the rainbow sprinkles because she thinks they taste like wax. I knew she was gonna end up eating half. That's why I got such a big one.

"Why you need to drown it in toppings I'll never understand," my mom says, more to herself than to me.

If I told her about Allan, she'd think I was being ridiculous and dramatic. I'm sure she'd say, "Of course you can see him on your own," but then when the time actually came, she'd forget about this conversation and assume she was invited. And then I'd have to disinvite her and that would be even more complicated.

Around us, people weave down the sidewalk, winding around trash bags and parking meters. Some people hold hands with their friends and some walk alone, listening to their headphones and tuning out the real world. Everyone is trapped in their own heads and their own routines and their own sets of friends, just like me. Here I am: trapped in between two parents who hardly know each other and forced to swing across the empty space between them alone.

## Chapter 8

My mom and I went to LA two summers ago so that she could do a Yoga workshop with an old dancer friend of hers. We stayed at her friend's mansion near Hollywood, and every day, my mother did Yoga and I lay by the pool, bored.

Then, on the second to last day, me and my mom made a plan to have lunch with Allan. It was going to be the first time I saw him in over five years.

We met him at an outdoor Mexican restaurant. Everything in LA seemed weird and half empty, like you were on the outskirts of a city instead of in the middle of one.

All through lunch, I couldn't stop staring at Allan. When I was little and I saw him, I thought he was big and tall and weird looking, but now I saw that he was handsome. His features were strong. He had wide-set, heavy-lidded gray eyes and full lips. It occurred to me for the first time that I actually looked more like him than my mom.

My whole life, I wished I looked like my mom with her high cheekbones and her delicate nose. I would watch people's gazes flick from her perfect face to mine, trying to do the math—how did *she* make *me*? Realizing that I looked like Allan was exhilarating. In a way, looking like him felt like belonging to him.

At lunch, when Allan caught me staring, he flinched as if my gaze stung. It seemed as though he could look at me, and he could speak to me, but he couldn't do both simultaneously.

The whole time, my mom kept doing this weird thing where she filled the air with all this useless chatter, which is really unusual because she's such a quiet person.

When Allan got up to go to the bathroom, my mom grabbed my hand.

"You okay?" she asked.

"I'm fine," I snapped. "You're the one who's being weird."

That night, I couldn't sleep. I lay in bed next to my mom in the unfamiliar guest room and watched patches of light glide across the ceiling when a car passed by on the street.

Finally, I got up and tiptoed downstairs through the dark house. I crept through the back doors and walked out to the tennis court. I lay down on the smooth, soft ground. California wasn't hot like New York. The night air was mild and damp. I looked up and watched as the clouds moved by too quickly, skating across the sky. Somewhere far away, a red searchlight drew circles in the dark.

I thought about Allan and wondered if he was thinking about me. Did he leave New York because he loved LA so much? Or did he just want to get away from me and my mom?

I wondered what his house was like. I couldn't understand why anyone would want to leave New York to live somewhere that felt so much like nowhere.

The next day, Allan stopped by where we were staying unannounced. I was still in pajamas and my mom had already gone to take her Yoga workshop so he and I were alone. It was the first time since I was nine years old that that had happened, when he lived in New York.

"I have something for you," he said when I answered the door. We were standing in the shadowy foyer of my mom's friend's house. "I figured I'd just leave it if you were out."

"What is it?" I asked.

"This," Allan said. He was holding a camera in a leather carrying case that fit it tight as a muzzle. "My old camera."

My heart felt as if it were literally expanding. "Really?"

"Yeah. Come outside. I'll show you how to use it," Allan said.

Allan and I sat side by side on the front porch. Looking up at him in the white LA sun, I could see him clearer than ever.

He took the camera and unscrewed the lens from its base. Without the lens, the camera was a simple rectangle with a hole in the middle. In the opening was all this tiny, delicate machinery.

"This is the shutter," Allan explained. He pushed a button and the shutter opened and clapped so quickly, I almost missed it, like the batting of an insect's wings.

"What you just saw, that's how pictures happen. That fraction of a second when this hole opened, that is when light gets in and exposes the film," he explained. "This is really basic, but basically the wider the opening, the less time you need to expose the film."

I wasn't following everything Allan was saying, but I didn't mind. At lunch the other day, his attention had been scattered and nervous, but now, he was patient and clear.

Everything about the camera felt ancient and magical. I looked through the viewfinder and practiced releasing the shutter. I loved the way that it sounded when I pressed the button, like a tiny heartbeat or a gasp of breath.

"You'll spend a fortune getting your film developed," Allan said. "But it's worth it. Good to participate in these dying art forms. Who knows, maybe your school even has a darkroom. It takes institutions a while to overhaul them and put in digital labs."

Everything Allan said came from a place of so much knowing, I suddenly became immensely curious about what else he knew. What kinds of things had he taught his students that he'd never had the chance to teach me?

I loved my new camera and even more, I loved that it came from Allan. Here I was, my peeling black pedicure exposed on my barefoot toes, and I was happy. Nothing about this world was familiar, the wide lawn and the rows of palm trees, their elegant trunks all bending gently to the left like the arms of dancers in the corps de ballet. It was all new and strange.

I looked up at Allan. His mouth was in a straight line but it felt like a smile. We hadn't spent the same amount of time together as most fathers and daughters, but suddenly that didn't matter so much. Now that I had his camera, we had a bond that was stronger than time.

# Chapter 9

Monday afternoon, I'm the last person in the photo lab. Benji is in his office doing work, but all the other students have left. I could leave if I wanted to, because we don't have any assignments to work on. But I stay because I'm dying to develop my film from the weekend and see the pictures I took.

Alone, I step into the light-safe closet where we go to unload our film. Even a tiny bit of light could damage the image, so it's completely sealed up. There is no darkness in the world like the flat, black darkness of this space. I fumble blindly until my fingers, now familiar with the procedure, pop the film canister open. I feel the negatives uncoil quickly, wings flapping in my palm. Gently, I work my way through the process. When the canister has swallowed up the whole roll, it's safe.

Then, I set out treating it in the chemical baths. While my film processes, I sit at the desk in the photo lab and thumb through one of the old stained *PhotoPro* magazines that's been in here forever.

When I finally look up from the magazine, it's four o'clock. If I left now, I could still catch some daylight. I could walk home the long way and get an iced coffee and get lost in the throngs of people stripping down to swimsuits on the grass at Tompkins Square Park. But I can't bear the idea of leaving without seeing my new photos.

I always liked photography. But ever since I started taking Benji's class, it's as if everywhere I look, I see photographs. There are two worlds now—the real world, and then this other world on top of it, or underneath it, which can be frozen and framed and lasts forever.

I see this other world all the time now. I see it when I'm waiting for a bacon, egg, and cheese at the greasy bodega on the way to school. I fall in love with the way the cook's crisp white apron contrasts against his dark, worn hands—leathery and ropy with old age. I saw it the other day when my mom asked me to go to the store to buy cinnamon. I was standing in front of the spices, and suddenly I felt as if the whole wall of jars was splitting open and jumping to life. Each jar had an identity and a history. There was a person who had designed the label, and a factory where the glass was molded, and each one had traveled around the world to end up in front of me. I knew it wasn't an unusual sight and that this was just like any other aisle in the fluorescent-lit grocery store. But for some reason it felt miraculous. And this morning, while I was zoning out eating cereal at the kitchen table I saw a sliver of white light tremble on our shiny hardwood floors. It slipped from side to side like it was alive, and I felt compelled to take a picture.

When I walk around with my camera, I feel certain that

what I'm doing is important. I'm solving a mystery, but I don't know what the mystery is. It's as if my pictures are contributing to some story that needs to be told and I'm just a vessel, that some other force bigger than me is using me to channel its message.

My phone lights up and I glance at the screen. At first, I think it's just another Google alert about Allan, but then I do a double take. It's an e-mail. I grab the phone and wait for the message to load, every fraction of a second an eternity. And then there it is: an e-mail from Allan, *RE: Visit to NY?*

It reads, "Yes, I am headed to NY in July. Install starts Monday the 12th. Drop by the gallery anytime that week. Looking forward, XX, Allan."

I touch the screen lightly to close the e-mail, zinging with excitement.

While I wait for my film to dry, I daydream about Allan's visit. Maybe I should invite him to come to the darkroom one day while he's in town. I imagine myself giving him a tour, showing him our different stations. I always feel so grown-up down here, adjusting all the timers and managing my film. I would love for Allan to see me like this. I can practically hear him telling me he's impressed. "Sadie," he'd say, "this is really something. You are really something."

When the negatives are dry, I make proof sheets in the darkroom and then finally sit down with a magnifying glass and inspect my work. There it is: the last week of my life, compressed and chopped up into a grid of one-inch stills.

Some are bad, like this series of my mom's breakfast from the other day that I thought was going to be brilliant. But things that I don't even remember taking came out well, like this photograph I took of the side of a bus with a stupid advertisement on it. I was trying to photograph the advertisement, but what I didn't realize is that I took a picture of one of the passengers on the bus: a white-haired woman staring out the window.

In real life, the world is a jumbled mess. But in here, it has an order. As neat as a string of beads. There's a message in these pictures, I'm sure of it. Like Morse code or fortune-telling tea leaves. I just wish I knew how to read it.

# Chapter 10

Willa got a 102 percent (a grade I didn't even know was possible) on her AP Bio test, and to celebrate she wants to go see the worst, most overproduced, biggest budgeted, 3-D action movie of the summer, *Stellar Warrior 2*.

We're meeting at Union Square, but I'm early so I watch strangers pour out of the throat of the subway station. People are always moving in the city, twisting up and down stairways, and gliding to the tops of high-rises in elevators. Sometimes, I think this place is nothing more than an ocean, with layers of interlocking life.

"Congratulations!" I squeal when I see Willa, throwing my arms around her neck. "You're so smart. How does it feel to be so smart?"

"Get off of me." She laughs.

We walk and get candy at Duane Reade so we won't have to buy the expensive kind at the movie theater.

On the way there, I tell Willa about Allan's e-mail. I didn't want to tell her that he was coming to New York until he had e-mailed me himself, otherwise I knew she would reprimand me for stalking.

"Wow," Willa says when I'm done telling her. "How do you feel about that?"

"How do I feel about what?" I ask.

"About seeing your dad," she says.

"I'm excited," I say, though isn't it obvious? "It's really good timing because I'm obsessed with my photo class and I can't wait to show him what I'm working on. It's gonna be so different than it was when I was younger because now we have stuff in common. Like, real stuff."

Willa nods carefully, and then says, "That's great."

"And you're finally gonna meet him!" I squeal. "You have to come to his opening. It's gonna be amazing."

Willa purses her lips.

"What?" I ask.

"Nothing," she says, blinking away whatever was on her mind.

"I wonder if he's gonna be like how you imagine," I say. "How do you picture him?"

"I don't really picture him being any way," Willa replies.

Willa is being sort of hard to read, so I say, "You want to meet him, right?"

"Of course," she says.

I must look skeptical, because she smiles brightly, loops her arm through mine, and says with a little more enthusiasm, "Come on! You know I'm excited to finally meet your dad! His show is gonna be so great."

I follow Willa through the revolving doors into the bright, fluorescent-lit Duane Reade.

"Izzy was really funny about it because she didn't know who Allan was when I told her, because no one knows artists by name. Unless, they're like, van Gogh or whatever," I say. "But then she said she Googled him the other day and she was like 'Sadie, I had no idea your dad is famous.'"

"Izzy Tobias," Willa says cryptically.

"What?" I ask.

"Are you guys, like, becoming friends?" she asks.

"I don't know, maybe," I say. "The beach was really fun last week, you should have come. Phaedra Bishop was there and she's so cool. She's so down to earth even though her family is who they are."

"Down to earth?" Willa scoffs. "Yeah, right."

"You don't even know her," I reply.

"Neither do you," Willa quips. "Besides, I just don't get why you idolize people so much. She's not any cooler than you. Even if her godmom is Beyoncé or whatever people say."

"I don't idolize *people*," I reply, putting air quotes around the word people. "But she's Phaedra. Everyone idolizes her."

"I don't." Willa shrugs.

"Yeah, but you're abnormal," I say. "You're . . . I don't know. You're *you*."

"Aw, you're making me blush," Willa teases, rolling her eyes.

We've arrived at the candy aisle, and Willa puts her hands on her hips and examines our options.

Watching Willa decide between Junior Mints and Hot Tamales, it occurs to me that we haven't done this nearly enough lately. We've both been so busy with our separate summer programs. It feels good to be reunited.

*Stellar Warrior 2* takes place in outer space, and with our 3-D glasses on, we zoom through black holes and swim through the galaxy. Broken pieces of spaceships float right out in front of our noses. The air-conditioning combined with the candy sugar-high combined with the way that Willa looks like such a cute nerd with her regular glasses and her 3-D glasses on at the same time makes it a perfect night. Halfway through the movie, I take a selfie of the two of us and post it online. And then the people behind us shush me and tell me to turn off my phone and that makes me and Willa crack up.

After the movie, we stumble out of the theater into the carpeted lobby that smells like greasy popcorn and cleaning supplies. I'm about to suggest that Willa and I play a round of pinball when I notice a group of boys walking toward us and I freeze.

I recognize him right away. He's unmistakable: tall and lanky with that lock of dark hair in his eyes, shadows forming in the hollows beneath his cheekbones.

His eyes lock onto mine as he gets closer, and a half smile breaks on his lips.

"I know you," he says.

"Hi, Noah," I say. And in that instant when I hear myself say his name out loud, it's like I'm right back at that rooftop party a year and a half ago.

"How are you?" he asks, his black eyes swallowing me up so that the rest of the world gets blotted out.

"I'm good," I say.

"Come on, Bearman," one of the other boys shouts. "Let's move it."

Noah nods at his friend. To me he says, "See you around?"

And then, just before he walks away he tosses me one last smile. There's a bottle in my heart full of all the things that I want even though I know I shouldn't. Noah's smile smashes that bottle and everything that I've tried so hard to keep contained spills out.

On the street outside the theater, I try to breathe. The sun has gone down and the sky is dark. All the natural daylight has been swapped for too bright, artificial nighttime lights.

Willa puts a hand on my shoulder. "Are you okay?"

"I can't believe that just happened," I murmur.

"He's the worst." Willa sighs. "Sadie. You are *so* way too good for that guy."

"I know," I reply. "Totally."

Willa frowns. Then she says, "He doesn't deserve you." As if she didn't hear what I just said.

Later, I lie on top of my covers and stare at the ceiling in the dark. Not seeing anything, just listening to my blood pump between my ears.

That night a year and a half ago, after I followed Noah in from the roof, we went to the living room where there were people drinking and loud music was playing. We sat side by side on the couch and swapped stories about stupid things, like what bands we'd seen live and where we went to elementary school. He told me he also had Mr. Lewis for math in ninth grade, and then I told him about how I accidentally found Mr. Lewis's YouTube account where he posts nightly videos of his cat. He didn't believe me. He said, show me. I said, my phone battery is low. He said, "C'mon, we'll find a computer."

Noah led me into some random bedroom and closed the door behind us. It looked like a guest room slash office. There were no decorations on the wall or clothes on the floor. There was just a big plain bed and a desk with a computer on it.

Noah walked over to the desk and sat down in the swivel-y chair. I stood behind him, looking over his shoulder.

Noah jiggled the mouse to wake up the computer. It wheezed and then the black screen lit up and a log-in page appeared.

"Damn," he said. "I guess no cat videos."

"Oh no," I said, biting my lip.

Noah sighed and stood up. But then, instead of leaving, he sat down on the edge of the bed. I stood there, unsure of what to do.

"Come here," he said softly.

I didn't move right away, so he reached out and took my hands and pulled me gently toward him. His hands were strong and soft, and I wondered if he noticed how much mine were sweating.

A lock of brown hair fell into his eyes, and he looked down at my shoes and then up at me. His eyes were underwater. He pulled me close to him. One of his knees was in between my legs. His hand slipped up under my shirt, under my bra.

We hadn't even kissed and he was touching my breast. If he had been even the tiniest bit less certain, I would have been grossed out. But his abandon was contagious. I could feel my own thoughts growing disorderly.

He stood and grabbed me and flipped me around so I was lying on my back on the bed. He hovered over me on his hands like he was at the top of a push-up. The overhead light on the ceiling was a blinding white bulb behind him. His face was in shadow. His lips were damp. His body was a tent that I was hiding underneath, and it was warm and dense and slow in the tent. He kissed me in a way that felt like so much more than a kiss. It felt like we were talking or dancing or seeing through each other's skin to our insides.

It all felt so right. The way he pulled my jeans off with the light still on. The feeling of his hands on my stomach, my thigh, my knee, my ankle. He was easy to do things with. I thought I'd have been afraid, but Noah was so unafraid that I just followed his lead. We got closer and closer together, kissing and rolling around, and I was pulling him toward me as if I'd known him my whole life. Then he lifted off of me, and I opened my eyes to see him put on a condom. That was the only moment I really saw any of the parts of him I'd been touching.

When we were having sex, I felt certain that Noah loved me. He held on to me like he needed me, like he'd been seeing me in the hallways every day and wondering about me. I felt as if he knew everything about me, even things about my mom and our little apartment. It was like he knew I barely had a father and he could see the hole that Allan left in my heart, and he cared about all of it. It felt like he wanted to make it all better. And it seemed like he could. At one point, I felt him grab on to my foot and it felt small in his hand, and he squeezed it so tight he cracked the knuckles in my toes.

## Chapter 11

When we show up for class the next day, Benji has scribbled a quote from the night's reading across the board. *"A photograph is a constructed object. What it shows the viewer is not necessarily the truth. It is, after all, nothing more than an arrangement of light and shadow."*

"What does this mean?" Benji asks, tapping his marker against the whiteboard.

Nobody raises their hand.

"It's from the reading," Benji presses. "Did anyone understand the essay? What does it mean that a photograph doesn't necessarily show the truth?"

I raise my hand and Benji waves his marker at me. "Yes?"

"I took it to mean that a picture is a real thing. Like it's a piece of paper and it actually exists, but the image on it could be made up or not totally real," I say.

The truth is, I thought about the essay all night. I read it twice and lay in bed wondering if all the things the writer said about the photos were true. It seemed to me like he was saying that photography shows us the world but also lifts off and away from the world at the same time.

"Great, Sadie," Benji says. "Nice explanation. Can anyone add to that?"

Izzy looks at me and rolls her eyes.

"What?" I whisper.

She mouths something back, but I can't understand her at all.

After we discuss the reading, we pin up our photographs from the street photography assignment. Today is our first real group critique. Everyone's pictures all together are so similar they practically blend. Other than me, everyone took pictures on the street. I took mine inside of a subway car on the ride back from Willa's last week.

At first, I had been afraid to pull out my camera on the subway. I didn't want some creepy old guy to start talking to me and asking me questions about the Leica. But, it was a quiet afternoon and I could tell no one in that car was going to bother me. So I took out the camera, and I even pulled out my light meter and my gray card, and took a whole roll of film between Eighty-Sixth Street and Astor Place.

The best picture from that roll, the one that I printed for today, ended up being this one I took of a little boy sleeping on his grandmother's lap, his cheek smeared sweetly against her thigh. I was surprised when I printed the photograph to see how good the lighting looked. I think of subway light as being really bad, but in my photograph, the light seemed liquid. It pooled in the empty seat next to them and slid down the slick surface of the metal pole.

Benji singles out my picture right away.

"What do you guys see here?" he asks the class, pointing to mine. "Sean?"

"A boy on a train," Sean grumbles. Sean fell asleep twice today already.

"I like the pole," this girl Alexis says. "I like how shiny it is."

"I like the kid's sneakers," Cody with the long hair adds. "They look brand-new."

Benji jumps in. "It seems like there's lots to look at in this picture. When there are so many things happening, how do you know what the picture is really about?"

"Maybe it's about a lot of things," Alexis adds.

"Maybe it's about *light and shadow*," Izzy says.

Benji lights up. "Yes!"

He looks at the photo, temporarily turning his back on us, and Izzy takes the opportunity to stick her tongue out at me. And then she laughs, which makes me laugh, too.

Benji hears us laughing and turns in our direction, locking eyes with me. "Is something funny, Sadie?"

My laughter stops abruptly, a car screeching to a halt. My face burns as I shake my head *no*, too shamed to speak.

"Good," he says.

When he turns away again, Izzy rolls her eyes at his back, like *Benji is so uptight*. I try to smile in agreement, but I'm worried that Benji thinks I was laughing at him when really, all I think is that he's wonderful.

When I get home, my mom is sleeping on the couch in the front room.

I tried so hard to find interesting people to photograph for this assignment, but now, seeing my mom resting there with wide stripes of afternoon light lying across her body like tropical leaves, and her gold bangles slumped drowsily down her wrist, she's the most amazing subject in the world. I pull out my camera and take her picture.

She must hear me rustling because she wakes up.

"Hey, honey," she says, rubbing her eyes with the backs of her hands. "Wow. I just touched bottom."

"Guess what?" I say, putting down my camera to untie my shoes. "Benji loved my photo this week."

"Who is Benji?" she asks, sitting up.

"Benji is my photo teacher. How could you forget that? I talk about him constantly."

"Oh, right. Gosh, how did I forget that? I'm just really out of it today." She sighs. "I need some tea. Maybe that will make me feel more grounded."

Whenever my mom is stressed she gets super spacey. For some reason, it annoys me more than if she just snapped at me.

"I'll make it," I grumble, heading to the kitchen.

If Allan were here, he would want to know everything about what Benji said. He's probably even read the essay that Benji assigned over the weekend.

I put a pot of water on the stove and lean against the refrigerator. The kitchen window is propped open with a stained cookbook and soft, humid air seeps in from outside.

Every day, the days are getting longer. Summer is opening up like a flower. Soon, Allan is going to be here and then everything is going to finally be the way it's supposed to.

## Chapter 12

Allan lived in the city for a year when I was in fourth grade. I had barely ever seen him before then and, at first, when he told my mom he wanted to see me, I said no because I was so scared.

That was back when I used to take Saturday morning ballet class from my mom's friend. I always felt like a real ballerina warming up in that room, the out-of-tune piano banging out music as we stretched. Something would stir inside of me when I clutched the worn wood of the ballet bar, the wet sleety city outside all cold and hard and ugly, and everything inside hot and kneaded and beautiful.

Even though I was afraid to meet him, my mom said it was important that I did. So one Saturday morning, we ate breakfast with him before ballet and then they took me to class together. Allan was strange and unfamiliar. He didn't look anything like the button-nosed boys in my class who everyone thought were cute. But he had a kind of authority that not even my teachers had. It was hard to make him smile, but because of that, when he did, it mattered more.

We did that for a few weeks, and then Allan volunteered

to take me to class alone. Soon after that, he decided he wanted to use my voice-over for a film he was working on so I started going back to his studio with him after class for weekly recording sessions. He gave me this French philosophy book to read, and I didn't speak French so I just spat out the words as best I could, and made up *a lot*. No matter what I did, though, Allan loved it. He told me I was doing a great job all the time. He gave me coffee and doughnuts, two things I was never allowed to have at home. I think if I'd asked him for a glass of wine, he would have said yes.

My favorite part, though, was riding the subway together after class. I loved sitting side by side on the yellow and orange bucket seats of the train. In everyone else's eyes, to all those strangers on the train, we were a normal father and daughter. Feeling normal felt extraordinary to me.

"Is Daddy coming today?" I asked my mom on the way to my Spring Ballet Recital that March. The sky was a mixture of rain and sleet. The two of us huddled together under her umbrella as we shuffled up 125th Street toward the subway.

"Since when is he Daddy?" she asked, squeezing my hand through her gloves. "Oh, forget it, let's take a cab."

My mom yanked me with her into the street. I had to jump over a puddle to not drench my shoes. Rain sloshed in the gutter. She stuck out her arm until a yellow cab swerved over to us. "Get in."

"Is he coming?" I asked again, once we were inside the cab.

"I'm pretty sure he is," she said.

I smiled, satisfied. I wondered if Allan would bring me

flowers. Not that it was that kind of recital; it was just in the classroom. But he might not know that some parents brought flowers.

"Sadie?"

I looked at my mom. Behind her, icy sludge slid across the cab's window.

"Don't call him Daddy, okay?"

"Why not?" I ask.

"I just don't think it's appropriate."

"What's appropriate?"

She sighed and then, with a forced patience in her voice, asked, "What does the word appropriate mean or what is appropriate in this situation?"

I wasn't sure what I was asking either, so I just shrugged and turned back to my own window. I touched my bun to make sure it was still perfectly in place.

## Chapter 13

"**D**o you want to go to the New Museum right now and just get it over with?" Izzy asks as we pack up our bags at the end of class on Friday. Benji is making us go see art over the weekend and write about it for homework. Teachers always make us go to museums when they run out of ideas.

"I was supposed to go over to Willa's," I say, biting my lip. "Lemme ask her and see if she wants to come."

I text Willa and she writes back:

> ur teacher is making you go to a museum? What is this,
>
> fifth grade?

I write:

> I kno rite

She writes:

> I'm just gonna stay home and be boring. Have fun tho.

When Izzy and I step outside, storm clouds are blooming overhead, carving out dark shapes in the summer sky.

During the school year, Izzy and I were secret darkroom friends who never spoke outside of the photo lab. We always stayed long after the first bell to print. We didn't talk those afternoons, we just listened to Tom Waits and The Cure and watched our pictures emerge in the chemical baths, using the tongs to gently rock the photos against the plastic walls of the tubs. Sometimes we stayed past the late bell at four thirty, until the lab supervisor came in to dump the developer and lock the doors at six. In the winter, when you go outside at six o'clock it's already dark. Icy air freezes all the traces of chemicals in your hair.

The first time Izzy and I really spoke outside the darkroom was on the first day of class earlier this summer, when Benji paired the two of us up for an icebreaker assignment. We had to photograph each other and do interviews.

The picture Izzy took of me ended up being not very good. She thought it would be interesting to photograph me alone in a classroom. It was a good idea in theory, but in reality, the room looked washed out and I looked like I was posing, but I'm not supposed to be posing, so it's awkward.

My picture of Izzy turned out really well. I had her lean against this metal door in the hallway by the girls' bathroom in the back of our school. I chose that spot because the light back there is amazing. It's one of those spots where, if you go there in the middle of the day, everything—even the thick swarms of dust in the air—is illuminated. Light bounces off the adjacent white wall and makes the whole space glow. In the photo, the light seems to emanate from Izzy herself.

The funny thing is, nobody ever uses that bathroom because it smells and the sink is permanently stained. But in the photo, lots of things got erased. Photography is powerful that way. If you want it to be, it can be the best liar in the world.

When I interviewed Izzy, I learned that she dyed her hair for the first time in fourth grade, and that she let her cousin pierce her ears. I learned that her mother is a fashion designer from Algeria and her father is an architect. Her favorite food is dumplings and her favorite movie is *Heathers*. Also, I learned that, like me, Izzy wants to go to art school next year.

Izzy learned that I'm an only child and that my mother once danced ballet at Lincoln Center. Also, that's when she learned that my father is an artist.

Now, walking down the street with her, I'm aware this is the first time we've been alone together outside of photo.

"So, you and Phaedra are best friends?" I ask.

"Basically," Izzy says. "I mean, I have a lot of best friends. Most of my best friends graduated already."

"Oh really?" I ask. "Like who?"

"I was really close with a lot of people two years ahead of us," she says. "Like Madison Mills and that whole group. Reeny and Wyatt and Noah and all them. I wish that our grade was like that. There's no one exciting in our grade."

Noah. Would I go up in Izzy's esteem if I told her what happened with us? Or down?

"Anyway, to answer your question, yes, Phaedra is probably my best friend in the city," Izzy continues before I get the chance. "I'm really close with her whole family, too. I went with them to Italy during winter break last year. It was amazing."

"That sounds amazing," I say. "Phaedra is so mysterious."

"Pssshhh." Izzy scoffs. "Everyone treats her like she's made of porcelain or something. But she's totally not. She's actually really regular."

"She is?" I ask.

"I know it can be hard to tell because she's kind of reserved or whatever," Izzy explains. "People always think she's a snob or something, but she's actually just shy."

What I want to say is *Why in the world would Phaedra Bishop have any reason to be shy?* But instead, I say, "That makes sense."

"But I also made some really good friends at RISD last summer," she says. "I did their precollege program and I became friends with all these amazing kids who live in Boston and all over. I think those people are kind of my real best friends."

"Their summer program looked fun," I say, faking a casual, indifferent tone. The truth is, I had wanted to do the RISD precollege summer so badly, but it was seven thousand dollars and my mom said no way. We had one of our biggest fights ever over it.

"Oh you should have done it! It would have been so fun to be together," Izzy chirps.

A hot wind curls down the street and the first thick drops of rain splatter on the pavement.

"Yay!" Izzy cries. And then she throws her arms around my neck, hurtling herself onto me in an almost football-player tackle and I laugh.

Izzy and I duck into a deli to buy umbrellas. Izzy grabs one of those super energy drinks out of the fridge and places it in front of the cashier.

"This is very bad for you. This poison," the old man behind the counter says, in a thick, foreign accent.

"I know, it's horrible," she says, batting her dark lashes at him.

He smiles. He likes her. After he gives her change, he tells her she looks like his sister who still lives in his home country. She asks him where he's from and he says, "Turkey. Where are you from?" and she says, "Nowhere. Just here." And he says, "New York. Best city in the world." And she says, "Yeah yeah yeah whatever." And he laughs.

Even with our umbrellas, Izzy and I are sopping wet when we stumble into the New Museum lobby twenty minutes later. Inside the museum is dry, quiet, and antiseptic white. The exact opposite of the storm that churns outdoors.

The show we came to see is a painting exhibition on Level 3. As we wander up through the galleries, we pass strange sculptures and text pieces, and a silent film projected in a big darkroom. I don't understand what I'm seeing, but I like how each object in the museum is meant to be meaningful. In the real world, things that are important and things that are unimportant are all shuffled together, but here, everything is worth looking at and considering and the rest is erased.

Izzy sets the pace, deciding when we move from one room to the next. She looks like she belongs here, the way she doesn't second-guess how much time she spends in front of any one artwork before moving on.

Finally, we reach the painting exhibition that we came

here to see. The paintings are much smaller in person than they looked on the Internet. Each one is a still life of flowers. They are painted really simply; a child could have made them. Still, the combination of pinks and lavenders is mesmerizing. No matter how bright their colors are, all the flowers look sort of sad.

There is one that shows a single red rose in front of a bright blue background, and the rose's shadow looks kind of like a lollipop. It reminds me of a birthday card I made for my mom when I was little that she had framed. I wonder what happened to it. It hung on the wall at our old apartment, but I haven't seen it since we moved. It's probably in one of the boxes we put in storage in a warehouse somewhere deep in Queens. It's strange, how just looking at a painting of a rose can make me think about my old apartment, and things I've lost, and dark rooms in large faraway buildings.

"What's your dad's art like?" Izzy asks as we ride the wide elevator back down to the first floor after we're done seeing the show.

"It's . . . hard to explain," I say. "He's having an exhibit in New York this summer. You can come with me to the opening if you want."

"Omigod, really? Yeah, I'll come," she says. She leans against the wall and inspects me from across the elevator, smiling. I wish I knew what she was seeing.

In the bathroom before we leave, Izzy refreshes the makeup that the rain washed off, putting on sky-blue eye shadow.

"Pretty color," I say to Izzy. "It's so blue."

"You like?" she asks. "I've been really into it lately. It's so out it's in, you know? I think the key to being fashionable is just to do the opposite of whatever the magazines tell you to do. Want to try some?"

Izzy hands me the case, and I lean in toward the mirror and paint the eye shadow onto my lids, just like Izzy did.

"What are you doing after this?" I ask Izzy.

"Don't know," she shrugs. "Phaedra's meeting me here now."

"Phaedra is coming here?" I repeat.

"Yeah," Izzy says. "She's actually being really annoying about plans. She keeps flaking on me and then she does this thing where she's, like, 'where are you?' She acts like I've been being hard to reach, but I'm totally not."

"Oh, really?" I say. "That's annoying. Are you gonna say something?"

"Say something?" Izzy laughs. "Yeah, right. That's just how friends are. The more you love them, the more mad they make you."

"I guess so." I want to ask her more but she's engrossed in her reflection again.

Izzy gives her hair a final tussle and then turns to me and smiles. "Ready?"

Outside, the rain has momentarily stopped. Phaedra is leaning against the wall. She's perfectly dry, as if she brought her own mild weather with her.

Izzy gives Phaedra a hug. "Were you waiting long?"

"Just got here," Phaedra replies. To me she says, "Hi, Sadie."

This is the first time Phaedra has ever said my name.

"Hey," I reply, trying to sound normal. "We just saw this painting exhibit, it was really good. You should see it."

"Oh really?" Phaedra says. She smiles, which lets me know I said the right thing.

"It was great," Izzy agrees. "Anyway, did you hear from Paul?"

Then, Izzy and Phaedra start texting and making plans for tonight on their phones. They speak to each other in the code people use when they're friends, saying things like *"last time"* and *"the other guy"* and *"the one whose sister went to my camp."*

"What are you guys doing after this?" I ask.

Izzy looks up. "Meeting up with some people."

I want to ask who and if I am invited, but then Phaedra steps into the street to flag down a taxi and one careens over to the side of the road and screeches to a halt.

"Bye, girl," Izzy says. "See you Monday."

And then they're gone, tumbling into the cab and laughing and going who knows where. I stand there for a moment on the curb, stunned to be left behind.

Izzy and Phaedra are good friends and they probably had these plans for a long time. Still, I wish I was going with them. I wish it so badly that it's as if I can feel the ground burn beneath my feet.

# Chapter 14

Allan came to my recital, after all.

There were ten girls in my class, and ten sets of parents watching us from behind a strip of red masking tape that Anyeshka had put on the hardwood floor. It felt amazing to have my mom and my father there.

Waiting in line before my solo, the pianist banging out our songs, I felt like something important was about to happen. Arms in first position, my right toe pressed to the ground, just waiting to burst across the stage. I knew the moves by heart: sashay-sashay-leap, then fifth, then élevée, and then curtsy.

There were only two girls in front of me and my heart was starting to race. I looked out at the parents. My mom smiled as she watched the girl who was doing her solo. And then Allan turned abruptly and left the room. *No. Come back*, I willed him with my mind. He didn't know it was almost my turn.

He missed my solo. My limbs felt heavy as I skipped across the stage. My mom had seen me practice a million times at home, but Allan had never seen me dance. At the end we curtsied and all the grown-ups flooded across the tape and embraced us.

"Where's Dad?" I asked. The word regained its unfamiliar sound, tasting ashy in my mouth. The best girl in the class was standing next to me. I just wanted her to hear me say it once.

"I'm not sure," my mom replied calmly.

We walked out of the classroom into the damp, linoleum-floored hallway. Allan was leaning against the turquoise wall, typing on his phone.

When he saw us he put his phone away.

My mom stood behind me, her hands resting on my shoulders.

"Good job, Sadie," Allan said.

"Did you see my solo?" I asked, suddenly hopeful. Maybe he had watched the performance from the hall.

Allan shrugged. "I got this phone call I had to take so I left right after the part where you were . . . you know . . . twirling."

"That was before my solo," I said lamely. I stared at the floor. The tips of my pink ballet shoes were scuffed up and graying, and the elastic band that stretched across my foot looked homemade and pathetic. My feet looked nothing like the beauty of a real ballet dancer's feet.

"Hey," Allan said.

I looked up at him and he reached out and ruffled my hair a little. "You were great. You were fantastic."

And then he bent down so his face was close to mine.

"The whole show was like your solo because I was only watching you," he said seriously.

"Really?" I said. Allan's words parted the clouds that had settled over me, and now the sun burst through.

"Can we get ice cream at Luigi's?" I was asking both my mom and Allan, but I was looking at Allan.

Allan straightened up and looked at my mom. "I have to go, actually."

"But you like Luigi's," I protested. "Remember? You said the coffee ice cream tasted like real coffee."

Allan's eyes met mine for a fraction of a second and then they flicked back up to my mom. "I can't."

"That's fine, Allan." My mom sighed.

"But—" I started to object.

"I'd love to but I can't. But great job, today. You're a star," Allan interrupted. He squeezed my shoulder quickly and then he turned.

I stood there, frozen in place, and watched Allan disappear down the hall. While he walked, he wrapped his scarf tight around his neck, preparing for the cold outside. I could feel myself sinking into a hole in the linoleum floor.

"Come on, Sadie," my mom was saying. "Let's get you changed."

But I could barely make out her words. All I could hear was the silence that Allan had left behind.

*July*

# Chapter 15

The world seems half-empty on the Fourth of July weekend because so many people are away. Most of the rich bankers and the real estate agents are at their country houses, and everyone else is at home with their families or at the beach. It's funny knowing a place so well that you can feel its pulse change, like your own breathing slowing down in the moments before you fall asleep.

Willa and I walk around her neighborhood in I-don't-care clothes and drink Frappuccinos as the summer day fades to dusk. We stroll down a leafy block, past a big brick school with a grid of darkened windows, and then a row of brownstones. I can see inside to living rooms with paintings and bookshelves, warm lamps flicking on as the evening sky grows dark outside. The sounds of someone practicing piano music, playing the same few bars over and over again, emanates from deep within some building.

This is the best thing: walking around on a warm night and letting the world envelop you. When my mom and I lived near the park, we used to walk around the reservoir every night when the weather was good. We'd do as many loops as we needed to until we stopped feeling worried or tired.

Tonight, Willa and I have a destination. We are going to Video World, the old movie rental store that's somehow still in business. It's the only video store I know of, and Willa and I love it there. We spend more time picking out movies than watching them. We even love the cases that the DVDs come in, all plastic and greasy with these low-res pictures of the stars taped to the front.

I'm walking in the DRAMA section when I see *Heathers*. "What about this?" I ask Willa.

Willa looks up and wrinkles her nose. "What's that?"

"It's Izzy's favorite movie," I say nonchalantly.

Willa raises an eyebrow.

"I think I've seen it, actually," Willa says, after a minute.

After a half hour of cruising the aisles, we leave with two things that we've both already seen: *Pitch Perfect* and the whole first season of *Game of Thrones*. It's a perfect combination for a sleepover.

We ride the elevator up to Willa's floor with her upstairs neighbor Miles. Miles is a year younger than us but a foot taller, not including his curly hair which adds another three inches. He's bone skinny and pale, with huge blue eyes and glasses, like a not-cute Harry Potter. He goes to an uptown prep school and he's such a genius that he skipped a grade, so he's going to be a senior next year, too.

"I see you guys are having about as wild of a Friday night

as I am," he says, and he nods at our bag of videos and sloppy stay-at-home clothes.

"We're party animals. What can I say," Willa deadpans.

Back at Willa's, we order pizza and curl up on the big, soft couches. Everything about Willa's apartment is perfectly worn in: framed school photos on the wall and scratches in the guest bathroom marking her and her sister's growth every year.

We're halfway through the second episode of *Game of Thrones* when Willa's sister, Danielle, comes home.

"Hey, kids," she says, dropping her purse on the floor. "What are you watching?"

She's wearing tight black jeans that show off her long skinny legs and a white tank top that makes the tan on her arms glow. Danielle and Willa have matching features and the same straight brown hair, but everything comes together on Danielle in a way that it all falls apart on Willa.

"Sshh," Willa says. "None of your business."

"I'm going to open a bottle of dad's wine. Don't tell," Danielle says, traipsing into the kitchen.

Danielle is one of those girls who is equal parts sweet and scary. She went to one of the uptown all-girls high schools, and for some reason she always looked like even more of a bad girl in that old-fashioned plaid uniform. When Willa and I were younger, we used to go through Danielle's drawers when she was out and tally all of the condoms and cigarettes, speculating about all her secrets. We'd spend hours wondering who she liked and when she'd first had sex.

"Cute shoes, Sadie," Danielle says when she comes back.

"Thanks," I say, proudly peeking at my vintage sandals.

"Willa, why don't you ever wear cute stuff?" she asks, swatting the back of her sister's head.

Willa ducks away. "Leave me alone."

Danielle looks back at the screen.

"Lemme guess," she says. "They all die."

"Stop talking, we're watching," Willa whines. "You're being so annoying."

"I just wanted to tell you—"

Willa grabs the remote and pauses the TV show. Then she glares at her sister. "Fine. Speak."

"I wanted to tell you I'm going to a party tonight at someone's apartment from your grade," she says. "Do you guys want to come?"

I'm shocked and excited that Danielle invited us to something. Danielle has never once included us in anything before, in all of history. College must have made her nicer.

"Our grade?" Willa scoffs. "Wow. That must make you feel like a real loser."

"I know, it's embarrassing," Danielle says. "But Katie wants to go."

"Whose party is it?" I jump in.

"This guy Justin Chang," Danielle says.

My heart leaps into my chest.

"Justin?" I repeat. "I know who that is. He's friends with Phaedra and Izzy and everyone."

What I don't say is *that means Noah might be there, too.*

Willa looks at me, not smiling. I try to act normal, slump

down onto the couch, and look at the TV like I don't care.

"I don't want to go out," Willa says.

"Okay. Well if you change your mind I'm not leaving for a while," Danielle says, turning so quickly that her shiny brown hair fans over her shoulders like a girl in a shampoo commercial.

After Danielle goes to her room, I can't concentrate on the TV show anymore. There's a party and everyone will be there. Why does Willa have to be so above it all the time? Why can't she be normal and get excited about a party for once?

It must be a full twenty minutes because we're into the second act of the next episode when Willa pauses the TV, and her eyes bore into me in the silence.

"What's wrong?" I ask.

She glares at me.

"What did I do?" I repeat.

"Just go with Danielle if you want to go so bad," she says, as if she'd been inside my head this whole time.

# Chapter 16

"Do you think Willa is happy?" Danielle asks in the taxi. She brought a SmartWater bottle full of vodka and orange juice and she takes a sip. And then she says, without waiting for me to answer, "It's rad you are old enough to party with. I wish Willa would party with me. What's with her?"

"She's just Willa," I say.

"You're so right," Danielle says. "That's such a little sister thing. To just, like, do what you want all the time and not care if other people are making everything easier for you."

I tug on the hem of the tight black dress Danielle let me borrow. It's too small for me, but Danielle said it's too small in a good way. It feels like just yesterday that she was screaming and literally throwing shampoo bottles at us when she found us trying on her clothes in eighth grade. Now, I'm wearing her dress with her permission, going to a party with her on a Friday night.

"Here. Have some," Danielle says, shoving the bottle at me.

Danielle is watching and I don't want her to regret bringing me so I take a sip. It tastes terrible.

"Anyway, Willa is still awesome. I can't wait for her to

come to Yale," she says. "I'll be a junior when she's a freshman. That will be amazing. She's going to love college. You're going to love college, too. It's so much better than high school. Where do you want to go?"

"I think I want to go to IACA," I say. "In California."

But Danielle isn't listening. She taps on the plastic that divides the backseat from the driver. "Excuse me? Sir?"

The driver doesn't turn around, but says, "Yes, ma'am?" with a thick accent.

"Can I smoke in here?"

"No! No smoking! You cannot smoke!" he replies. I can see him trying to catch Danielle's gaze in the rearview mirror. She sinks back into the pleather seat and rolls her eyes.

As the taxi curves onto Central Park West, the velvety black trees zip by to our right, blending into the night sky. To our left, the looming apartment buildings stare down at us, their stone faces hard as armor.

Justin lives on the corner of Eighty-Third Street and Riverside Drive. It's one of those huge, almost block-size brick buildings that look like a thousand others in the city, including the one we lived in when I was really little. There's something so strange about walking into an unfamiliar building that is almost identical to a familiar building. The tiny differences between each one, like the placement of the elevator and the smell of the walls, seem dangerous.

The metal jaws of the elevator open and Danielle and I ride up to the ninth floor. The hallway that leads to Justin's apartment gives me the same strange feeling as the lobby. I feel an uneasy kind of déjà vu. Like when you dream about a real place but everything in the dream is altered in ways that you can't name.

Someday, I'm going to do a photography project where I take pictures of people's hallways. I could take a trillion and no two would be exactly the same. And if I hung them side by side, all the differences between them would pop out.

Danielle pushes open the door to Justin's apartment and we are immediately sucked into the party. People's faces slur together, music and laughter and heat erasing all the eerie surrealness of the hall.

"Ugh, everyone here is in high school," Danielle complains.

"How can you tell?" I ask.

"I just can," she says. "I'm gonna go find Katie."

There's a dance party in the living room, and Phaedra Bishop is sitting on one of the couches talking to a girl I've never seen. She catches me staring at her and she smiles and beckons to me. I walk up to them, standing awkwardly.

"Hey, you," she says, patting the sofa next to her.

"Is Izzy here?" I ask.

"No, she left for the country," she says. "I'm going tomorrow 'cause my dad had to work late. I'm so sick of the city. It's so gross in the summer."

I nod in agreement. I'm used to people around me acting like certain things are normal—like country houses and private school tuitions. "Where's your country house?"

"Cape Cod," she says. "It's so beautiful. It's been in our family forever; it's really old. I think it's haunted."

"Wow," I say.

"Hey, actually, I wanted to ask you," she says, her eyes focusing on mine for the first time. "Izzy mentioned that your dad is an artist. I didn't know that."

"Oh, she did?" I stammer. "Yeah. He is."

"What's his name?" she asks.

"Allan Bell?" I say, swallowing. And then I add, "I don't think you'd have heard of him."

"Allan Bell . . ." she repeats it to herself. "I'm gonna ask my mom. My parents are really involved in the arts. And I love art, too. I'm not talented at anything, but I think I'll probably be an art history major in college. What kind of stuff does your dad make?"

"He's made a lot of things," I say. "He makes sculptures and does performances. He's been in the Whitney Biennial a couple of times and both times he made installations and videos."

I think I see a flicker of approval flash in her eyes, but it's gone as quickly as it was there. Is it possible that Phaedra Bishop is curious about me just like I'm curious about her?

The girl on her other side holds out a glass of a clear liquid, offering it to Phaedra. Phaedra shakes her head no. Then she says, to me, "You want some? It's vodka soda."

"No thanks," I say.

"I don't drink either," Phaedra says.

I don't correct her—I do drink, sometimes. But it feels good, being on Phaedra's team.

"I'm back," Danielle announces, grabbing my arm above the elbow. "Katie isn't here. She left. Let's go."

"Already?" I ask. "But we just got here."

"I'll take you home. I'm going to meet up with Katie. She's at a bar, but you need IDs to get in so I can't bring you," she says.

"Oh," I say, deflating.

Embarrassed, I wave good-bye to Phaedra and follow Danielle through the party back toward the entrance.

The front door to the apartment swings open as we approach it and more people pile in. Danielle walks past them all, determined to leave.

I notice him before he notices me. *Sam-from-somewhere.* He doesn't smile, but something else registers on his face when he notices me and it feels better than a smile.

"Hey," he says. "Are you leaving?"

"Yeah, we were going to." I look at Danielle, who isn't happy that I'm stalling.

"Bummer. We're just getting here," Sam says. And then he grins and gently flicks my arm with his thumb and forefinger. "You should stay."

*Stay.* The word expands, blooming into the wonderful and scary possibilities of *staying.*

"What now?" Danielle groans.

"Maybe, um . . ." I begin. "Maybe since you're going to a bar anyway and I can't go, maybe I'll just . . . stay."

"Fine," Danielle says, seeming a little relieved to be free of me. "See you later. Don't get kidnapped or whatever or it'll be my fault."

I look up at Sam. His eyes don't look as green in the dim lights as they did the other day at the beach. There is a peeling sunburn on his nose. I wonder if he got it the day we met or in the week since then. I wonder about what he has been doing since I last saw him.

"So," I say, shrugging nervously.

"So," he replies. "How's it going?"

"Okay. How's it going with you?" I ask.

"All right," he replies.

"That's good," I say.

Maybe it's because I remember how real things felt when we talked last time, but the conversation between me and Sam feels really extra small now.

"Wanna go in?" he asks.

I nod. We wander through the apartment silently, which feels better than forcing stupid party chatter. We walk past a bedroom where people are crowded together with the lights off and the music turned up too loud. We walk past the line for the bathroom where girls are huddled in groups of three, whispering. Somehow, me and Sam are outsiders together. Sometimes he leads the way, and sometimes I do.

It's strange, this weird comfort we have, like old friends. On the way here with Danielle, and whenever I'm with Izzy, I feel compelled to keep the conversation going. That if I stop asking questions and saying witty things, they'll remember that they don't actually want to hang out with me. Around Sam, it feels safe not to talk.

After a loop, we end up back in the living room. There's a small balcony outside of a set of sliding glass doors and I follow Sam onto it. A few smokers are huddled in the corner.

They ignore us and we silently agree to ignore them, too.

Sam leans against the wall and stares out at the Hudson River and to the New Jersey skyline on the other side. A big ship that looks like a party boat, with red, white, and blue lights popping on and off, glides down the surface of the slick dark water.

"Are you doing anything fun for the Fourth of July weekend?"

His words snap my attention back to him. "Not really. Are you?"

"I'm going to New Hampshire tomorrow," Sam says.

"Nice," I say. "How do you get there? Do you have to fly?"

"We drive," he says. And then he adds, "Driving is this thing that people do where they sit behind the wheel of a motor vehicle and it moves and . . ."

"Oh, right . . . driving," I say, scratching my head theatrically. "I've heard of it."

He smirks. "I didn't want to assume."

I roll my eyes, trying not to laugh.

"Yeah, we'll leave at the crack of dawn tomorrow," he continues. "To beat the traffic."

"Who's going?" I ask.

"Me and my mom," he says. "Her boyfriend is staying because he says he has to work. Which pisses me off."

"Why?" I ask.

"He's never been to New Hampshire," Sam says. "They've been dating for two years and we moved to New York to live with him, and he hasn't once seen where she's from."

"Oh," I say. "Is he very busy?"

Something sad blazes in Sam's eyes. It's so quick, I almost don't see it happen, like the shutter snapping open for a fraction of a second inside a camera lens. For that moment, I'm seeing straight through him to his heart.

But all he says, is, "Yeah. Really busy."

"I can't imagine my mom having a boyfriend," I say, after a minute.

"She never has?" Sam asks.

"No," I say. "And my parents were never even married."

"Mine neither," Sam says. "They had me in high school. So dumb."

"They had you in high school? Wow," I say. "How old is your mom now?"

"I don't know." He shrugs. "What—thirty-three? No. No, she's thirty-four. That's right."

I feel my jaw drop. "Omigod. That's so bizarre. My mom is fifty-seven. She didn't even have me until she was forty."

Sam nods slowly. He moves away from the wall and rests his forearms on the banister of the balcony. I stand next to him and do the same. The edge of my arm is touching the edge of his, and I can feel the exact shape of where our skin is making contact, like a clothing iron, searing its shape onto a blouse.

"Good for her," Sam says. "I always feel so bad for my mom. Like she's wasted her whole life raising me."

"I'm sure that's not how she sees it. I always wish my mom was younger," I say. And then I add, "It's weird how I keep telling you things I never tell anyone."

Sam doesn't react to what I just said, and I'm worried I

went too far. But then he turns his head and his eyes find mine in the darkness.

"I know."

I try to hold his gaze, but he looks down. "Going back is gonna be weird."

"You're not excited?" I ask.

"Not really," he says. "My friends there . . . it all feels different than it used to."

"Different how?" I ask.

Sam sighs, and gazes out at the view. On the street, ten stories below, a taxi pulls up in front of Justin's building and a family piles out. They look like toys, all shrunk down to miniature by the distance.

"I mean, I spent most of this year feeling like New Hampshire was home and I was just visiting here," he says. "I had a girlfriend there, and all my real friends were there. But then . . . I don't know. Things changed. Now, this is more like home in some ways."

My chest tightens at the word *girlfriend*.

"A girlfriend?" I repeat. "Do you still . . . ?"

Sam looks at me but he's not seeing me. His eyes are far away.

"No," he says. "We broke up a few months ago. But we're still friends, I think."

"So you're gonna see her this weekend?" I ask, trying to sound like I don't care.

"Yeah, probably," he says. "I don't know. It's weird."

"What's her name?" I ask.

He elbows me a little. "You don't know her."

"Yeah, never mind," I murmer, tucking my hair nervously behind my ears.

"Mandy," he says. And then he corrects himself, sounding a little sadder this time. "Amanda."

Sam bites a nail, stares out into space, and then he shakes his head like he's shaking off a thought. He turns to me.

"What about you. You have a boyfriend?" he asks.

I shake my head no.

"Why not?" he asks, a teasing smile breaking on his lips. "Nobody good enough?"

"Yeah, right," I scoff. "I've never had a boyfriend. I had this one thing with this guy, but we were never, like, together."

"I get that," Sam says vaguely.

"Can I tell you another thing that I've never told anyone and that I probably shouldn't tell you?" I say, trying to make him smile again.

"Please," he says, not missing a beat. He looks amused.

"I've never even had a friend who is a boy," I say. "Like a guy friend."

"No way."

"For real."

Sam's eyes rest on mine, and he lifts his chin in this really cute way so that he has to look down his nose at me.

Then he pulls his cell phone out of his pocket. "What's your number?"

I tell him and he types it into his phone. Then, he keeps typing.

"What are you doing?" I ask.

A minute later, my phone vibrates in my back pocket. I

pull it out. There's a new text message from an area code I don't recognize. I open the message and read. All it says is: hi friend.

"So now you do," he says. "Have a guy friend."

Suddenly, I wish I could reach up and touch that piece of peeling skin on his nose. I wish I knew all the things that his ex-girlfriend knows about him, how his skin smells, and what it's like to feel his hands. I wish I knew how he kisses. The thought of Sam with a girl makes my stomach turn over.

But Sam isn't into me. He just said we're friends. Still, there's something about the way he's looking at me that makes me wonder if he's wrong.

I pry my eyes away and look out at the view. The party boat on the river flashes blue and red and white.

The doors to the apartment open and loud music momentarily billows up like a wave as a group of people tumble onto the balcony, shredding our private moment. The only one I recognize is Justin.

Justin spots Sam and hands him a paper bag with a bottle of something tucked into it. Sam takes a sip. It stains his lips wine-red. He hands it to me, but I don't feel like drinking. When I hand the bottle back to Sam our fingertips touch.

"I should probably leave soon," I say.

Sam doesn't make a move to come with me. He takes another sip of the wine and says, "Okay. Well, I'll see you soon. Right, friend?"

"Right," I say. *Friend.* The word swirls around me, like someone's flipped a coin inside my heart. It's a quarter spinning through midair, and I have no idea how it will land.

I take a cab back and then climb carefully into bed beside Willa without waking her. I lie under the sheets and close my eyes and I imagine I'm still standing on the balcony next to Sam. It's just the two of us there, hovering above the crowded city and beneath the planes and satellites in the sky. The quarter is still spinning: *friends or something more*. Maybe it will just spin and spin forever and all I'll ever feel is my own dizzy longing for it to stop.

# Chapter 17

The next morning, I wake up alone in Willa's bed. A siren wails outside, growing louder and louder like it's right on top of me before it fades away.

Willa emerges from her bathroom, freshly showered and dressed for her family trip to Martha's Vineyard. She's wearing a white dress and open-toed sandals. I'm so used to seeing her in sweatpants, it almost looks like she's in drag. I notice she's got her contact lenses in, instead of her glasses, which is rare.

"You look fancy," I say. "Very summer-house chic. Are you excited?"

But Willa doesn't smile or laugh.

"How was the party?" she asks instead.

"It was so crazy," I say, sitting up a little. "I ran into that guy Sam. The one I told you about who I met at the beach."

"Why is that crazy?" Willa asks.

"'Cause," I say. "It was just, I don't know. We talked for a while. I feel like he really gets me. I think we are gonna hang out again. He took my number."

"Wait, really?" she asks, focusing on me. "So, you're gonna go on a date or something?"

"No, I mean, we're just friends," I say. "It was actually really funny. I told him I'd never had a guy friend before and he was like 'I'll be your guy friend.' But it was kind of flirty, too," I say, searching for the words.

"He said he was your friend?" she asks. "That doesn't sound flirty."

It's like Willa is being deliberately obtuse and it's starting to make me mad.

"Just never mind. I can't explain it."

Willa picks up a comb and starts yanking it through her wet hair. "Just be careful, okay, Sadie? I feel like you shouldn't be so trusting of those people."

"Those people?" I repeat, wanting to roll my eyes.

"Like that whole scene," she says. "City kids trying to be badasses. All those rich kids my sister hangs out with. Phaedra and Noah and everyone."

"Rich kids?" I ask. I hate when Willa calls people rich. It makes her seem so spoiled, like she doesn't know that she is one of them. Or that in the grand scheme of things, pretty much everyone we know is.

"You know what I mean." She sighs. "Those kids are just the worst. They're obsessed with being hip or whatever and it makes everyone act so fake."

I find my jeans on the floor and pull them on, yanking the zipper shut.

"What's your problem this morning?"

Willa stops combing her hair and looks at me, and I can see her doing that thing she does where she formulates a complete sentence before she speaks.

"You left me at home alone last night to go to a party with my sister," she says, putting her hand on her hip.

My mouth goes dry the way it does when I'm in trouble.

"But you told me to go," I object. "You said, literally, 'go to the party.'"

"Because you were sitting there sulking," she snaps.

Hearing myself described like that hurts, but I try not to show it.

"I'm sorry, all right?" I say, knowing I don't sound sorry at all. "I shouldn't have gone."

Willa sinks down into her chair and faces me. Half of her wet hair is combed into neat ruler straight lines and the other half is a tangled mess.

"It's not a big deal," she says. "I shouldn't make it weird. We're just . . . different about social things, I guess."

Different. The word sizzles. I can tell Willa thinks she's more mature than me, but I don't want to argue with her now. "I'm really sorry," I repeat.

"Thank you," she says. "Apology accepted."

After that, Willa packs for her weekend while I DJ music off of her laptop. I try to forget about the conversation, but I can't help feeling bothered. How come Willa has to make me feel like any time I want to go to a party I'm being weak or a follower? It's easy for her to say no to things: her big sister is Danielle Davis-Spencer. Even if she doesn't care about any of that now, Willa can be as much a part of the elaborate social hierarchy of the city as she wants. Anytime she wants. Not everyone gets to have that privilege.

I think about what Izzy said the other day: the more you love someone, the more mad they make you. It hadn't seemed true to me at the time, but watching Willa pack for her fancy Fourth of July weekend, I think I might know what she means.

# Chapter 18

The first day back after the Fourth of July break is the Portrait Assignment critique in Photo. Izzy is going first. She walks up to the front of the room and pins her three work prints to the corkboard. Izzy is wearing a canvas frock with a blinding floral print and no shape. It's the kind of *if-you-don't-realize-this-is-cool-you-aren't-cool* look that Izzy can pull off because she exudes so much confidence.

Benji blows his nose and walks up to the board, stuffing a dirty tissue in his back pocket. He has a cold and he's in a bad, scary mood, the way that teachers always get when they're sick.

"I see," Benji says, examining the photos. I can't see his face, but I can tell from his tone of voice that he's not impressed. "What do you guys think about these pictures?"

In the three photos Izzy decided to print, Phaedra is sitting by a window. In one, she's staring out of it. In the next, she's looking at the camera, and in the third she's standing up pressing her forehead to the glass. There are a lot of problems. For one thing, the way she cropped them makes her body look truncated and flat. Plus, Phaedra is lit from some ambient light behind her that makes her look gray. All the things that Benji tells us over and over again to consider—light source, composition, scale—have been neglected.

I'm feeling nervous and protective of Izzy, so I raise my hand. When Benji looks at me, I say, "I like them."

Benji covers his mouth and coughs. "Okay. Why?"

"I think," I start, searching for the right words, "I don't know. I think they have an interesting . . . mood."

"Mood?" Benji repeats.

"They're just pictures of a pretty girl," Cody says. "They're not even really portraits."

"What do you mean by not a portrait?" Benji asks.

"Because. There's no, like . . . identity to the person in the photos," Cody says.

I wish I didn't, but I know what he means. If I took Phaedra's picture, I'd want to capture so many things about her. Not just the planes of her face and the shape of her eyes, but the way that she can seem simultaneously so nice and so cold. I wonder if it's possible to capture something like that in a photo.

Benji rubs his eyes. "Did you use the light meter?"

Izzy nods.

"What were your settings? Where's your middle gray?" Benji asks.

Izzy fidgets. "I think it was her tank top, but I wanted it to be more contrast-y because—"

Benji slams his finger down on Phaedra's tank top. "That? That's your middle gray? It's practically black."

Izzy tosses her hair.

"Look, I know this is the point in the semester when everyone starts to slack off. But this photograph does everything I've told you not to do," Benji says. His finger is pressed so hard to her picture that it begins to turn white. "The light is sloppy. The composition is sloppy. And you broke my number one rule. I said on the first day of class the one thing I never want to see is pictures of you hanging out with your friends. This isn't beginning photo. Save the photos of your friends for Instagram. This is an academic class."

A heavy silence rolls through the classroom. Everyone is frozen, not shifting in the foldout chairs or even breathing.

I glance at Izzy. Her face is bright red. Finally she manages an imitation of a casual eye-roll. "Fine."

Izzy stands up and walks with forced calm to the board to take her pictures down, her ugly-chic frock not moving. Her hand trembles as she yanks the thumbtacks out of the board.

Benji's bad mood is a weight that doesn't lift. Normally, he wraps all of his criticisms in thoughtful compliments. But today, he just stands up there and tells people what they could do better. He even takes out a red pen and circles three different areas on Alexis's prints where the light settings were off.

Finally, it's my turn. I'd been excited to share my photograph, but now I'm really nervous.

For my portrait, I took a picture of my mom sitting on our couch, underneath this framed photograph of her that hangs on the wall. The framed photo is her headshot from when she was a dancer. It appeared in the program next to her name when she performed, and in it, she looks strangely blank and doll-like.

She's nineteen in that picture. Nineteen. I remember being little and looking at that picture and thinking I would never reach that age. But now, I'm seventeen, which touches eighteen. And eighteen touches nineteen. Plus, Danielle and Noah are nineteen and they don't seem old. Realizing that an age that I thought was grown-up is actually really young gives me a weird queasy feeling like vertigo.

"A picture within a picture," Benji says, gesturing toward my work. "What do you guys think that tells us?"

"The picture on the wall looks really different from Sadie's picture," Sean offers.

"Can someone add to that comment? How would you describe the difference between the two pictures?" he asks.

"The one on the wall is clearly taken by someone who doesn't know the woman in the picture, and in Sadie's picture, you can tell they know each other," Alexis says.

"How can you tell?" Benji asks. "I agree. But I wonder if you can describe that."

"Maybe it's because the woman on the couch looks less perfect," Alexis adds. "Her hair is a little messier and there is a hole on the sleeve of her sweater. So it looks like they're comfortable together."

Benji steps closer to the picture and stares at it hard, as if it's an ancient artifact that he's trying to decode, instead of just a picture. "You're right. There is a real sense of intimacy here, between us and the woman on the couch."

"It's her mom," Cody scoffs. "Of course she's comfortable."

Benji looks at Cody and his expression grows serious. "People don't necessarily feel comfortable with their parents."

For the first time, I wonder about Benji's family.

"Ultimately," Benji continues, "whether or not there is intimacy between these two people in real life doesn't matter. What matters is whether or not the photograph makes us believe that there is."

Benji is still looking at Cody, but I feel like he's talking to me. "One of the things that's interesting about photography is that intimacy can be faked. Film gets exposed in a fraction of a second, so if you can capture even one fleeting moment of connection between yourself and someone, it becomes preserved, and to an outsider, it will look real."

After that, Benji talks about my technique and tells me I need to work my shadows better. But I keep thinking about what he said: a fleeting fraction of a second can be preserved and turned into something that lasts forever. I wonder if that's a good thing at all.

"Benji was being such a dick today," Izzy says on the sidewalk after class. She already put her sunglasses on so I'm forced to look at her mouth instead of her eyes. "He doesn't get me at all. He's not as smart as he thinks he is."

"You don't think he's smart?" I ask.

"My teachers at the RISD Summer Program last year knew so much more than him and they were really into my pictures. Benji is very old-fashioned."

"Oh," I say dumbly.

"Anyway, when is your dad's opening?" Izzy asks. "Is it this weekend?"

"Next weekend," I tell her.

"Okay, good, don't let me forget," she says. And then she blows me a kiss and walks in the opposite direction.

After we've parted, I walk home and think about what Izzy said about Benji. I agree with almost everything Benji says, even the critical things. Does that make me old-fashioned, too?

Waiting for the light to change on the corner of Fourth Street, I notice three identical yellow taxis lined up behind the crosswalk. To my left, a man in a white chef's apron smokes a cigarette near the entrance of a restaurant, the smoke unfurling like a white ribbon. Overhead, a weave of delicate black telephone wires slices through the thick blue summer sky. There's a pair of dirty sneakers draped from one of the wires, and a pigeon swoops in and nips at the laces, mistaking them for food.

There's so much going on around us all the time that we don't see. I wonder if that's what Sam meant about not being able to describe somewhere you've lived your whole life because you're too close-up. But with my camera on, I feel like I can see everything. I can see things that are so mundane and familiar that they are invisible to everyone else.

I take out my camera and photograph the pigeon and the shoes and the knotty, sagging wires and instantly, everything I was thinking about Izzy disappears. There's just me and this fleeting, mysterious everyday-ness of the world.

## Chapter 19

The night before I'm going to see Allan at his gallery, I can't sleep. Outside my window, the sky is clotted with clouds. We're in a cycle of hot muggy days and even hotter stormy ones.

It's been a week since the party at Justin's and I haven't heard from Sam yet. I wonder if he changed his mind about wanting to be my friend. Every night, I stare at my phone and will it to light up with his name, but it remains dark.

I told myself I wouldn't do this, but I can't help it. I log-in to Facebook. I don't know Sam's last name but I find a Sam who is friends with Justin Chang pretty quickly and his hometown is in New Hampshire.

Sam's profile picture is a sloppy, low-res picture of a figure from faraway in the snow. I can't tell if it's a picture of him or someone else. And the rest of his profile is equally lazy and untended. He doesn't have any other pictures of himself and it looks like he never logs in, because the posts on his page are a mix of spam and advertisements. But there is one girl who has posted a lot to his wall. The most recent post is dated in January, but as I skim down his timeline, I can see that they span back in time for years.

I click on her name and find myself on her page. Amanda Muller from Newberg, New Hampshire.

She has tons of pictures and tons of friends. She has strawberry blond hair and big dark brown eyes. She has her septum pierced with a shiny dumbbell, but other than that she has sort of a plain style. The more pictures I look at her though, the prettier she gets. Even the nose piercing sort of grows on me. It's so hard and tough looking that it makes her face look even more angelic in contrast.

And then I see something that makes me stop.

I'm staring at a series of webcam pictures of Amanda and Sam together. In the first one, they're sitting side by side. Sam looks a lot younger. His hair is blonder, probably from the sun, and so long that it's tucked behind his ears and a little natty. I look at the date. These were posted two years ago. Sam was fifteen. Amanda is looking right at the camera and Sam is staring off into space. In the next one, Sam is leaning so close to the camera that the computer lights up all the crystals in his eyes. In that one, Amanda is behind him, laughing and covering her face with her hands. She has peeling black nail polish on her pale fingers and a woven bracelet on her wrist. In the next photo from the series, Amanda is sitting on Sam's lap. I can't see their bodies, but I can tell because her head is higher than his, and his chin rests on her shoulder. And in the last one he's holding her head in his hands in a play-fighting move, and she's squirming and laughing.

I know Sam said they broke up, but you can tell that at the instant that this picture was taken, they were in love. I think about what Benji said earlier: photography can fake intimacy. A half a second of love can turn into something that lasts forever. Looking at this picture, I know I might be seeing something that didn't really exist, but it looks so real it's blinding.

I snap my computer closed and stare up at the ceiling, neon bulbs floating around my field of vision.

What am I trying to find? When I'm walking around with my camera on, I feel this constant itch as if I'm longing for something I've never seen. Something I've only dreamed of. But with the Internet it's the opposite, the way it sucks me into holes instead of leading me to new parts of the world. So often, I go online and scroll around until I find something that hurts me enough to turn it off. I wonder if that's what I'm looking for: someone to pinch me and wake me up.

The next morning I get ready with a zinging flutter in my chest. Today, I'm going to see Allan at his gallery after class.

My mom is making coffee when I emerge from the shower.

"I'm done early today if you want to do something," she says. "We can go to the movies. Or I could take you to a museum? You could show me what you've been learning."

My hands grow hot and sweaty in my pockets as I try to casually shrug. "I can't, actually. I have to stay late today."

In the stairwell outside our apartment, I sink against the wall and close my eyes. Lying makes me feel sick. I know I should go back inside and tell her the truth.

But I don't.

The neighborhood Allan's gallery is in, Chelsea, is quiet and bright when I arrive there after class. Some galleries boast big flashy signs, and some are discreet, unmarked.

Allan's gallery, Kaplan and White, is an old, prestigious gallery, with a location here and another one in Switzerland (thank you, Google). The only other time I've been here was when I was nine, when my mom and I came to see a screening of the film I narrated. I don't remember the art, or even Allan from that night. I just remember the stuffy room packed with too many people. I remember black high heels and red lipstick and sweat. I remember burying my face in my mom's dress when she tried to introduce me to someone.

Now that I'm here, I see it's bigger than I remembered. The gallery takes up almost half of a block on Twenty-Seventh Street, stretching all the way to the corner of Eleventh Avenue, where the city gives way to the wide highway.

When I reach the door, I hesitate. The door is open and two guys in hoodies haul a ladder out, not noticing me. I peer inside. I can see a few people milling around the enormous, bleached rooms. One of them is Allan. His back is to me, but I recognize him right away. Even from far away and behind, he looks smaller and older than I remember, his hair more gray than brown.

He turns in my direction but he doesn't notice me. Seeing his face makes my heart pound between my ears. I'm suddenly dizzy. Why didn't I bring my mom? I should have done this with her. I shouldn't be here alone.

"Can I help you?"

A stylish woman steps out of the gallery. She has shiny blue-black hair, and she wears a green-patterned dress that looks vintage.

I comb my hair nervously with my fingers. "Um. Yeah. I'm here to see Allan Bell?"

I say it like a question, even though it's not a question.

Her expression reveals no understanding. She smiles intimidatingly and says, "Is he expecting you?"

"I think so," I say. "I'm his daughter."

"This way," she says, her neat smile staying perfectly in place.

I walk with this woman through the space back to where Allan is examining a few pieces of paper that he's arranged on the concrete gallery floor. Her high heels *click-clack* loudly in the almost empty rooms.

"Allan. There's someone here for you," the gallery girl says.

Allan uncrosses his arms and then turns and sees me. When his eyes clasp on to mine he stays perfectly still for a moment while the woman walks quickly away.

I'm frozen in place. It's taking so much effort for me to try to smile naturally that I don't even have the ability to say hello or walk toward him.

"Sadie," he finally says. "Wow. You look really well."

He stands there, staring.

"Hi," I manage.

And then he steps toward me and gives me a long, firm hug.

"So, this is all new work," Allan says, gesturing broadly

to the cardboard boxes that are leaning against the walls. "We're just unpacking now. I haven't shown these pieces anywhere."

"Cool," I say.

Allan continues. "I think it's going to be good. I mean, what I really wanted to do was have the dancers that Marla and I have been working with in LA come out here and do a performance. But that's not going to happen. Elaine doesn't think it will work in this space."

"Oh, really," I say, as if I know what he's talking about.

"Do you remember Elaine? You may have met her years ago," he says.

"I don't think so," I say, smiling eagerly.

"She's my dealer," he says. "She's going to be back in a minute; you'll meet her. She just had a lunch."

"Oh, okay," I say.

"Do you want to have a cup of coffee in the office? You can leave your backpack here. No one will take it," Allan says.

"Thanks," I say awkwardly. I let my backpack slide off and drop it gently on the floor. The Leica is buried in there, wrapped in a sweatshirt for safety. I didn't want to wear it around my neck today because I didn't want to seem like I was trying too hard.

I follow Allan to the back of the gallery where there is a small room attached to the main space. Inside, floor-to-ceiling bookshelves are lined with art books. More art books than I could have ever have dreamed of in one space. The beautiful gallery girl sits behind one of the three sleek desks, typing on her computer. She ignores us as we walk past her.

Allan sits down at an adjacent desk. He pours us each a cup of coffee from the pot that's sitting there.

"Sit," he says, pointing to another desk chair that's positioned sort of awkwardly between the two desks.

"So," Allan says, looking at me across the desk. He pulls his cell phone out of his pocket and places it on the desk. He looks at me, and then immediately picks up his phone and flips it over so the screen is facedown. He's nervous. So am I.

"So, are you excited about the show?" I ask. My voice is about an octave higher than normal. I hate that the gallery girl is still sitting within earshot, even if she's pretending she can't hear us.

"I think so. We have a lot of work to do between now and Saturday," he says.

"That's cool," I say, for the millionth time.

"How's Johanna?" he asks.

"She's good," I say.

"Is she dancing at all anymore?" he says.

"No," I say.

"That's too bad. She was a really interesting dancer. Too intense for ballet," he says. Then he sinks back into his chair and wipes his hands over his face. "Why am I telling you about Johanna? You know her."

"No, it's okay, it's interesting," I say. "I like hearing you talk about her."

Allan looks at me, maybe surprised that I reassured him, and he smiles. He lets out a long, whistle of breath. It might be the first time he's seemed even a little relaxed since I got here.

The landline rings and the gallery girl answers promptly. "Kaplan and White . . . Hi, Elaine . . . I'll tell him . . . Okay."

She hangs up and turns to Allan. "Elaine is going to be here in five minutes and she's bringing the Shulmans."

Allan stands up. "Okay, then. Sadie, I have to get ready for these people who are coming by. I'll walk you out."

I sit for a moment, stunned that our visit is over so quickly. Blindly, I follow Allan away from the desk.

I pick up my backpack from the gallery floor and Allan walks me out.

"You've really grown up," he says, when we're outside. For the first time, we are safely out of earshot of the lurking gallery girl.

"Thank you?"

"I can't wrap my mind around how much you've changed since I saw you last summer," he says.

"You mean two summers ago," I say.

Allan shakes his head. "No. I saw you last summer in LA. I took you and your mom out to lunch. I picked you up at her friend's house in Hancock Park."

"Yeah, that was two years ago," I say, trying to keep my tone light. "That was the summer after ninth grade."

Allan's phone beeps and he reads a text. Then he looks back up at me.

"I'm sure I saw you last year," he says firmly.

"Oh, okay, maybe," I say, forcing a smile.

"Anyway. Listen, sorry today was so short. I know Marla

would like to see you. Can you meet us for lunch tomorrow?" he asks.

"Um, yeah," I say. "I have class, so it will have to be a late lunch. I'm taking advanced photography. I actually wanted to tell you about it."

Allan's phone beeps again and this time he types a text. When he's done, he looks back at me. "So, tomorrow? Late lunch. I'll e-mail you later when Marla tells me what her schedule is."

"Right. Okay. Great," I say with a smile, trying to show just the right amount of enthusiasm.

I'm trembling as I walk back toward the C train. My nerves unwind slowly as I get farther away from the gallery. *That was good*, I tell myself over and over. *That went well.*

That night, my mom drags her fabric samples out of the closet and places them on our couch. Whenever she has a little free time, my mom likes to daydream about reupholstering our couch. I kind of think she'll never do it, she just enjoys the project.

"I like the green one," she purrs, taking a sip of her tea.

"I like the red one," I say, playing along. I can't believe she doesn't know I saw Allan. I can't believe I'm really not going to tell her.

"You're right," she says, frowning. "The red. I want the red."

"You're crazy." I smile.

I wonder if she and Allan ever spent time like this—just puttering around their apartment, talking about nothing.

It's strange to have almost no memories of my parents being together. Imagining them interacting is like imagining how a celebrity couple might behave when no one is watching. If I didn't exist, I don't know if I'd even believe they were ever together.

Later, I climb into bed beside my mom. She has her ruby earrings on and gold bangles circling her wrists even now. My mom sleeps in jewelry; she wears it like tattoos.

I burrow into her side and she wraps her arm around my shoulders, pulling me closer.

"Why did you and Allan break up?" I ask.

"Why are you thinking of that right now?" she asks.

"I just am," I reply.

"You know why it ended," she says.

"Tell me again."

She sighs. "Fine. But the story hasn't changed. There's no secret about me and Allan: We were together, I got pregnant, and I was thrilled. I'd always wanted a baby and I didn't think I could have one. Getting pregnant was the best thing that ever happened to me. I didn't care that Allan and I were already kind of over. It didn't matter."

I've heard this a million times but it always feels like something is missing.

"Over how?" I ask. "Like not in love anymore?"

"You could say that," she says. "It's hard to explain."

"Did you fight a lot?"

"Constantly," she replies quickly. "And when we weren't arguing, we were just ignoring each other."

"So you ended it. And you and me moved out of his place."
I know the story. "But what about before? You must have
had some good times, or why were you even together?"

My mom pauses, and then when she speaks, her tone is
firm. "What is this really about?"

*Allan is here.*

"I think I might like someone," I say instead. "Like *like*
him."

Which is part of the truth. The whole truth is that it took
me forever to stop liking someone who rejected me over and
over again, and now I like someone who thinks I'm just a
friend. The truth is that my heart might be cursed.

"Well, I guess you could say what I liked about Allan was
that he was incredibly smart. Which is probably why you
are so smart, too. I've always had a lot of respect for smart
people," she says. "So, that was a good thing about us."

I stare at my mom's left hand, resting on top of the blanket, her fingers absently combing over a loose thread in the
fabric. My mom's skin is as young looking as someone her
age's skin can be. But still, it's starting to soften and wrinkle, like crushed silk.

Back in my room, I pull out the one photograph I have of my
mom and Allan together. My mom's friend took it before she
got pregnant with me. In it, Allan's hand is resting on my
mom's back and she is staring up at him. She isn't smiling
but she's looking at him like she adores him. I know she did.
She loved him. Why can't she just say that? Why can't she

just admit that they had something good and that she made a mistake by giving up on him so quickly?

I wish I could travel back in time to the moment this photo was taken and see them together that day. What did they talk about? Did they laugh? If my mother hadn't had me, would they still have drifted apart?

The longer I stare at the picture, the more frustrated I become. No matter how hard I look at it, I can't figure out what I want to know.

*Chapter 20*

The next day, I find Allan and Marla at a table in the back of the Japanese restaurant where we are meeting for lunch. They stand up to greet me.

"Sadie, you remember my partner, Marla, right?" Allan asks.

"Hi, Sadie," Marla says, looking even more mousy and unremarkable than I remember. She gives me a small, brittle hug. She feels like a pebble.

Marla must be in her mid-thirties because I know she's about twenty years younger than Allan. But Marla isn't a cliché younger woman. She's more old-ladyish than my mom.

They sit down and hold each other's hands on top of the table.

"It's sushi and small plates," Marla says.

"Okay, thanks," I say. *I know how to read, Marla.*

Allan studies the menu carefully and then looks up at her.

"I think I just want soup," he announces.

"Fine," she says.

Allan is dressed plain, same as yesterday, wearing a beige polo shirt and an odd, lightweight, neon green Windbreaker.

He has a strangely simple style. Nothing like the artists you see in movies with their black turtlenecks. Allan is dressed like a regular guy.

Marla has more of an intellectual look, with her makeup-free face, messy hair knotted on top of her head, and loose-fitting maroon blouse.

"Tell us about your summer, Sadie," Marla says. "Are you going to camp?"

I laugh, and then stop myself at the look on her face. "Sorry. It's just, I'm seventeen."

"I went to camp until I was nineteen," Marla replies calmly. "I was a counselor."

"Well, I never went to camp, not even when I was little," I say. Then I drag my gaze forcefully away from Marla's and look right at Allan. "I'm taking an advanced black-and-white photography class this summer."

"At your school?" Marla says.

I don't respond because I wasn't talking to her.

"How is IACA?" I ask Allan.

"Good," he says, taking a sip of tea.

"Do you teach the same classes every year?" I ask.

"Pretty much," he responds.

"Do you think IACA is a good school?" I ask. This would be the perfect time to tell Allan that I want to go to IACA for college, but I don't want to say it in front of Marla.

"Of course," he says. "Right, Marla?"

Marla nods.

"What are you learning in your photography class?" Marla asks. "I've taught a few undergrad photography classes over the years. Does your teacher talk about contemporary issues or is it more of a technical class?"

I wish it was Allan who asked, but I'm glad to have the chance to tell them about Benji.

"It's both," I say. "Benji's really into making us print good quality pictures. The only thing he gets mad about is when people have bad darkroom techniques. But he also talks a lot about what stuff means."

"I can't imagine teaching darkroom photography today," Allan says. "It's so outdated."

"Yeah, but that's part of what's cool about it," I say. "It feels ancient."

That makes Marla laugh, and, as if Marla's laughter gives Allan permission, he laughs, too.

"What are your assignments like?" Marla asks.

"They're different every week," I tell them. "We did portraits last week. And I think we're gonna do landscapes next week. Usually, we have to shoot over the weekend and we print during the week."

Marla's eyes glaze over but she forces a smile. "Great. Do you have any of your pictures with you?"

"Yeah," I say. I put my backpack on my lap and riffle through all the junk in there to try to find my photos. I place a few things on the table, two unopened rolls of film, my cell phone, the I LOVE NY souvenir postcard I've kept in there for years.

Allan picks up the postcard. "What is this?"

"Oh, nothing, just a random cheesy postcard." I blush. "I collect them."

Finally, I find the manila folder where I keep all the pictures I've taken and place it on the table in front of Allan.

But Allan is still holding the postcard, staring at it.

"So, these are just test prints, but you can see what I'm up to," I say, nudging the folder closer to him.

Allan ignores it. He says, "You have a landscape assignment coming up?"

I nod.

"You know what I would do if I were you?" He smirks. "I would just hand in this postcard."

Marla claps her hands together and laughs.

"Yes! That would be brilliant," Marla agrees.

"But, I didn't even take the picture," I say softly. "I don't even know who did . . . it's just a postcard."

"Don't worry about that. That's all part of the piece," Allan says.

He hands the postcard back to me and sinks back into his chair.

"I don't know if my teacher would be okay with it if I just handed in a postcard," I say.

"He'll love it. And if he doesn't, tell him artists are supposed to challenge ideas of authorship," Allan says. "It helps prevent the constant commodification of ideas."

"You think?" I ask.

Allan and Marla are glowing, awake with the energy of their creativity.

"I'm going to order a beer," Allan announces, looking right at Marla.

"You think you should drink?" she asks. "I thought you weren't feeling well."

"I'm fine. I think it's fine," he says. Then he turns to me. "Do you want a beer?"

"Um, okay?"

Marla crinkles her forehead disapprovingly. "She's seventeen."

"She's mature. Right, Sadie?" he says, and he gives me an almost conspiratorial wink.

I've never had a drink while it was still light out, and when I step outside after lunch, I feel fizzy and woozy. Allan offers to walk me home. He tells Marla he'll see her later.

Allan and Marla kiss quickly. She's not as homely as I first thought. When she was talking about art, she lit up. I get why Allan likes her. I guess I like her, too. And liking her feels a lot better than hating her.

Walking down the street with Allan, I get that feeling I haven't had since I was little and he lived here for that summer. That intoxicating "just me and my dad" feeling.

"Everyone complains about New York being so different now, but I love it," Allan muses as we walk past another fancy boutique. "Does Johanna like it?"

"Like what?" I ask.

"That New York has become this giant mall," he says, like it's common knowledge.

"I don't know," I say. "She works so hard."

Allan nods. "She was always very serious about her work, if that's what you mean."

"I think I'm like that, too," I say. "I'm serious about my work."

"You're in high school, it's different. Don't worry, you won't have to work so hard when you're older," he says.

Which confuses me because that's not really what I meant.

After that, we barely talk. I glance up at Allan, strolling down the street with his hands tucked into his pockets. No one would stop and notice him. A stranger walking past would never guess that he has met celebrities and billionaires and journalists and that his artwork has been shown in museums that tourists wait in line to visit.

When we're a few blocks from our apartment, I stop. I can't risk us running into my mom, so I say, "This is fine. I'll just say good-bye here."

"Is your mom home? I'd like to say hi," he says.

"She's teaching until late," I lie.

Allan nods, like he understands.

"Great seeing you, Sadie," he says. "Will I see you at my opening on Saturday?"

"Of course." I beam.

"Good," he says, and he pats my upper arm once more before leaving.

## Chapter 21

"**P**haedra wants to come to your dad's thing this weekend, too," Izzy announces before class on Friday morning. "That's okay, right?"

"Of course," I say, opening the classroom door. It occurs to me as I do it that this is the first day the door has ever been closed. Benji always leaves it wide open.

Izzy sees before I do. She clasps her hand to her chest and mutters, "OMG."

The photo lab has been transformed. All the chairs and desks are gone, and instead, there are ten four-by-five cameras on tripods, each tagged with a yellow Post-it with a name. I find the one that says my name and stare at it, hypnotized.

I'd seen a large-format camera once before, when one of the seniors returned it to the photo lab while I was working last year. But I'd never been this up close to one.

The camera is as big as a human head, and the long skinny tripod legs make it look like a spidery robot. I reach up and touch the giant mechanical lens gently, as if I'm stroking a sleeping monster who might wake up.

"I didn't know we were gonna get to use these," I murmur.

"Me neither," Izzy says.

"Don't get too excited," Alexis says, in her usual know-it-all tone. "I'm sure Benji won't let us take them home."

"Actually, you'll all be taking them home over the weekend."

We turn and see that Benji is standing at the back of the room. Maybe he's been there the whole time but we were too distracted by the cameras to notice.

"These cameras aren't just valuable," he says. "They are part of the history of photography. They connect us to the past."

Once everyone is in class, Benji explains how the camera works. The negative is four by five inches, the size of a postcard, so that you can capture more detail than with a regular 35mm camera. While he talks, I marvel at the camera. I love how black and silent it is, like a piece of a spaceship that has fallen right here into the classroom.

"You are going to use these cameras for your landscape project. You'll take ten pictures with it over the weekend," Benji says.

"Is it even really gonna make a difference if the negative is four by five inches or 35mm?" Sean asks when Benji's done lecturing. "It's not like we are going to print enormous pictures. So, what's the point?"

Benji smiles cryptically. "You'll see. This camera captures

so much detail. Everything becomes so clear. Clearer than reality in a way. More real than real. It crystallizes the world."

I touch the camera tenderly, wiping away a smudge of dust as Benji's words sink in.

I go home after class and the afternoon melts away as I move around the apartment taking pictures with the camera. I don't notice the minutes or hours sliding by. When my mom comes home at six, I'm setting up a still life in the living room. I stop long enough to show her the camera and try to explain what Benji told us. When I'm done, she doesn't say anything, just gives me a tight, long hug.

My mom reheats leftovers and I take a break from working just long enough to eat with her. Then, while she's doing dishes, I make her pose for me with her rubber gloves on so I can take a picture of her with the sink full of dishes behind her.

After dinner, we go up to the roof so that I can try and take a landscape.

I set up the camera for a long exposure, while my mom stretches her arms up to the sky and breathes in all that muggy summer air. The day has faded to dusk and the city lights glitter beneath the wide pale sky. If I can capture what I'm seeing, this will be the most beautiful photo ever.

To take a picture with the four by five, you have to cover yourself with a blanket to protect the film from light. So I throw the cover over myself and focus the camera, watching the image of the city appear on the screen, a tiny replica of the real world.

The craziest thing about the four by five is that when you look through the lens, the image appears upside down. I can't remember Benji's explanation for this. All I know is that right now the real world is blotted out entirely and I'm staring at an upside-down picture. And it feels right. Finally, the city lights can become the wild, messy stars they were always meant to be.

Later, I lie in bed and do the reading that Benji gave us as homework over the weekend.

My phone rings, interrupting my thoughts. I close the magazine and reach for it.

*Sam.* I sit bolt upright in bed.

"Hello?" I say, trying to sound not too excited.

"Hey, did I wake you?" he asks. I can hear noise in the background.

"No."

"So, I'm at this diner with some people," he says. "I think it's near where you said you live."

"What diner?" I ask.

"Warszawa. On Avenue A," he says.

I know Warszawa. A memory surfaces and I push it down.

"I know it," I say. "It's close."

"Want to come meet us?" he asks.

I wait a second before I answer so I don't sound too eager. "Sure. I'll see you soon."

After we hang up, I slip into my shoes, careful to be quiet so I don't wake my mom. She's a deep sleeper anyway. Sneaking out won't be hard.

# Chapter 22

I swore I'd never go back to the Warszawa Diner. That's where I was when I realized, I mean, really understood in my bones, that Noah was over me.

In the weeks after we had sex, Noah and I barely spoke. When I passed him in the hall at school, he'd given me low fives and smiles and a part of me thought he was flirting. He didn't ask me out, or add me on Facebook or anything, but he looked at me in a way that he never had before. And that gave me hope.

The Upper School Winter Concert was at the end of January. I normally wouldn't go to music department events, but I knew that Noah would be there because he played in three different bands and I wanted to see him outside of school.

I blow-dried my hair so it was shiny and neat and wore my favorite lace-up boots even though it hurt to walk for more than three blocks in them.

I sat in the back of the auditorium with a girl from my science class, Elizabeth, and watched Noah play.

Onstage, Noah never smiled. The spotlight did amazing things to his already amazing face, moving over his bones like liquid, so you could really see his cheekbones, his deep-set eyes, the dark hole of his mouth. I know the clarinet isn't considered a super-sexy instrument, but I couldn't even look at his hands on it without thinking about his hands on me. Every time his fingers moved or pumped the buttons, I wondered how he knew what to do. Everything about Noah was silent and instinctual.

The girl in the chair next to Noah was named April. She was in my French class and she always wore one of those big puffy winter jackets with a hood, and knotted her hair in a bun. I always thought of her as kind of plain, but onstage April looked beautiful. Her hair was down and the spotlights made it so shiny. Even her frumpy, long-sleeved black orchestra dress seemed somehow elegant on her when she performed. At one point between songs, Noah leaned in and said something to her and she smiled. Envy torched my heart.

After the concert, we walked in a big group to Warszawa. Everyone always went there after plays and things because they serve alcohol without carding.

It was a wet, cold night. The snowstorm the week before had melted and then froze and then melted and then froze and the result was that mountains of old snow, brittle as Styrofoam and as brown as coffee, were stuffed into all the gutters and pressed up against the walls of buildings. My toes froze and grew numb inside the thin leather of my boots, and I had to remind myself that the pain was worth it.

At the restaurant, we filed in and took over five of the big red pleather booths. I sat with Elizabeth. I wasn't in Noah's booth. He hadn't seen me. He didn't even know I'd come.

At one point, he got up to go to the bathroom. I went, too, timing it so I could run into him in the hallway.

When he came out of the bathroom, I pretended to not know he was coming.

"Oh, hey," I said, smiling.

"Oh, hey," he repeated. But it sounded totally different the way he said it.

"You were really good tonight," I said.

His eyes jumped to something over my head and then he looked back at me.

"Uh. Thanks," he said.

"So . . ." I said. "Which is your favorite song?"

"Hmm? My favorite what?" he asked.

"Your favorite song," I repeated. But the brightness was draining out of my voice as Noah's indifference landed harder and harder.

"I don't have one," Noah said, glancing behind me again.

I looked at his hands. Those clarinet hands. He had a Band-Aid on one of his fingers that I hadn't noticed when he was onstage.

"What happened to your finger?" I asked.

"Aw, nothing," Noah said, and then slid his hands into his pockets. "Hey, I gotta get back to my table."

"Oh, right, yeah," I stammered, trying to roll my eyes like *silly me.*

He patted me on the shoulder as he scooted past and said, "Be good, okay?"

*Be good?* I watched him walk back to his table across the restaurant. *We had sex!* I wanted to scream at his back. *You singled me out. You saw all of me. You reached inside me and held my heart; you felt it beat in your palm.*

He slid into a booth with some other kids in his grade and took a slug of a drink from a big glass. Laughed at something someone at his table said. He didn't care about me. I could see it with my own eyes. And there was nothing I could do to change that. His words played over and over in my head. *Be good. Be good.*

# *Chapter* 23

Twenty minutes later, I'm sliding into a booth at Warszawa next to Sam. He scoots down to make room for me, but the booth is tight and I can feel the side of his leg against the side of mine. I wonder if he can feel it, too.

"These are my friends, Allison and Greg," he says, introducing me to the people at the table. They aren't kids I could pigeonhole as being from one part of the city.

"We ate already, I'm sorry," says Allison. She has dyed blond hair and bad skin, and her eyes are the purest blue I've ever seen.

"It's fine," I say. There are swivels of grease and ketchup on the empty plates. "I'm not hungry; I ate earlier."

"We were starving," says Greg. "We just walked for two hours."

"It was beyond annoying," Allison adds. "We tried to get into this eighteen-and-up show and they carded, and they never card. So we ended up just walking around forever doing nothing. That's how we got so hungry."

I look at Sam. His chameleon green eyes have shifted

again to matching the mint green walls of the diner. It's the first time I've let myself look right at him since I got here.

"You were with them?" I ask.

"Yup," Sam says.

"Cool," I say stupidly.

Sam looks at me and a smile cracks on his face. He bangs my knee with his knee under the table. I'm not sure if it was on purpose or if he was just shifting his weight, but it makes me blush.

The boy, Greg, scoots out of the booth with a wad of cash to pay at the front. Allison sinks into the booth, closing her eyes.

"How was New Hampshire?" I ask Sam quietly.

"Okay," Sam says, his eyes doing that camera-lens thing where a real emotion flashes in them for a second. "I'll tell you about it later."

"Paid. Let's go," Greg announces.

Allison folds forward, resting her head on the table dramatically. The boy yanks her ponytail flirtatiously but she doesn't react.

Outside, on Avenue A, people are tumbling down the street in big groups. It's after midnight, but it's a warm, clear Friday night and people are out. Allison steps into the street and hails a taxi. Car headlights light up her white legs so she glows against the dark, dirty city. She and Greg climb in.

"Did you walk here?" Sam asks me.

"Yeah," I say. "I live like ten minutes from here."

"Which way?" Sam asks.

And then we're walking side by side.

Sam and I don't talk about the fact that he's walking me home. At each corner, I wait to see if he needs to start heading in another direction, but at each corner, he crosses with me.

I lead us the long way back because I want to stretch out our time together. In the low light, the street looks grainy and dim. Black water glistens in the gutters.

Sam tells me about his week in New Hampshire and I tell him about my week here, catching up like old friends. He tells me there were thunderstorms every day that he was home, and I tell him it only rained here once. Sam says he went swimming every afternoon, and I tell him that I spent every afternoon in the darkroom, besides the day I had lunch with Allan and Marla. We both can't believe the summer is already half over.

Before I'm ready, we're back on my block. My steps begin to slow down. There are still so many things I want to know about Sam and his trip. Did he see Amanda? Did he think about me?

I stop walking across the street from my apartment and stare up at my bedroom window. From this angle, even if the light were on, I could only see the ceiling. A strange, small unit of measure of me and my life.

"That's my apartment," I say, pointing to my window.

"Are you tired?" he asks.

"Not really," I say. "Are you?"

"No," he says.

"Do you . . . do you want to come in?" I ask, my heart racing as I say the words.

Sam looks up at my window, not answering me.

I panic as I realize I said the wrong thing. I rack my brain for ways to make it better. I could say "Just kidding" or "That's a stupid idea."

But then Sam says, "Sure."

Sam and I tiptoe past my mom's room and into my bedroom. I close the door behind us and turn on my desk lamp. The large format camera rests on its spidery tripod legs in the middle of my room. My bed is unmade and even my wall of postcards is looking sloppy because three of them fell off this week and I forgot to re-pin them. Now I'm seeing my room through Sam's eyes, and I'm embarrassed that it's such a mess.

I linger awkwardly by my desk. Was it a mistake to invite Sam in? Does Sam think I'm throwing myself at him? Or is this what *just friends* do?

"This is the camera you were telling me about?" Sam asks.

"Yeah, it's pretty amazing," I gush.

"How does it work?"

"Come here," I say, stepping toward the camera. "I'll show you."

I pick the lightproof blanket up off the floor and drape it over Sam's head and the camera, giggling at the site of him half covered in a blanket.

"Are you messing with me?" he asks, but his voice is muffled.

I laugh. "I promise, I'm not. Watch."

I open the lens and he gasps. I know what he's seeing: the world flipped upside down.

I lift up the edge of the blanket and peer underneath to check if it's in focus. I'm so close to him, I can feel heat coming off his body.

"I have to focus it," I say. "Look."

Then, Sam lets me step all the way in so we are both underneath the blanket. I'm standing between him and the camera so that the whole front of Sam's body is pressed against my back. I can feel his breath in my hair, his chest expanding and contracting. I try to focus on the camera, but my body is dissolving.

The image on the viewfinder shows my desk. All boring stuff, just my laptop, a half-drunk cup of tea, and a stack of handouts. But everything looks magical through the camera's lens.

"Why is it upside down?" Sam whispers. When he speaks, I can feel the air of his words like a breeze.

"It has to do with the mechanics inside," I explain. "The way that light is being reflected. Regular cameras have mirrors that make things look right side up. There's no mirror inside of this camera. So, that's it."

"Hmm," he says.

Sam reaches out and touches the viewfinder with his pointer finger. I can feel his arm over my shoulder. His face is practically in my hair. He places his left hand on the side of my hip, as if he's holding me steady, as if he can feel how much my body is melting. We are so close, if he wanted to, he could turn my whole body toward him and we'd be kissing.

But then he steps back and pulls the blanket off, and we are back in my bright bedroom. My face is burning. I wonder if he can see how he transformed my body from the inside out. I stare at my feet, afraid to meet his gaze.

"That camera is sweet," he says.

I look up at him. His cheeks are flushed, too.

"Yeah," I say.

He sits down on the edge of my bed. There are holes in his jeans and I can see the skin of his sharp knees behind the ripping white threads of denim.

"What do you think your mom would do if she came in and saw me in here?" he asks.

"Omigod," I say, laughing at the thought. I sink down onto the floor, leaning my back against the door. "I can't even imagine. Honestly, we've never even talked about whether or not I'm allowed to have a boy in my room or whatever. It just hasn't come up."

"My mom never let me be in my room with the door closed when Mandy used to come over," Sam says. "It was so stupid. She can't control what goes on."

I feel a pinch when he says her name but I try not to show it. What did they do, alone in a room together? I try to push the thought away but it rises up in my stomach.

"But you know, I guess my mom is extra paranoid since she got pregnant with me in high school, or whatever." Sam shrugs, oblivious to my jealousy.

"Do you miss her?" I ask.

"Who? My mom?" Sam blinks innocently.

"No," I say. "Mandy."

Sam frowns. "No. I mean, yeah, but as a friend."

"Did you see her when you were in New Hampshire?" I ask.

Sam cocks his head. He doesn't answer my question, just looks at me curiously, like he's assembling a puzzle. Then, he says, "Did you show your dad this camera? It kind of makes the one he gave you look small."

I laugh. "No. He hasn't been over here or anything. And we just got these today. So . . ."

"He's gonna be impressed, though," Sam says.

"I hope so," I say. I pull my knees to my chest and wrap my arms around them, holding myself tight.

"You're lucky. You know that, right?"

"Lucky how?" I ask.

"To have parents who you respect," he says simply.

It's late. It must be almost two a.m., but I don't want to ask Sam or check my phone because I'm worried if Sam realizes how late it is, he'll leave.

"Wanna see some pictures of Allan's work?" I ask.

Sam nods.

I crawl over to my desk and pull out the old *Artforum* magazine with Allan on the cover.

Sam slides off of the bed onto the floor and I scoot back over to him. We sit side by side, our backs against my bed, and I open the book so it's on both of our laps. Again, we are close enough to kiss. Again, the places where our bodies are touching, our elbows and our ankles, feel electric. All of our fumbling keeps bringing us closer and closer together but never quite close enough. Is he as aware of it as I am? Is it possible that this feeling could be one sided?

The more I get to know Sam, the more the things that I don't know about him, like how he kisses and what he looks like without his clothes on, grow heavier and more distracting. The closer I get to him, the closer I want to get.

Sam thumbs through the pages slowly. He isn't reading every word, but I watch his eyes scan the images and read the pieces of text that have been pulled from the article. There's a photo of Allan with the caption, "When I work, I'm reaching for things that are always present."

"This is impressive," Sam says. "But it's all over my head."

"It's not over your head," I say. "It's just the kind of writing that is supposed to make you feel that way."

I take the *Artforum*, and stretch across my floor to deposit it back in my drawer. Then, I turn and face Sam.

"I'm embarrassed," I say.

"About what?" he asks.

"That I made you look at Allan's article," I say.

"Why?" he asks.

"'Cause. I don't want to seem like I'm bragging," I say. "Or like I'm obsessed with my dad or something."

Sam half smiles. "I know it's not like that."

I scoot closer to Sam. He puts his arm around my shoulders and I tip my head onto his upper arm, letting him hold me. I shut my eyes, feeling his shoulders rise and fall as he breathes.

Then, I feel his fingers moving through my hair, so gently

at first I don't know if it's happening. Seconds, minutes, maybe hours pass, with my cheeks burning and my body beating like one giant heart. I don't know how long we sit there because the moment is elastic, expanding and contracting. A second isn't a second, it's an eternity. We're sinking lower onto the floor, until we're lying down, my head resting on Sam's hard chest, right at that bony place where his collarbone and shoulder meet. I close my eyes, feel him breathing beneath me, feeling his hands in my hair, the subtle smell of his skin, and the cotton of his shirt beneath my cheek.

I wake up when a garbage truck grunts loudly on the street outside my window. I open my eyes, disoriented. I'm lying on the floor on my side, and Sam is on the floor, too, also asleep, his knees a little bent. I rub my eyes. The light in my room is a dusky lavender. Outside my window, there is a rim of glowing orange light over the city. The sun is coming up. I panic as I reach for my phone. We might never have talked about it, but I know if my mom came in now and saw that a boy slept over that it would not be okay.

"Sam," I whisper.

He doesn't move.

I gently touch his arm and he stirs. When he opens his eyes, there's a blank moment before he remembers where he is, and then his eyes pop open.

"What time is it?"

"Maybe five? It's getting light out," I whisper.

He sits up. "Wow. Are we good? Did your mom come in?"

I shake my head *no*. His shoes are sitting on the floor next to him. When did he take them off?

"I don't remember falling asleep," I say, blinking.

"You passed out," he says. "I didn't want to wake you."

Sam grabs his shoes and gets up before I do. His cropped hair is crooked from the way he slept and his shirt looks wrinkled.

I stand up, and we're face-to-face, not touching.

"I should go before we get caught," he says.

Then he taps my calf with his sneaker, breaking the invisible wall between us.

"Yeah," I say. "You're right."

I open the door, check that the coast is clear, and give him a nod.

He walks past and then he stops and looks down at me. He's only a foot away from me now. If my mom opened her door, she would see us here.

"Sadie," he whispers. His green eyes see straight through me.

"Good luck at your dad's thing tonight," he says.

I swallow. Nod. "Thank you."

And then he's gone, out the door. I'm not tired now, though. I lie on my bed and watch the sky turning from lavender to white to pale blue as the day arrives. And then, just when it's so bright out that it looks like a normal morning, I fall asleep.

# Chapter 24

When I wake up again, my mom has gone to work. I roll out of bed and head to Willa's, stuffing a change of clothes in my backpack. We're going to spend the day at her apartment and then go to Allan's opening together.

On the subway ride, I know I should feel tired since I basically didn't sleep, but instead, I feel energized. My night with Sam is a good secret, something that gives me strength. I keep reliving all the ways we did and didn't touch. The only thought gnawing at the edge of my mind is why he didn't kiss me. If he liked me, wouldn't he have tried?

As soon as I walk into Willa's room, I sit down at her computer and open it up to Amanda's Facebook page.

Willa watches with her hands on her hips. "What are you doing?"

"Do you think this girl is pretty?" I demand.

Willa looks at the screen, and then at me.

"Who is this?" she asks suspiciously.

"Sam's ex-girlfriend," I reply.

Willa reaches out and snaps the computer closed.

"Okay, fine, I know, I'm being bad," I say. "I just wanted to know if you think she's prettier than me."

"Of course I don't," Willa says gently. "Obviously I'm gonna think you're prettier than some stranger."

"I don't mean it like *that*," I protest. "I mean, like objectively pretty."

Willa doesn't answer me. She turns, crosses to her bed, flops down on the mattress facedown, and screams a muffled scream into her pillow.

I can't help laughing. I climb up on the bed next to her and poke her pale arm with my pointer finger so it turns pink. Willa bruises the easiest of anyone I know.

"Please. Just tell me."

She rolls onto her back, her glasses are crooked on her face.

"I refuse to condone this crazy behavior," she says, staring straight up at the ceiling. "First of all, if she was his girlfriend, I think it's safe to say he thinks she's pretty. And guess what else? There are probably a lot of other things about her that he likes, too. Maybe things that matter to him even more than what she looks like."

"I know." I sigh. "I'm just curious about her because I'm curious about him. I think I like him for real. He came over last night, and we stayed up for hours, just talking and doing nothing."

Willa looks at me and her eyes grow enormous. "Wow! Really? He came over? What did you guys do?"

"*Nothing*," I say. "I can't explain it. We just talked and then, like, didn't talk. He's just really comfortable with himself. He's just easy to be around."

I picture Sam in my bedroom and my body turns hot at

the memory. I press the heels of my hands into my eyes. I don't know if I can stand not knowing what's going on between us.

Willa takes her glasses off and rubs the bridge of her nose. "I'm so tired from this week. I hate my science class. My teacher is a fascist."

"Why do you have to do this to yourself?" I ask. "You know you're going to get into Yale. You're a genius, plus you're a legacy. You'll be fine. "

"I don't want to go to Yale," Willa says. "Yale is just a party school for rich city kids."

I groan. "Now who's the one being crazy?"

"I'm not being crazy. Everyone knows it's true," Willa insists.

I slap her arm affectionately. "You don't honestly believe that."

Willa lets her eyes meet mine and all the laughter drains out of them. "Fine. I don't want to go to Yale because I don't want to go to college with my sister."

"Really? Why not?" I ask.

"I just know how it will be." Willa sighs. "I'll end up writing her papers for her, like I did in high school. Besides," she says softly, "if I go there, I'll be 'Danielle Davis-Spencer's little sister' for the rest of my life."

Willa and I are lying side by side and now I wrap my feet around her ankles.

"You'll never be Danielle's little sister to me," I say. "She'll always just be Willa Davis-Spencer's big sister."

Willa smiles. "Aww. Thanks, Boo."

Later, we are making pancakes, trashing Willa's kitchen, when Izzy texts me.

*Where and when r we meeting?*

"What does Izzy want to know?" Willa asks, glancing at my screen.

"She wants to know what our plan is for tonight," I say. "You know, for going to Allan's show."

Willa drops the spatula and pancake batter splatters in a ring around it on the floor. She crouches down quickly and picks it up. Then, she tosses it in the sink, grabs a paper towel, and starts wiping up the mess.

"I'm surprised you invited Izzy to your dad's opening," Willa says, rubbing too hard on the floor. "It seems, like, kind of personal."

"It's no big deal. They wanted to come," I say.

"They?" Willa repeats, still looking at the floor. Her tone is fake-natural. "You mean Phaedra is coming, too?"

The mess is totally cleaned up. So I say, "I think you got it all."

Willa stands up and starts doing dishes, her back is to me.

"Are you okay?" I ask, turning off the faucet.

Willa hovers over the sink, still not looking at me.

"Maybe I'll just skip tonight," she says softly.

I laugh. "Come on. You're kidding, right?"

She shakes her head no.

"What are you saying?" I ask, stunned.

She looks up at me. She has a smear of pancake batter on

her forehead. "It just doesn't seem like you need me there."

"What are you talking about?"

"You'll have Izzy and Phaedra there. I'm sure you guys will have fun."

"But it's my father's show," I protest. "You've never even met him. You were going to meet him."

Willa sighs, choosing her words in her irritating, measured, Willa way. "If having me meet your dad was so important to you, then why are Izzy and Phaedra coming?"

"'Cause they're my friends, too," I say, getting annoyed.

Willa rolls her eyes. "Come on. Those girls are not really your friends. You know that, right?"

Humiliation rises in my chest, like a wave swelling in the ocean before it crests.

"That's not true," I protest. "They are my friends."

Willa lets out an exasperated groan. "Ugh, you're driving me crazy. It's obvious they've decided that being into art is cool, so now they're trying to adopt you like you're a pet or something. It's all so fake and I don't know why you're pretending it's not."

Willa makes my friendship with Izzy and Phaedra sound small and pathetic. I feel like she always does this: she sucks all the fun out of my life and spits it back onto the floor.

"Whatever," I say. "You're just jealous that they want to be friends with me and not you."

"Jealous? I am not even the tiniest bit jealous," Willa says, rolling her eyes. "Those girls are gonna ditch you the second they realize you don't even know him."

She doesn't have to say who "*him*" is.

Dizzying hurt crashes on top of me, flooding my brain with blinding heat. "You don't know what you're talking about," I snap. I leave the kitchen, rushing down the hall to Willa's room. Hot tears streak my face. I'm crying. And it's the bad, embarrassing kind of tears that I can't make stop, like when you're crying in front of a teacher or on the street and everyone is trying not to stare.

I can hear Willa following behind me and I whip around so we are face-to-face.

She reaches out to touch me but I push her away.

"Don't," I manage through my sobs. "Don't pretend to be a good friend."

"I'm sorry if I sounded mean," she says. But she doesn't sound sorry at all.

"You're just bitter," I spit, "because Danielle is your sister and you're nobody."

Willa halts. "Excuse me?"

"You heard me," I say, with more certainty now. "You're jealous. You're jealous of Danielle because she's so much prettier than you. That's the real reason you don't want to go to Yale. And now you're jealous of me because I'm making new friends. You're just a bitter, jealous loser."

Willa's face goes white.

We stand in silence for a moment, and the horror of the mean things I've said settles on my heart like dust after a burst of wind.

Then, I'm on the street outside of Willa's. I slip into the narrow alley between her building and the building next door and clutch my backpack to my chest like a shield. Our fight exploded so fast. I wipe away tears and lean against the brick wall. My mind is zinging and bruised from all the insults Willa and I just threw at each other and I can't make sense of any of it.

I stare up at the seam of blue sky between the two buildings. I wish I could be up there, far away, somewhere deep in outer space. If I were looking down at the city right now, I wouldn't see me, or my problems, or any of the mean, crooked, shameful things in my heart.

# Chapter 25

Three hours later, I'm back at home getting ready for Allan's opening. I have to keep suppressing the memory of my fight with Willa, stomping down on it hard like crushing an empty soda can. I change into the outfit I've been planning to wear. It's a simple pale blue cotton dress that belonged to my mom. Then I put on dark red lipstick that flattens my mouth and looks dramatic with my pale skin. I think Izzy would approve, since it's the kind of anti-fashion fashion move that she likes.

*I don't need Willa*, I think, as I walk toward the West Village under a smudge of pale clouds. It's better this way. A new life is emerging out of my old one, and it might even be an upgrade.

Phaedra lives in the prettiest part of Manhattan. The cobblestone streets are lined with unbroken rows of manicured redbrick brownstones and each perfect, cozy home promises to contain one equally perfect family. The people in these houses seem out of reach of the rough, dirty grasp of the city, as if the whole neighborhood floats above the rest of us.

I text Izzy when I get there, and she comes down and lets me in.

"Phaedra used to live on the second floor with her little sister, but last year she moved to the top floor which is basically an attic," Izzy explains as we walk up the Bishops' winding marble staircase.

"Hey," Phaedra says when we reach her room. "I'm just about ready to go."

Phaedra's room is darker than the rest of the house. The floors are made of planks of worn, dark wood, and the walls are papered with patterned wallpaper that looks Indian or Thai.

"I'm excited about your dad's show," Phaedra says, slinging a super-soft-looking leather tote bag over her shoulder. "I love going to openings."

"Me too," Izzy says.

Izzy perches on the edge of Phaedra's king-size bed, texting. Phaedra's bed is unmade in a way that looks inviting and sexy, not sloppy like mine or Willa's. Instead of a closet, Phaedra has a free-standing antique wardrobe. I'm trying to memorize everything I see. These are the choices that Phaedra Bishop makes in her own space. And I'm surprised by how much I like Phaedra's style. Her taste is so rustic. It occurs to me that my mom would fall in love with this room, too.

"Oh, and by the way, my mom wants to meet you, Sadie. It turns out she used to know your dad or something," Phaedra says, checking out her reflection in the mirror. Then she turns to face us. "Ready?"

"Mom! Mo-om!" Phaedra calls as Izzy and I follow her down the stairs.

On the third floor, Phaedra knocks on a door and screams, "Mom, don't be naked, we are coming in!"

The master bedroom looks like a hotel room, all matching and bland.

"Stacey! Wonderful to meet you!" Phaedra's mom says, stepping out of her walk-in closet. She's wearing a black dress and high heels.

"It's Sadie," Phaedra corrects.

"Nice to meet you," I say.

"I'm Lucy," she says, clasping my hands in hers. She looks exactly like Phaedra, except older. The diamond studs in her ears are so big they sag a little. "We are huge fans of your father's work. We've met him a few times over the years because we are collectors. We know Michael Meyer well. I used to work in a gallery ages ago, long before you girls were born. It doesn't even exist anymore."

"Oh, wow," I say. "So you know him?"

"Listen, Stacey," she begins.

"Mom, I just told you, it's *Sadie*." Phaedra rolls her eyes.

"Right. Of course. Sadie," Lucy tries again. "I'm on the board of City Art Works and our annual fund-raiser gala is next week. It's a really wonderful organization and we raise a lot of money every year at the event. This year it's being held at the Park Avenue Armory."

I don't answer because I don't understand anything she just said. It takes me a minute to realize she's waiting for a response. So, I venture, "Oh, really?"

"We'd love it if you and your father would come," Lucy continues. "There are two seats available at one of the best tables."

"One of the best tables?" I repeat, trying to keep up.

"You have to come," Izzy jumps in. "It's gonna be amazing. And I'll be there. And Phaedra obviously. You'll know people."

"It's been sold out for months," Lucy continues. "But we'll make room for Allan Bell. It would be such an honor to have him. Ask him about it tonight."

"Ask him what?" I ask.

"Mom, no, we're not going to ask him at his opening," Phaedra whines. "That's embarrassing."

"Fine. I'll send you an e-mail and you can forward it along," she says to Phaedra. Then, her blue eyes flick back to mine and she smiles. "Lovely to meet you, Sadie. I'll be looking forward to seeing you next weekend."

We get off the subway at Eighth Avenue and walk west. The street is busier than when I came last week. People linger in front of the big metal doors of warehouse buildings, talking to one another softly, the smoke from their cigarettes unfurling extra slow in the muggy summer air. A woman in high heels walks straight down the middle of Twenty-Third Street, as if this whole block were her private driveway.

I catch my reflection in a window and I feel a jolt of pleasure. I feel powerful walking with Phaedra and Izzy. I wonder if maybe it's a good thing that Willa didn't come tonight, after all.

Now, I lock eyes with my reflection. I look like the kind of girl who never gets hurt. Not the pathetic kind I was earlier who cries when her friend flakes on plans. I never want to be that girl again.

The gallery looks different than it did the other day. All the boxes have been put away and the lighting is brighter and more direct. Allan's photographs hang in small black frames on the wall.

Allan's photos are just pictures of computer printouts full of text. You can see the texture of the crinkled page and the three-hole punches along the left edge. The text looks like words but up close it's just scrambled letters—nonsense.

We're nearing the back of the gallery when I see Allan. He's sipping wine from a plastic cup and wearing the same boring clothes I've seen him in both days, a Windbreaker and jeans.

He sees me and waves, beckoning us toward him.

"It looks amazing in here," I tell him.

"Thank you," he says. "Where's your mom?"

"She's at home," I say, confused.

"Oh. Did you show her the e-mail? I was hoping she would come," he says.

"I don't remember," I lie. "But, I want you to meet my

friends." I'm careful not to address him as Allan in front of them. "Phaedra and Izzy, this is my father."

"Phaedra," Allan says approvingly. "Interesting name. Daughter of Minos."

"That's 'right." Phaedra beams.

"Phaedra's mom thinks she might know you," I say. "Lucy Bishop?"

Allan thinks. "Sounds familiar. Is she an artist?"

"No, she's crazy, you'll never remember her," Phaedra says. "She worked for Michael Meyer in the nineties."

"Oh, right. I know those people pretty well. Lucy . . . Lucy . . ." he says. Then he scans the room behind us. "Have you seen Marla?"

"No," I say.

"She wanted to say hi to you," he tells me. "I thought she was just right there . . ."

"I'm Jen," a blond girl who has been hovering just behind Allan interjects. "I was a student of Allan's at IACA. How fantastic to have Allan Bell as your father. What's that like?"

I look at Allan, unsure what to say, and he looks back at me blankly.

"Tell her," he says.

I stare at him. What am I supposed to say? The only word that pops into my mind is *nothing*. That's what it's like having him as a dad.

"It's cool," I say dumbly.

"You girls are all so chic," Jen continues, blathering on as if any of us want to talk to her. "You're in high school? I was so not as stylish as you guys when I was in high school."

A hand on my shoulder gently pushes me aside, and a tall, bony-faced man steps in and gives Allan a hug.

Allan turns to me, his eyes not focusing on mine as he says, "Great to see you, Sadie. Don't leave without saying good-bye."

*Don't leave without saying good-bye?* I've been dismissed, and it feels like a slap.

I walk through the crowd, my face burning with shame. I can't believe how much time I spent looking forward to tonight. Choosing the right outfit and planning exactly what time we'd arrive. And none of it mattered anyway because Allan barely looked at me. His eyes skimmed across my face like a stone skipping on water.

I'm pushing through the crowd when Izzy grabs my hand and pulls me to a stop. "Omigosh, Sadie, Look who's here!"

"Who?" I ask.

"Benji!" she squeals.

Benji steps forward out of the crowd, a beer in his hand. He gives me a warm, crooked-tooth smile.

"It's so great running into you girls here," he says. "I love seeing students out and about. Especially doing artistic 'horizon-rising' things."

"Yeah," I agree vaguely.

"Sadie, can I ask you . . ." Benji smiles shyly. "Are you related to the artist? Bell and Bell?"

My eyes snap up to meet Benji's.

"Um, yeah," I say, hoping he won't ask me to introduce them. "He's my father."

"Wow," Benji says. "Interesting."

"You didn't know that until just now?" Izzy asks Benji.

"Well, I had wondered," he says. "I wasn't sure. I thought Allan Bell lived in LA, so . . ."

"Yeah . . ." I say. "I need to get some fresh air."

"Okay, take care," Benji calls as I walk away.

Outside, I lean against the exterior wall of the gallery.

A man and a woman with matching shaved heads and minimal outfits stroll past me into the gallery holding hands. Each person I see looks more fashionable than the last. Earlier, that made me excited. But now I can see the way I look to the people here: I look like a nobody. I must have seemed liked a nobody to Allan, too.

"There you are. I thought for a second you'd left," Izzy says. She's talking to me, but her eyes are drifting around behind me, people-watching as newcomers arrive. "This show is so amazing."

Phaedra arrives beside Izzy. She doesn't stare at people as they come in like Izzy does. Instead, everyone who comes in stares at her. I watch her for a second and I almost can see her enjoying the attention.

Izzy pulls out her phone and takes a selfie, angling the camera so that the gallery is in the picture behind her.

Suddenly, I wish Willa were here instead of these two. But then our fight spins through my mind, the dial landing on the mean things I said to her, and my stomach seizes with guilt.

"Are you okay?" Phaedra asks me, sensing the shift.

"Yeah." I swallow. "I just . . . I was supposed to call my mom. I think she's waiting for me."

Even though it's a lie, as soon as I've said it, it feels true. And thinking about my mom widens the toxic pit of anxiety that's growing in my chest. I lied to her about coming here tonight, and for what? So that I could get in a fight with Willa? So that Allan could blow me off? So that I could linger around the gallery like a pathetic hanger-on? I miss her so much it aches. Now, I'm terrified I'm going to cry for the second time today.

"I have to get home," I blurt.

"Already?" Izzy asks, looking perplexed.

"I promised my mom I'd get home early." I try to smile. "I'm just gonna walk to the subway. You guys should totally stay, though."

Izzy shrugs and looks at Phaedra. "What do you want to do?"

"I could stay a little longer," Phaedra says casually.

On the walk home, the sky is clotted with clouds, reflecting the orange and yellow lights of the city back onto itself. Rain is coming, if not tonight, then tomorrow.

Today feels like it was ten days combined into one. I can't believe that it was only last night that Sam stayed over. All day, as the hours slid by, I could feel the memory slipping steadily away from me. Sam never called or texted to see how I was. What if it didn't mean anything to him?

When I get home, my mom is sitting on the couch watching TV and eating frozen yogurt. She seems normal, which is weird for her.

"How was your night?" she asks. She's wearing glasses instead of her contacts, which she almost never does and they make her look older than usual.

"Okay," I say.

"Did you do something special?" she asks. "You look nice."

I should tell her the truth. I should tell her I saw Allan earlier in the week and that he invited me to his opening. But then I'd have to tell her how he treated me, and the fight with Willa, and the pain and humiliation is too fresh to relive.

"I went over to this girl Phaedra's," I say. And then I quickly change the subject, adding, "Is there more froyo?"

She blinks. And then she smiles.

"Yup," she says. "In there."

In the freezer, I find the frozen yogurt. She got my favorite kind: vanilla with rainbow sprinkles and cookie dough.

I sit down next to her. "What are you watching?"

"Some detective show." She sighs.

"Can I watch with you?" I ask.

"Of course," she says, and then adds with a laugh, "I'm not following any of it. Maybe you can explain it to me."

My mom presses play and I've just sunken into a comfortable position on the couch beside her when my phone vibrates. I snatch it off the coffee table and read the screen. My insides somersault in a tumble of relief and joy when I see that it's a text from Sam.

How was tonight?

I write back: Okay not great. My mom is willfully ignoring the fact that I'm texting, but her curiosity is an electric current coming off of her skin.

My phone pulses again. oh no. are you ok? I write, I'm fine. It wasn't bad. My dad was just busy. And I got into a fight with my best friend. But am good. Happy. Had a good night. Shouldn't complain. And then just to make it extra clear, I pile in some emoticons. I put in two smiley faces with hearts for eyes and a starry night sky.

After a minute, he writes, That bad? That makes me laugh out loud.

My mom pauses the TV show and looks at me.

"Who is that, honey?" she asks. Even my mother isn't disciplined enough to not want to know.

"Nobody," I say. "Just my friend."

"Well, are you gonna play on your phone all night or are we going to watch this show together?" she asks.

"We're gonna watch, I promise," I say, and I can feel myself smiling and blushing, a mix of excitement and shame. "I just have to write back really quickly."

I have so much to say to Sam, but I have to keep it short.

I write back: I know. Gotta go tho. Ttyl. And he writes back: K. Last night was fun btw.

"Okay, I'm done, I'm ready to watch, I'm sorry," I announce. I feel better than I've felt all day.

But my mom doesn't push play yet. Instead, she looks at me really hard. Then, she reaches out and pushes my hair back off of my forehead. She lets her hand linger on my head and scans my face for something.

"What?" I ask.

"You look really beautiful," she says.

For the second time tonight, I contemplate telling her

everything. But then she turns away and pushes play and the TV bursts into action. My phone is next to me and I gently run my fingers over the screen, staring at Sam's words again. He said last night was fun. I pick up my phone and squeeze it tight, feeling it grow hot in my hand.

# Chapter 26

Returning the camera to Benji on Monday sucks. As I develop the pictures from the weekend, I promise myself that someday I'm going to have my own large-format camera. Maybe, I'll even have my own darkroom. A darkroom would be a really fun place to make out with Sam. I push the thought away, but it only comes back stronger.

I rock the tub of developer and watch my picture emerge, the image rising out of the white paper. It's funny, with all the technological advancements in the world, that I still think this simple, old-fashioned one is the most amazing.

Ever since he texted me on Saturday night, all I've been able to think about is Sam. Sam in my bedroom. Sam on the sidewalk. Imaginary Sam in my imaginary darkroom in my imaginary house, pressing me up against the wall. Sam coming up behind me where I'm standing right now and wrapping his arms around my stomach.

Someone pokes my side, interrupting my fantasies and making me jerk so that developer splashes onto my jeans.

I look up and see Izzy, smiling mischievously.

"What's up?" I ask her, trying not to feel annoyed.

"Want to come with me to Phaedra's after class?" she asks. "We had so much fun at your dad's thing."

This is the first invitation I've gotten from Izzy that is a one hundred percent normal hang out. There's no special occasion, just friends spending time with friends.

"Okay," I say, feeling better about my jeans.


Phaedra opens the door to her house wearing cutoff shorts so tiny the white lining of the pockets hang out beneath the fringe, and an old T-shirt with the collar ripped out.

We follow her upstairs and she collapses onto her bed, starfish-style.

"I'm a waste of space today," Phaedra says, staring up at the ceiling. "All I've done is eat pizza and watch TV."

Even acting like a slob, Phaedra seems like a princess, with her clean nails and shaved legs.

"What did you do last night?" Izzy asks.

"I went on a walk with Justin," she replies. "We had to talk."

"Did you finally dump him?" Izzy asks.

"You broke up with him?" I ask. "I didn't even know you were together."

"Oh, believe me, you can totally dump people who you aren't together with," Izzy says. "Phaedra does it all the time."

Phaedra sighs. "I feel really bad. He was so sweet."

"So, what happened?" I venture.

"I just wasn't into him in the way that I want to be into someone," she says. "I was, like, I don't know . . . I know this sounds awful, but I was bored."

"Phaedra has this problem where she gets every guy she has ever liked and then she gets bored with them," Izzy explains.

"All I want is someone to challenge me, you know?" Phaedra asks, looking earnestly wounded. "Do you know what I mean?"

I nod, even though I'm not sure I do.

Then, abruptly, Phaedra props herself up onto her elbows and says, "Sadie. My mom is serious about you and your dad coming to the gala on Saturday. Did you ask him?"

"I haven't yet," I say.

"Did you get the invite? I thought I sent it to you," Phaedra says.

"Um, yeah, I think so," I say. The truth is, I saw the e-mail yesterday but I wasn't sure yet how or when to ask Allan.

"Check," Izzy says.

Izzy and Phaedra watch expectantly as I scroll through my e-mails on my phone.

"I got it," I say.

"Forward it to him," Phaedra says. "My mom is so excited for him to come."

Usually, I'm very deliberate about writing to Allan. I time it so that I hadn't written to him too recently, and I craft my sentences to create the right tone, but Phaedra and Izzy are waiting so I have no choice but to scribble something quick. I forward the e-mail and click send.

"Done," I say, trying to smile.

"Good. It's gonna be so fun," Izzy says. "There are always lots of people there from school. Do you remember Noah

Bearman who graduated last year? He's so hot. He's always at these things because he and Phaedra are family friends."

"I know Noah," I say.

"Yeah, duh, everyone knows Noah," Izzy snorts.

"We . . . hooked up," I say. "In tenth grade."

Phaedra was typing something into her phone, but now she stops, sits upright, and stares at me. "Are you serious?"

I nod.

"You and Noah Bearman?" Izzy repeats. "Really?"

"Really."

"He is so beautiful. You are so lucky," Phaedra says softly.

The fact that Phaedra Bishop thinks *I'm* lucky makes the world swing momentarily upside down.

"What happened? What's the story?" Izzy demands. She pats the bed next to her commandingly. "Sit down and start talking, girl."

"There's not that much to tell," I say. "It was at that big New Year's party in tenth grade. Did you guys go to that?"

"Hooking up at a party is different than actually hooking up," Izzy says. "Was it like a dare or something?"

"No, actually," I say, feeling a little insulted that it's so hard for Izzy to believe. "We were alone. We talked for a while and then yeah . . . it was definitely . . . real."

"You slut!" Izzy laughs. It's supposed to sound funny and affectionate but it stings.

Phaedra is staring at me.

"How far did you go?" Izzy asks.

"We went all the way," I say. And then, looking at their wide eyes, I can't help giggling. It's surreal to have Izzy and Phaedra staring at me with so much unchecked envy.

"Wow. No offense, but I thought you were a virgin," Izzy says. "I just assumed."

I shake my head no. "Are you guys?"

Phaedra shakes her head *no*. She doesn't take her eyes off of mine.

"I technically am," Izzy scoffs. "But I've done everything but. So I'm practically not a virgin."

I look at Izzy. It's funny, I've always assumed Izzy was more grown up and experienced than me in every way. It's strange to realize that there are things that I've been through that she never has.

"Sex is different from everything else," Phaedra says. "Right, Sadie?"

I don't have a basis for comparison but Phaedra seems so certain. So I say, "Sex is different."

I look at Phaedra and I think I see something burn in her usually placid blue eyes. Maybe some guy made Phaedra feel the way Noah made me feel: like I was the center of the world one second, and then the next second, that I didn't exist. Could someone make Phaedra Bishop feel like a nobody? It seems impossible because she's the girl who has everything. But for some reason, looking at her now, I feel certain that somebody did.

"Anyway, enough Noah," Izzy interjects, scooting off the bed. "Didn't you say your mom had a bag of clothes we could go through?"

"There." Phaedra points to a bulging black trash bag in the corner.

"I think I should go home. My mom is getting home early tonight so we were going to have dinner together," I say.

"Oh, come on, just stay," Phaedra pleads with a smile.

"You are going to freak out when you see these clothes," Izzy says. "When Lucy Bishop cleans out her closet . . . I mean, this is serious business. She's going to donate this stuff to charity, but we get first dibs."

"That's really tempting—" I start to say.

"I'm going to order us sushi for dinner. This might take a while," Phaedra says, reaching for her cell phone. "Sadie, are you sleeping over?"

All I want to do is go home and eat leftovers and watch TV with my mom. I want to help her choose fabric samples and listen to her getting-ready-for-bed sounds while I read.

"You have to stay," Izzy says. "We can go to this amazing coffee place before class tomorrow."

This is the invitation I've been waiting for. Once Izzy and Phaedra and I become real friends, I'll be able to turn down plans with them. But until then, my position is precarious. I have to be sure to play my cards right until I'm officially in the group.

When it's time for bed, Phaedra walks me downstairs to get me an extra toothbrush and towels in case I want to shower.

"Thanks," I say, taking the brand-new toothbrush. "This is perfect."

Phaedra smiles and nods, lingering. Her hair is pulled into a ponytail and she's already washed off her makeup and put in the retainer she sleeps in. Standing under the fluorescent lamp, she seems alarmingly young. It's funny how easy it is to put people on pedestals. Up close, everyone is kind of the same.

"I'm really glad I'm getting to know you," Phaedra says, lisping a little because of her retainer.

"Me too," I say.

"Good," she says. "And I just wanted to say I think it's really awesome how you don't try and get attention for all this stuff, like who your dad is and who you hooked up with and everything. I like that you want people to like you for who you are."

"Oh, thanks," I say, but I wonder if that's true.

"I'm like that, too," she says. "I feel like we're kind of similar."

I'm stunned. "Oh, wow! Thank you." It feels so good to get her approval that I only feel a little bit guilty about the fact that Izzy wasn't included in the moment, too.

Phaedra clicks her retainer in and out and in and out, fidgeting for a minute. Then she says, "You need anything else?"

I shake my head no, and she smiles like a little kid.

Back in Phaedra's room, I sleep on the couch while she and Izzy sleep together in her bed. I haven't heard from Willa since our fight. What would she think if she could see me now?

I check my e-mail before I fall asleep and I see that Allan responded.

"S. Thank you for coming to the opening. I'm going back

to LA soon and would love to see you again. How about lunch, just you and me, on Saturday?"

I write back quickly, "Yes to lunch. Exciting. Also, did you get my e-mail about my friend's mom's art gala? We can go to that afterward." After I click send, I place my phone on the dark floor.

Streetlights from outside wash in through the giant trapezoidal window and cast a geometric pattern on the dark wood attic ceiling.

It feels empowering to be getting so close to Allan that not every e-mail has to be a formal letter. Soon, I think, we are going to be as close as normal fathers and daughters. Who knows. Maybe I'll turn into one of those girls who makes fun of her dad for being a dork. I always knew it wasn't too late for us, and it's turning out I was right.

## Chapter 27

The next day is our four-by-five landscape critique. Izzy and I walk to class together from Phaedra's house. Even at nine a.m. it's so hot I'm sweating.

I tell Izzy about Allan's idea for my landscape project as we suck down our iced coffees.

"That's rad," she says. "Just a postcard? That's so badass."

"I don't know." I sigh. "Benji might not be into it."

"Who cares? You should do what your dad suggested," Izzy says. "Seriously, if you could take art advice from Benji Whateverthefuck or Allan Bell, I think you know who to listen to."

"What if Benji thinks I'm just trying to get out of doing the assignment, though?" I ask.

"No way. Benji loves you," she says.

While Benji critiques other people's pictures, I debate what I'm going to do. The landscape photograph I took with the four-by-five from the roof the other night turned out beautiful: sparkling and detailed. I know Benji would admire the range of grays. But what about Allan's suggestion?

Benji calls my name when it's my turn, and Izzy gives me a thumbs-up.

"Be strong," she whispers.

I nod and swallow. I walk up toward the front of the classroom, gripping my postcard in my trembling hand. I hold my breath as I pin it up and return to my seat, waiting to see what Benji will say.

An uncomfortable silence rolls through the room.

"Are you just handing in a postcard?" Cody winces. "That's so weird. You didn't even take it. That doesn't count."

"Who says that it doesn't counts?" Izzy asks. "If she found it, that means it's her artwork."

Benji looks at me. Then he carefully walks up to the corkboard. He plucks the thumbtack out of the wall and picks up the postcard. I watch as he slowly walks over to my desk and places it on my desk in front of me.

"I can't accept this," he says. "You didn't do the assignment."

"It is technically a photograph of the city, though," I say, but my voice wavers. I can't remember any of the things Allan said that made this seem smart.

"See me after class," is all Benji says. And then walks back to the front of the room. I can feel everyone's eyes on me, radiating fear.

"I'll wait for you outside," Izzy whispers to me, as everyone's packing up. "Remember, Benji is an idiot."

Benji waits until the room is empty and then he sits down at the desk next to mine.

"What happened?" he asks. "You didn't have time to take your own pictures?"

"I took my own pictures!" I exclaim. "They came out well. But I wanted to show the postcard because I thought, I don't know . . . I thought it would be interesting."

Benji frowns. "Sadie. It was incredibly disrespectful to the whole class to hand in a postcard in the middle of a critique."

"Why?" I ask.

"Because everyone worked really hard to get the assignment done," he says. "It's a—pardon my French—kind of a *fuck you* to the whole class."

It stings to hear Benji curse and I suddenly feel really bad.

"I'm disappointed," he says. "I'm not going to lie to you. You're too smart for that."

"But, that's not how I meant it," I object. "I love the class. I just, I collect postcards. I love postcards. And then my dad suggested that it would be interesting to hand in a postcard. And he's an artist. I mean, you know that. You were at his opening . . ."

Benji leans back in his chair, contemplatively. Then he says, "Your father is a really important artist."

"I know," I say.

Benji's face doesn't reveal what he's thinking. He says, "He lectured at Yale when I was in graduate school there. The auditorium was packed."

"That's good, I guess," I say, unsure what Benji is getting at.

"His work changed the way people think about photography. And sculpture," Benji continues, as if he's reading a Wikipedia page.

"I know," I say, squirming a little. "He's cool."

Benji doesn't smile. "He is cool."

The way Benji says the word "cool" sounds like it means something different than it usually means.

"Did you like his show last weekend? The new work?" he asks.

"Yes," I reply, although, I hadn't really looked at his work or thought about it for very long.

Benji looks at me. He tilts his head so that his swatch of hair shifts to the other side the way it does when he's thinking. Then he abruptly stands up.

"Give me your landscape prints," he says.

I take out my prints and hand them to Benji.

He looks at the picture I took from the rooftop on Friday.

"Look at that bird," he says. "Wow. You got so lucky. That's amazing."

"I know! I felt so lucky!" I gush, smiling for the first time all day. "I didn't even realize that bird was there when I took the picture. I didn't see it until I printed it. That's my favorite thing about the picture, how the bird on that billboard and the real bird are kind of looking at each other."

"You did a nice job with your light settings here. It's finally not too dark," he says, his eyes fixed on the picture.

"Benji?" I say.

Benji's eyes slowly lift off the photograph until they're meeting mine. He waits for me to continue.

"I'm sorry about the postcard," I say. "I didn't mean to be disrespectful."

He is stone-faced for a minute longer and then he nods. "You did the work. So I'll accept this print. But don't pull another move like that. I'm not kidding. Consider this a warning."

I nod.

"Is that clear?" he asks.

"Yes," I say, nodding so emphatically I'm getting whiplash. "Totally."


"I told you Benji was superconservative," Izzy says after I tell her what Benji said. "Don't listen to him."

We're standing on the cement sidewalk and the clouds are a matching gray. It's the kind of day that's hot but sunless. Everything is bathed in a milky light, so bright that my body doesn't even cast a shadow on the ground.

"You think?" I say. "The whole thing is confusing."

"He's probably just jealous that you're Allan Bell's daughter and he's nobody," she says.

"Right," I say.

"So. Anyway. What are you going to wear to Phaedra's this weekend?" Izzy asks.

"I don't know," I say, not listening.

"Well, let me know if you want to borrow something," Izzy says. "It's a big deal. People pay a thousand dollars a ticket to go."

And then Izzy leaves, heading toward the subway, and I know I'm supposed to be excited about a party with Phaedra and Izzy and Allan but something dirty and ashamed swirls around my heart. I can't put my finger on what it is, but I can feel it there, swinging around heavily, tugging like a fish that's been caught on the end of a line.

# *Chapter 28*

Sam and I make a plan for Friday. We plan it over text messages, because now, apparently, Sam and I are friends who text. I'm going to meet him near his apartment and we are going to walk to Randall's Island because he says I need to see it. He told me it's bad how Manhattan kids never leave Manhattan and I need to explore more. I told him it's bad how kids from New Hampshire think they know everything about city kids just because they've lived here for a year.

I meet him on the corner of 103rd and Lexington.

"You ready for this?" he asks.

"Ready as I'll ever be," I reply.

We walk to the eastern edge of Manhattan, where the island ends and the rushing East River and FDR highway tear across the landscape.

Sam points to a small footbridge that arcs over the river. It's bright white and delicate, almost fragile-looking, like lace.

Sam drags his fingers along the fence while we walk across the river, making a tinkling sound on the metal. Below us, the water runs shiny and dark. The cars on the FDR whisk by at regular intervals.

Sam's shadow on the white is a blue puddle under his feet.

"I got an e-mail from my mom's ex-boyfriend this morning," he says. "It was so random."

"What did it say?" I ask.

"Just, like, whatsup."

I wait for him to continue. When he doesn't, I say, "Is that a good thing?"

"I guess," he says. "He was basically my stepdad. He lived with us from when I was five to when I was thirteen. It's kind of messed up that we don't have a relationship anymore."

"Where does he live?" I ask.

"The town over from ours," Sam says. "Not far. He's a math professor at a community college there. It's pretty funny. He doesn't seem like a math person. He's got tons of tattoos and he's in a punk band and stuff."

"Oh really?" I say. "He sounds awesome."

"He is," Sam says. "He's the only adult I actually respect back home. Too bad I was such a little shit to him at the end."

"Why don't you tell him that?" I ask.

"Tell him what?" he asks.

"What you just told me," I say. "That you're sorry you were such a little shit and that he's the only adult you respect."

Sam looks at me and then without prompting, he springs across the bridge and grabs onto the chain-link fence, his feet dangling momentarily beneath him, one of his dirty sneakers pressing against the metal handrail. I look at him through my camera's viewfinder and take a picture. And then he pushes himself off and resumes walking.

"You're good at not talking about things you don't want to talk about," I say when he's back at my side.

"See. We're both good at things." Sam smiles. "You're good at photography and I'm good at not talking about things. And you thought I didn't have any skills."

I laugh. "But for real, don't you like anything? Don't you ever think about where you want to go to college? Or what you want to be when you grow up?"

"When I grow up?" he repeats. "What does that even mean?"

"You know what it means," I reply.

"Maybe," Sam says.

I look up at Sam. His hair has grown a little in the few weeks since I met him. It seems funny now that when I first saw him, I didn't think he was especially hot. I mean, I liked his green eyes and his cute ski-jump nose, but he's not like Noah with everything all styled and perfect. But now, the more I'm around him, the more handsome I think he is. Like a camera coming into focus on something you didn't see before.

"Why are you looking at me like that?" Sam asks.

"I have to confess something," I blurt. "I found Mandy on Facebook."

He stops and stares at me.

He blinks. And then says, "What? How?"

"Are you mad?" I ask.

"No, not at all. But how? You don't even know her last name," he says.

"I'm a pro. Trust me," I say. "Amanda Muller, right?"

"Wow. I'm impressed," he says.

"She's pretty," I say tentatively.

Sam elbows my side. "What's with you and pretty? You're always pointing out that things are pretty."

"No I'm not," I protest.

"Yes you are," he says.

"I'm a visual person," I say. "Besides. Don't you think she's pretty?"

"I mean, yeah, of course I do," he says. "She's beautiful."

The word choice surprises me and it makes something turn over inside of me.

"What about you? Who was this guy who didn't want to be your boyfriend?" Sam asks.

"Noah Bearman," I say. "He went to my school but he graduated last year. Do you know him? He's around."

Sam shakes his head no. "What happened with you two?"

"It was nothing. I mean, it was something. We hooked up at a party. And it wouldn't have been a big deal but it was like ..." I stop walking. I don't know if I can finish my sentence.

"Like what?" he asks.

"Like. My first. My first everything," I say.

Understanding spreads through Sam's eyes. "Oh. *Oh*."

"Yeah," I say. "And he was just really popular, and he was about to leave for college at the end of the year so he probably didn't want to be in a relationship. So it never happened again."

Sam looks away from me, shakes his head. "Fuck that. What a jerk."

"He's not that bad," I say meekly. And then I ask, "Did you and Amanda . . . ?"

He looks at me crookedly. "Did we what?"

I look at him, like *you know what.*

"Yeah," he says.

"So you were each others' firsts?" I ask.

He smiles a little sadly. "No. Actually. Neither of us."

"What? How old were you when you . . . ?" I ask.

"Fourteen," he says. When I glance up at him that solemn expression has returned to his face. The one that ends conversations.

After a few minutes, we reach Randall's Island. It's sleepy and quiet. We walk down a dirt path, trees and green lawns spreading around us. Trees canopy overhead and small diamonds of light and shadow swarm the world.

A mosquito buzzes in front of my face and I swat at it lamely.

"Yuck," I say, wincing.

"What?" Sam glances at me.

"Just a gross bug," I say.

"It won't hurt you," he says.

I roll my eyes, "Oh what, so now I'm a prissy city girl?"

"What did I say?" he laughs, surprised.

"I know what you're thinking," I say. "And you know what? I think this whole hike is pretty rugged of me."

"I didn't say anything," he says.

And then he pauses, turns to me, and flicks my arm with his thumb and forefinger.

"What?" I ask.

"Hike," he says. "Pshh."

He tries not to smile, but he can't help it.

We arrive at a patch of matted grass on the bank of the East River and Sam sits down and wraps his arms around his knees. I sit down carefully next to him.

We have an unobstructed view of East Harlem. The red-brick projects we were standing in front of a few minutes ago stare back at us, shrunk down to toy size by the distance.

There are a few other people, families sitting nearby with picnic blankets and sandwiches and sodas. I finished my roll of film on the bridge, so now we have nothing to do besides just sit here. A breeze passes over us and then the air grows still again. Across the river, Manhattan is silent.

A few summers ago, my mom and I went to her friend's house in Connecticut for the weekend. My mom rented a car and drove, which was already strange because I didn't even think she knew how to drive, and once we were on the road, I realized she barely knew how. Then, on the way there, we got a flat tire and pulled over on the side of the highway and got out of the car.

When we were in our car zooming along just like everyone else, the road felt quiet and even. But standing on the side of the highway everything changed. The cars were deafeningly loud and fast, all jangling parts. And the street was wider than I realized. The signpost we were underneath was massive and damaged. From the road, the signs looked small and neat. But up close, it towered over the road. Looking at the Manhattan skyline, dwarfed by distance, it feels so different than when you're in it.

"Hey."

I look at Sam. I was so lost in thought I almost forgot he was there.

"This is nice," I say.

He nods.

And then he says, "Philosophy."

"Excuse me?" I say.

"That's what I want to do," he says. "Study how people see things. Or whatever."

I look at Sam and he's blushing harder than I've seen him.

"You have no idea how hard my dad would laugh at me if he heard me say that," Sam says. "I can already hear him— what are you going to do with a degree in philosophy?"

I say, "I thought you don't care what your dad thinks."

"I don't," he says.

"I know you don't," I reply, but he knows I know he's lying.

Sam yanks a fingerful of grass out of the ground and tosses it in my direction, but the wind carries it away before it reaches me.

He lies down on his back and I lie down beside him.

And then, Sam picks up my hand and my breathing stops. He holds my hand carefully, moving his thumb rhythmically across my palm. I wonder if he can feel me coming apart. He isn't looking at me, but he doesn't let go.

"I can't believe I'm your first guy friend," he says.

"I like it," I say, because that's all I can manage.

"You like what?" he asks.

I want to say, I like you. I like everything about you. I like how it feels when you touch me and say my name, or even when you just look in my direction. I like you as more than a friend. Instead, I say, "I like that you're my friend."

After an uncountable number of seconds that feel infinite with longing, Sam lets go of my hand. He sits up.

I sit up, too. He looks at me and lets his knee knock against mine.

"Hey," he says.

"Hey," I reply.

I stare at the collar of his shirt. I'm burning up and I'm afraid if I look into his eyes I'll burst into flames.

Sam bites his lip so hard it grows red. He reaches out and brushes a strand of hair behind my ear. And then he leans in and kisses me.

Sam's lips are salty and crazy soft. His nose presses into my cheek, his hands hold my head like if he let go I'd crumble, and I might. His hands might be the only thing holding me together. Sam is making me go blindingly white-hot.

Then he stops, slowly letting go of me and pulling away.

I wonder if anyone in the history of the world has ever felt anything like that. I stare at him. What just happened?

Sam lies down and closes his eyes.

"Sam?" I say.

He doesn't open his eyes.

"What does this mean?" I ask.

"I don't know," he says.

"I mean . . . are we like . . . ?" I ask.

"Sadie," he says, flicking my upper arm.

"What?" I ask.

Sam is looking at me like he wants to kiss me again.

I hope he does.

But then he says, "You're great. I like being friends with you."

The word *friend* stings. Maybe the kiss disappointed him. Maybe I momentarily slipped out of the friend category and now he's pushing me back into it.

Staring at Sam's unreadable profile and those closed-camera-lens eyes, I know I'm not gonna get answers to any of my questions from him right now.

So all I say is, "I like being friends with you, too."


Sam and I don't talk about anything on the walk back across the bridge. When we get to the subway, he says, "Today was fun."

I say, "Yeah."

He says, "Have fun with your dad tomorrow."

"I'll try," I reply.

And then I leave. We don't talk about the kiss or when we are going to see each other again. We don't even hug.


When I get home, my mom is sitting at the kitchen table eating leftovers. There are books and file folders piled up on the table. Of course she still files her paperwork in cabinets instead of just doing everything electronically like the rest of the world.

"What are you doing?" I ask, slipping into the table across from her and taking a bite of her half-eaten samosa.

"Satya and I have been talking," she begins carefully.

Satya is her best friend and fellow teacher at the Yoga Center.

"Okay," I say. "About what?"

"She wants to go to India next fall. For three months," she says. "And she wants me to go with her. This is all the information on the residency she wants to do. There's a Yoga institute in Pune where we can live."

"That's incredible," I say.

"It might be good for me," my mom says, almost shyly. "Since, you know, you'll be off at college."

It's the first time I've ever thought about what my mom's life is going to be like when I've gone to college. I'll be living in a dorm with other students and probably a roommate. She'll be alone. The thought singes my heart.

"That sounds amazing," I say. "I hope you go."

After dinner, my mom takes a bath while I make dessert tea. We call it dessert tea but it's just coconut milk and honey, and sometimes a chamomile or ginger tea bag, too.

I sip my tea leaning against our small gas stove. The yellow overhead lamp casts long leaves of light around our two-by-six-foot kitchen. It's a dinky kitchen, with its worn wood cabinets and mismatched tiles, but I feel, suddenly, for the first time since we've moved into this apartment two years ago, that it's actually my home.

I wonder what Sam's apartment looks like. And what did his house in New Hampshire look like? Every thought leads back to him.

I always thought there were two categories of liking people: being attracted to them, or liking them as a friend. But now, Sam has shaken that whole paradigm. I know I'm attracted to him, but it runs so deep it doesn't even seem like it has to do with his appearance. It's like the invisible part of me is attracted to the invisible part of him.

I remember his kiss and my legs grow weak. If just kissing Sam felt that intense, what would it feel like if we went further? I try to fuse my memories of the things I did with Noah with my image of Sam. I want to picture Sam lying on top of me, holding my shoulders, pressing his forehead against mine. The idea of touching Sam like that makes me ache in a good way. I bite my lip to fight the feeling.

I steady myself on the counter and squeeze my eyes shut. And then a thought hits me like a splash of cold water and I stand up straight: what if Sam doesn't want me in that way?

My mom opens her creaky bedroom door and the sound shakes me out of my daze. I hear her walk into the bathroom and turn on the faucet to fill the bath. It's crazy that a year from now, I'll be preparing to go to college. And five years from now, I'll be done with college altogether. Is it really possible that I'll ever be twenty? Thirty? Forty? That mom will be sixty, seventy, eighty? Will there ever be a better day than today? This is perfect: I'm seventeen and my mom is down the hall taking a bath, and I just kissed a boy with green eyes. There are still so many things that I don't have and that I want, but I have the weirdest feeling that even if I got all the things I've ever wanted, I'd still choose this moment, right now, to be the one that lasts forever.

# Chapter 29

'm meeting Allan on the steps of the Metropolitan Museum of Art at noon. I climb the wide, bright stairs, passing a group of tourists taking selfies, their maps waving wildly in the wind like flags. Overhead, the sky is a shining blue dome.

When I spot him, I wave, and a gust of wind whips my hair across my face and in my eyes. I push it off, and see him smiling at me. I feel like the girl on the bow of a ship coming home at the end of a movie. I'm the star of that movie, I can just feel it.

As Allan walks toward me, I wish I could tell all the people around us who he is. *That man, my father, is a famous artist*, I want to shout. *This very museum that you have traveled around the world to visit owns two artworks that he's made.*

"Nice day," Allan says, his hands shoved into the pockets of his khakis. Without even trying, he looks smarter than everyone else in the world. "I like your dress. Your mom also looks good in red."

I've been to the Met a million times, so I know the rooms well. My teachers have been taking my classes here for field trips since kindergarten. Art teachers and history teachers and even math teachers can find a reason to visit the Met.

Allan doesn't talk to me while he looks. The only way you could tell that he is a real artist, and that the other people in the exhibit are just tourists, is that he never shows any signs of approval. Some people elbow their friends and point to things they admire. Others wear the audio guide and keep stopping in front of certain paintings to listen. Not Allan.

When we reach the modern wing, I see a sign that reads HENRI CARTIER-BRESSON: ROMANIA 1975 with an arrow pointing down the hall.

"Oh, can we go see that show?" I ask Allan. "That's one of the photographers my teacher had us study this summer. This girl in my class, Alexis, did a whole project on him."

Allan shrugs. "Sure."

In the photo gallery, I set the pace. I can feel him behind me, letting me decide how much time to spend in front of each picture. He gets it, I think. He knows I'm a real artist, too.

The pictures are all street scenes from a city I've never been to, from a time before I was born. But it feels as familiar as the world outside right now.

Some of these are photographs that I've seen in books, but they look different in person. The blacks are richer, but there's also some other harder to name quality that makes my heart flutter. I'm so used to seeing photographs on screens, unless they're mine or my classmates, and it's always magic to see the actual thing and to know that the artist touched it himself.

The last photograph in the gallery is one I've never seen before. In it, a man and two teenagers are sleeping on a train, and their bodies are intertwined. Even in 1979, there were teenagers like me and Sam, sneaking out, finding places to be alone together.

Allan doesn't want to eat lunch at the museum café so we walk together to a French restaurant on Madison Avenue that his friend told him was good. It's dark inside. An old man at the table in the front is drinking red wine and eating a steak. This is different from anywhere my mom and I would ever eat, especially for lunch.

While we read the menu, which is spare and expensive, Allan asks me what I thought of the museum. I want to impress him, and I grope for the right words.

"I loved the photo show," I say.

"Yeah." Allan shrugs. "That work holds up I guess."

"I love going to museums with you," I gush. "I wish you lived here and we could do it more often."

Allan scans the restaurant. He raises his arm in a kind of command as a busboy shuffles by.

Then he looks back at me.

"I could never live in New York again," he says, only responding to half of my comment.

"Well, at least I have your camera," I say, trying a different tactic. "So it's kind of like you're always here."

"I'm so glad you're using that thing," Allan says. "It cost

a fortune and I felt so guilty I never used it. Do you have it with you today?"

"No, because remember, we're going to go from here to my friend Phaedra's mom's party after this," I say.

He looks at me blankly. "Who?"

"My friend Phaedra? You met her at your opening?" I say, trying to jog his memory. "And I e-mailed you that invitation from her mom, it's a fund-raiser for this art program. So I thought we could just go there from here."

Allan is about to respond, but the waiter is walking by again and Allan's attention jumps away from me. He waves his arm over his head. "Waiter? Who is our waiter?"

"I'll be right with you," the waiter says, shuffling by holding a tray of plates.

"The service here is terrible," Allan says, looking back at me. "But the food looks great. Did you see that steak?"

"Right, yeah," I say. "Anyway, the party starts at four—"

"Yes. What can I get you?" The waiter appears next to our table.

Allan orders a steak and I get the French Onion Soup.

When the waiter is gone, Allan lets out a long, contented sigh. He sinks down in his seat and rests his hands on his stomach, seeming pleased and relaxed.

"So," he says. "Do you know where you want to go to college yet or is it too soon?"

I straighten up and smile. Here it goes.

"I want to go to art school," I announce. "IACA is my first choice."

"Oh, don't do that," Allan says, waving his hand away like he's swatting away a fly. "Art school is such a waste of time."

I'm too stunned to speak.

My silence must surprise him because he looks up at me and his eyes widen.

"Don't look at me like that," he says with a laugh.

"Like what?" I ask.

"Like *that*," he says, gesturing toward me.

"I-I-want to go to IACA," I repeat. "I want to be an artist. A photographer. And . . . if I went there . . . we'd be together."

Allan doesn't respond.

All of a sudden, I have a feeling I might cry so I focus on unfolding my napkin and laying it on my lap, smoothing out all the wrinkles over and over, trying to erase the creases entirely. The silence grows louder.

"Don't take it personally," Allan finally says. "It's not about you. I don't think anyone should be an artist anymore. The professionalization of art has ruined the field."

"But, you're an artist," I say, my voice trembling.

"You're too smart for art school," Allan says.

"You don't even know how smart I am or am not," I counter.

Allan laughs. "Point taken."

"This isn't funny," I say. "You're treating this like it's nothing, and it's not nothing."

"What do you want me to say? Go to art school? Fine, go to art school. Be an artist if you want. It's not up to me anyway," he says. "This has nothing to do with me."

*Nothing to do with you?* The words sink down into my gut, one by one. How could he not understand? Now my eyes begin to ache. I can feel the tears piling up behind them, my bottom lip trembling.

I look at my plate, which is bright white porcelain. I try to make my mind blank. Soon, the waiter brings our food and Allan eats. I just stare at my soup and listen to the sounds of him chewing.

Allan stops when he notices that I'm not eating.

"Look, you want to know my honest opinion? I told you. I don't think anyone should be an artist anymore," he says. "Be a business person. Be a computer programmer. Go to law school."

"But I love art," I say, when I can find my voice. "And I'm good at it. My teacher thinks I'm really good."

"So you're good at black–and–white photography, great." Allan sneers. "You're a sixteen-year-old girl. Go through a black-and-white street photography phase: fine. But you can't do that anymore. You can't be Cartier-Bresson any-more. The world already has that."

"I'm seventeen," I say. And now the tears burn my eyes. "I'm not sixteen."

"I said that," he says.

"No, you called me sixteen," I hiss, wiping tears away with the back of my hands.

Allan looks at me and sees the tears. I think he's going to apologize, but instead I see something grow cold and hard in his face, like water turning to ice.

~ ∘

After, on the sidewalk outside of the restaurant, Allan says, "Listen. I see you're upset. You don't have to tell me why. But I wish you'd calm down. Everything is fine."

I still can't speak because I'm so full of different feelings of anger and shame and I don't know what's going to come out of my mouth if I do.

"I need to get going," Allan says impatiently. "I really want to end this visit on a lighter note, but Marla and I are leaving for the country in an hour and I have to pack."

"But Phaedra's party . . ." I say.

"Sadie. Please," is all he says.

I drop my head forward and cover my eyes with the heels of my hands. I'm so mad at myself for messing everything up. When I finally let go and look back up at Allan, he is doing something on his phone.

"What are you doing?" I ask.

"Checking my e-mail," he says. "I'm waiting to hear from this museum curator. It's been such a headache."

Nothing I do is making Allan pay any attention to me and suddenly, I can't help it, I'm crying again.

"I can't believe I told you I wanted to go to art school and you told me it was a bad idea," I blurt.

"Well, if it takes one person to make you doubt yourself, you really shouldn't be an artist," Allan says with a self-satisfied smile.

"Stop laughing at me," I snap.

The amused expression on Allan's face vanishes.

"Okay. All right. Enough," Allan says. "This tantrum is boring."

"Boring?" I repeat. "That's really nice. That's really sweet of you, *Dad*."

Allan straightens up.

"Listen, Sadie," he says coldly. "This whole father-daughter melodrama you've concocted is ridiculous. It's a bunch of bullshit theatrics. You're not a little kid anymore, so stop acting like one."

I wipe away tears.

"Stop crying," he commands.

There are a lot of things I want to say. But mainly, I want to be away from him. So I smooth out the front of my dress and take a deep breath.

"I'm sorry. I made this lunch really awful. I should go."

Allan doesn't disagree.

"Look. I know I'm distracted. My mind is in a million other places, with this MOCA show coming up and everything," Allan says. "But your mom said you seemed disappointed when you came back from my opening the other night, so she thought I should try and make it up to you."

I stop crying. I'm too shocked.

"My mom . . . what?" I whisper.

"Yeah, she said you were out of sorts," he continues.

My mom knew I went to Allan's opening? I'm dizzy, out-of-body wobbly as Allan gives me a weak hug. He tells me to *take care* and to *stay in touch*, but none of his words reach my ears because I'm underwater.

And then I'm alone. I slump back against the brick exterior of the restaurant. The gorgeous summer day has turned sour.

Allan was an asshole, but I suddenly don't care. I guess, deep down, I expected to be disappointed by him. Maybe this was all theater, like he said. But my mom knew this whole time? I feel a chasm opening in my heart, between the half that is me and the half that is her.

# Chapter 30

I hide behind my sunglasses and walk toward the Park Avenue Armory. Around me, the world feels dirty. A yellow construction tractor tears up the ground, ripping up chunks of asphalt with its animal claws.

I step off Park onto a quiet, shady street. One of those Upper East Side brownstone blocks where the buildings are so old and the trees so dense, it's as if you fell through a crack in time to a hundred years ago. I pull out my phone to text Sam, but then I decide to just call him. It rings four times and then goes to voice mail. I don't leave a message, I just text him: can u talk? When I'm a block away from the armory, where the party is, Sam still hasn't called me back. I dial his number again. Again, it goes to voice mail. So I put my phone away and go inside.

There are security guards and photographers protecting the entrance to the gala. I make my way to the front of the line and the girl behind the table asks me my name.

"Bell . . . Bell . . . let me see here," she says, in her perky robot voice. "It says here Allan Bell and Sadie Bell. Is he with you as well?"

"He's coming later," I lie.

I stick my name tag to my dress and walk in. I peer into the reception, which is taking place in an elegant room filled with fancy-looking people. A team of photographers with cameras so gigantic that they could be weapons circulates through the crowd.

"You made it!" Izzy cries, tumbling into me. She's wearing a black dress and almost black lipstick. "Wait. Where's your dad?"

"He couldn't come," I say.

Her face falls and she grabs my elbow, pulling me out of earshot of the other guests.

"What? Why?" she whispers.

"We just, we had this crazy fight at lunch," I say. "It was so bad."

"That is so bad." Izzy's jaw falls open. "You have to call him and tell him to come. Phaedra's mom has told so many people he's coming. You guys are at our table."

"I can't," I say. "It's too weird."

"How can it be weird? He's your dad," Izzy hisses. "Just call him."

I look at Izzy. The mass of people behind her pulses with laughter and the clinking of champagne glasses. I say, "Okay. I'll call him. I'm just going to go somewhere quiet."

"Good." Izzy sighs. "Find me after."


I exit the cocktail room and find myself in the huge, vaulted ceiling armory where the dinner will be held. A sea of circular tables with china plates and floral arrangements stretches out for what feels like miles in every direction.

I check the number that's stamped on my name card and make my way to my seat. Wandering between the empty tables, I feel like I'm sinking into a maze. Finally, I find table 32. There are nine seats. *Isabelle Tobias. Lily Tobias. Terence Tobias.* Those must be Izzy's parents. And after that, other names I don't know. Until I come to *Sadie Bell.* And next to that *Allan Bell.*

Izzy thinks it's all so simple. She thinks I can just call Allan and tell him to come. The truth is, I have no power over him at all. Izzy doesn't know anything. But then I think about my mom and the fact that she knew about me and Allan all along, and I think *neither do I.* There are so many things I've been too blind to see.

I sink down into the chair that says my name and finger the embossed place card. I place it next to Allan's. They look so neat together: Allan Bell and Sadie Bell, father and daughter. But there will be no us. Maybe not ever.

I grab both place cards and wade back through the dining hall.

People are still arriving, wandering into the hall with their welcome packets and high heels. I'm climbing three small steps that lead into the cocktail room when someone taps me on the shoulder.

I turn and Noah is standing there. He's just come in with his parents and a girl who I recognize from the Internet as his older sister.

"Hi, Noah," I say.

His family drifts past us into the cocktail room, but Noah stays put.

"How are you?" he asks. I've never seen Noah so dressed up. He's wearing a black suit with a crisp button-down shirt. Something about the sharp white corners of his collar against the soft skin of his neck sends a jolt up my spine.

"I'm okay," I say. My voice feels far away from my body. "How are you?"

Noah steps toward me. He smells like soap.

"Fine. But, are you okay, really?" he asks, his eyes fastening on to mine.

I can't believe Noah Bearman is talking to me. He's looking at me closer than he's looked at me since that night. He's swallowing me with his bottomless eyes.

"I don't know," I tell him. "I'm. . . . I'm actually in the middle of kind of a terrible day."

"Do you want to talk about it?" he asks.

"It's a long story," I tell him. "I just had a fight with my father."

"Family." Noah sighs. "Family is tough."

"Yeah." We are still standing in the doorway and newcomers continue to pass us by, but I can't seem to move. I'm too hypnotized by the strangeness of everything that's happening: talking to Noah at this fancy party. I feel so far away from who I am. My fight with Allan divided the day and now I'm living in an alternate reality.

A caterer with a tray of champagne flutes walks by, and Noah grabs two glasses off the tray. He hands one to me.

"For you," Noah says. His eyes are doing their Noah thing, sparkling and smiling, but somehow not giving anything away. His perfect lips curl upward on one side, arcing into that perfect, apologetic smile.

"Thank you," I say.

And then he says, "I know a girl who could use a drink when I see one."

A big glass of champagne later and everything is starting to feel better. I'm in the cocktail room, surrounded by people who I don't know. Before I began drinking, the room seemed loud and the people looked anonymous and scary. Now everything feels bright and happy.

"Look who doesn't seem so sad anymore," Noah teases, handing me another glass of champagne.

"You're good at getting champagne." I giggle, accepting the drink.

"I have friends in high places," he replies, amusing himself.

"This is a pretty amazing party," I say. "Is that the mayor?"

Noah laughs. "You're funny."

"I'm serious," I say. "I honestly think that's the mayor."

Just then, I spot Phaedra talking to her parents. She catches me looking at her and she locks eyes with me. I can see her excusing herself from her conversation, heading over to me. I know she's going to ask about Allan.

I turn to Noah, grabbing his forearm without thinking.

"Can we go outside? I need to get out for a second," I tell him.

Noah doesn't ask any questions or seem surprised. Instead, he slips his hand into mine and we weave quickly through the crowd out to the front entrance and straight out onto the street.

It happens so fast and I'm reminded of how assured Noah is. That confidence, that thing that let him take my hand and pull me along, that's the same thing that sucked me in so deep a year and a half ago.

Outside, the line has dissipated. The party is beginning and arrivals are slowing down.

"You seem stressed," Noah says.

"I am," I reply. "Izzy wanted me to bring my dad, and I told her I would but then everything got all bad and weird and now he's not coming. And I feel like Izzy is gonna be so pissed."

"Wanna just get out of here?" Noah asks. "We could just leave right now. Fuck it."

I laugh. Behind us, the girl who checked me in is beginning to clean up the table, putting away the name tags of people who didn't show up.

It's only five. The sun is still shining. Noah's red lips bloom in the golden afternoon light. Going with Noah is a bad idea. But right now, doing something bad seems like it might feel really good. Maybe the day is still full of possibilities. Maybe you can just walk away from one destiny and right into another.

Three blocks and five minutes later, the armory and the fund-raiser and Izzy's scornful look are all starting to feel like they were just part of a bad dream.

"Where are we going?" I ask as we walk away from the armory.

"Dan Jackson's," Noah says. "It's a shithole but they'll serve us."

Dan Jackson's is a bar on First Avenue that smells like beer and has TVs in all the corners, stools and tables, and gross bar food and loud music. Everyone goes there because they'll serve alcohol to anyone. It's the kind of place Danielle and her friends love.

"So, you're here for the summer? Like back from college?" I ask.

"Yup," he says.

"Where do you go?" I ask. Like I don't know.

"Brown. It's all right," he says.

"Do you live around here?" I ask as we wait for the light to change, even though I know everything about him that you can know about a person from Google. When will I get to stop pretending I haven't stalked him?

"No. We live in Brooklyn. But my half sister lives up here," he says. "I can't stand this area. Oh, sorry, do you live here?"

"I live downtown. Kinda near school," I tell him. "But we used to live uptown. I moved a lot."

I can't believe I'm walking down the street with Noah. And it's occurring to me that this is the first time we've ever really spoken. He's not really how I thought he was. When he's talking, Noah is boring. But when he's not talking, when he's looking at me, or moving, or even watching other people cross the street, he's amazing. He's full of silent intensity. Maybe the things you can find out about someone from the Internet, or even from kissing them, don't really tell you what you need to know.

At the bar, Noah buys us each a shot of tequila and we swallow them, before sitting down at a sticky table in the back with big glasses of beer.

"How many drinks are you going to need before you start talking?" he asks.

"Not a lot, probably," I say. I feel drunk already. And being drunk is making it easy to keep drinking, making everything seem lighter and more slippery.

He leans back in his chair, keeping his eyes glued to mine. "You're so small. You must be a lightweight."

"I'm not small. Or a lightweight."

Noah jumps up. "I'm getting another. And another for you, too. Since you're not a lightweight."

Noah returns and sets two more beers down on the table. I take a sip.

"Brown is awful," he says, out of nowhere.

"Really?" I ask.

He pauses. "Okay, well not awful. That's an overstatement. All my friends there are from the city. I think if you grew up in the city, college just isn't that exciting."

I've never felt especially bonded to other people who grew up in the city, but I like the way Noah talks about us like we are somehow on the same team.

"We've just done everything already, you know?" he says. "There are all these kids who have just never seen the world. They're so sheltered."

I think about Sam. Sam is from a small town. But he knows so much stuff that I don't know.

"People from places other than the city know stuff, too," I say sincerely.

Noah looks at me like I've spoken in gibberish and then he cracks up. He laughs so hard that I can't help but laugh along, too, although I'm not totally clear on what's funny.

"You're hilarious," he says when he can speak again. He finishes his second beer in a big gulp. "Omigod. That was priceless."

I couldn't finish my second beer so Noah had it, and now we're back outside and we're drunk. The alcohol is making time collapse. The air is lava hot. The city is a volcano of color and noise. A woman pushes past me on the sidewalk, and I laugh. Why is she in such a hurry? Why is everyone so serious?

"Being drunk during the day is really amazing," I say.

Noah snorts. "Well, maybe you will like college, after all."

"Why? Is that what college is like?" I ask.

"No, I dunno," he says. He starts walking across Second Avenue and I follow him. The alcohol makes it easier to not stop doing things. We're hanging out. Stopping would be harder than not stopping. Talking is easier than not talking. Moving is easier than staying still.

"School's fine. Whatever. I've met some okay people, I guess. I took one class that was pretty good. But my best friends, and all my best memories, are still from here," he says.

I'm staring at Noah. He doesn't seem drunk, just sad. When he talks about his *best memories*, I can't help but wonder if he's talking about me and him. Does he remember us? Maybe all this time I was just too stupid to realize he liked me back.

"Hey," he says, looking at me and smiling. "Don't look so sad."

"I'm not sad," I say.

"You're feeling better? That's good," he says. "You have one of those faces that always seems a little sad."

"Do I?"

He's looking at me again, and it makes me feel beautiful.

Then, he resumes walking and I follow him, even though I don't know where we are headed. Our bodies knock into each other a little, sweaty forearms, and I step on his heels by accident a few times, but it's warm and easy, because we're drunk.

"I hate my father," I say.

Noah nods.

"He made me feel so small," I say. "And so stupid. Like I don't know anything. He doesn't know anything. He doesn't know who I am."

Noah smiles approvingly. "Let it out."

"I. Hate. Allan," I say, with so much conviction I'm almost yelling.

Noah laughs.

"He's so full of himself," I continue, talking right to Noah, as if he knows everything that's happened. The words are coming so easily now. "He could disappear and I could never see him again, and I wouldn't care. He's nothing. He's a washed-up old desperate loser with a snotty girlfriend and all they do is try be hip and smart. What's worse than a sixty-year-old man trying to be hip?"

"Damn," Noah says. "That's pretty real."

*And my mom*, I think. But the words freeze in my throat. I can't vent about my mom. I can barely think the words, let alone whisper them. *Why didn't you tell me? Why didn't you tell me you knew?*

"Hey, don't cry," Noah says gently. He pulls me toward him, sealing the gap between us with a hug.

I didn't realize I was crying, but I touch my face and it's damp from tears. I must be very drunk to not know I'm crying. I've never been this drunk. I lean into Noah, at first to steady myself, but then something changes. I am suddenly aware of how close to him I am. How close to all the parts of him that are hidden in his clothes. I pull myself away from him and we look at each other. Everything is different: I'm not crying and he's not laughing.

"You're good?" he asks, and his voice has none of that sarcasm in it. It's a simple, quiet voice. It's the voice he used that one night.

I follow behind Noah, looking up at his silhouette.

If this isn't fate, then what is? Today, on this cosmically bad day, it's Noah who has swooped in to make me feel better.

Sometimes life is a messy chaos, and sometimes it's a figure eight, with all the points circling back to the center.

Noah is leaning against a streetlight pole. Shade falls

across his face. He waits for me to look at him. His eyes are magnets.

"It's so funny that we are hanging out right now," I say.

His eyes sparkle.

"So funny," he agrees. And then he steps toward me and kisses me. In broad daylight on a public street corner. His face is pressed against mine, holding me close to him tightly. Just like last time. This is what I've wanted. Noah. The one who could complete the circle of my mind. My brain goes momentarily blank and then fear seizes up inside of me and all I can think is *SAM SAM SAM*.

I put my hands on Noah's chest and push him away.

He steps back, touches his lower lip with his hand. "I'm sorry."

"It's okay," I say, not sure what I mean, or what he's apologizing for.

"That was crazy. I just, you were looking at me like . . . and you're so . . . I'm sorry, I know that's not right," he says.

"No," I say quickly. He's leaving again. And even though I don't want him to kiss me, I really really don't want him to leave. "No. No. Don't leave."

Noah looks at me crookedly. He looks ashamed and sorry and cute again. Maybe I do like him still. Maybe I just need a little more time to get used to him.

"Let's go somewhere," he says. "Let's go sit down. We're too wasted to be walking around."

On Fifth Avenue, we sit on a bench in the shade with our backs to the park. It's breezy and quiet. An old woman with a walker inches down the sidewalk across the street.

I look at Noah. My thoughts keep swimming through the mess of everything and settling back on him.

"Noah," I say. "*The* Noah."

He looks at me sideways, maybe nervous. "Yeah?"

"Do you remember?" I ask.

He smiles lopsidedly. "Of course I do. Don't be crazy."

"I mean, what happened. Do you remember?" I ask. "That night?"

He shifts uncomfortably. Stares across the street then looks at me, giving me his best smile. He reaches out and tucks a strand of hair behind my ear. He says gently, "Don't."

"Don't what?" I ask.

"Don't make it weird," he says.

That makes me laugh. But not because it's funny. More like, it makes me laugh because it makes me so mad. Then I stop laughing. I fold forward, resting my chest in my lap so my fingers graze the sidewalk.

Noah puts a hand on my back.

"I'm sorry if I said the wrong thing," he says. "We're here now, you know? It's good to see you."

I sit back up, blood swishing around my head. My hands melting in my lap. I look at Noah. He has flecks of green in his eyes. Sweat forming around his hairline. He's handsome. I know he's handsome.

I want to feel something. But all I can see when I look at him is just a regular person, not the magical Noah I've dreamed of. I can't believe I let this person touch me. I can't believe I longed to be around him.

As if he can feel me shrink away, he takes my hand and massages it with both of his.

I pull it away. "I should go."

"You're too drunk to be alone. I'll wait until you've sobered up," Noah says. "We'll just talk."

"I don't even know you," I say. "I can't talk to you."

"Hey," he says, flirty and sweet. "I think you're amazing. I thought it back then and I think it now."

He pulls me toward him and I try to be glad that I'm finally hearing all the things I wanted to hear.

Noah kisses me again and this time I let him. I lean into him. I climb up onto my knees on the bench and he holds me tight. We're teenagers making out on a bench in the summer. This is perfect. This is Henri Cartier-Bresson. This is sunlight bleeding in my veins and alcohol fizzing in my brain. Izzy and Phaedra would be so jealous. Phaedra Bishop, the prettiest girl in the world, wants to kiss this boy. But how come I'm kissing Noah and I'm thinking about Phaedra?

I go limp in Noah's arms. Turn my head away. Force myself off of the bench with the slow painful effort of waking yourself up from a bad dream and walk away.

# Chapter 31

I n the stairwell up to my apartment, the walls warp and curve, and each step wobbles beneath my feet, as if I'm stepping on stones floating on a river. I wish I could become undrunk.

"Hi, honey. My evening private canceled so I'm home early," my mom says when I walk inside.

I try to focus on her but my vision keeps distorting.

"You're not home," I say. "You're at work."

And then I'm sinking down onto the armchair by the window, trying to get as close to the air conditioner as possible. Air is good. Cold is good. I'm sweating everywhere.

My mom's hand is on my forehead.

"What's wrong? Are you—oh my God. Have you been drinking?"

My mom grabs my shoulders. She's trying to get me to stand, or sit up, or look at her.

I open my eyes wide. There she is. All lies.

"How could you?" I ask.

My mom doesn't understand; she just blinks.

"You knew," I say. I want to explain but I can't find the

words. All I can manage is, "You knew I was seeing him. You knew about his show."

My mom gives me a glass of water with ice cubes in it that bang around. I don't know where it came from. When did she get it?

"No," I say, pushing the glass away. "Talk to me. Tell me why you did it."

"I can't talk to you like this," she says, and she doesn't sound happy.

"You never talk to me," I tell her.

And then I stand up to go to my room, but I don't make it. I crumble, hitting my knees hard on the ground, and then my palms on the floor and I'm on all fours. And then I'm throwing up on the rug.

An hour later, I wake up lying on the floor of the bathroom, my head in my mom's lap. She's got a cold towel on my forehead. There's a bottle of coconut water, her favorite kind, on the floor next to me. Next to that, a tray of melted ice cubes and a stack of crumbling saltines.

I reach for the coconut water, but my hand is shaking too hard so I give up.

"You're awake? How do you feel?" my mom asks.

"Better, I think," I say. I remember throwing up until my insides were so empty it felt like twisting a rope. I remember resting my forehead on the cold porcelain of the toilet bowl, and it was the only relief in the world.

I remember curling up on the tile floor and closing my eyes.

Now, I'm sober and weak. The taste in my mouth is rancid.

"I need to brush my teeth," I say. And then I see that a strand of my hair that's lying on the floor in front of me is waxy and bound together with throw up. So I add, "And shower."

My mom helps me sit up, and when she sees I can hold myself upright she nods.

"Shower. We'll talk after," she says.

And I can't read her face because there are too many different codes written on it, spelling out a story that I can't reconstruct.

After my shower, I feel a little better. When I go into my room, my curtains are open and I can see that the sky is only just getting dark. It's seven thirty. Early. And I've already had the longest day of my life. I thought at seven thirty today I'd be walking home from Phaedra's party with Allan, talking about my plans to go to IACA. That's the life I'm supposed to be living. This, what's happening, is just some accident. It's a black hole I stumbled into and took hold of my life. I wish I could rewind and start the day over.

When I'm dressed, my mom comes in.

"That was quite an episode," she says.

"I know," I say, eyes closed. And then I mutter, almost more to myself than to her, "I know, I know, I know."

My mom doesn't respond, so I open my eyes.

"That," she says, pointing to the bathroom, "is absolutely not okay."

I groan. I lie down and put the pillow over my ears so I don't have to listen.

She crosses the room, yanks the pillow off, and throws it on the floor.

"What's the matter with you?" she demands.

Now I sit up. "With me? What's the matter with *you*?"

My mom looks confused. "What are you saying?"

"How could you do that to me?" I say, and I'm yelling now.

She stares at me blankly. "I don't know what you are talking about."

"I saw Allan today. I know you know he's here and that I've been seeing him. He told me you've been talking to him about me," I blurt.

"I'm sorry you found out that way," she says innocently. "But I thought if you wanted me to know, you would have told me yourself. It's pretty clear you wanted me to stay out of it."

"Exactly!" I hiss. "I wanted you to *stay out of it*. You just need everything to be all about you. You hated that I was seeing Allan without you so you had to meddle. You had to come between us."

My mom doesn't speak at first, and when she does, her voice is thin and wiry. "That's what you think?"

"You can tell me whatever you want. But the fact is, you kept me and Allan apart my whole life and now we have no relationship. I hope you're happy."

My mom sits down at my desk chair. She says calmly, "You're angry."

"I hate you," I reply. I watch her to see if she reacts, but she doesn't. "I wish I'd been raised by Allan and never even met you."

"That's okay," she says. "You can scream at me. I know everything is a mess."

I glare at her and wait for her to continue.

"I should have told you I was talking to Allan. But what happens between you and Allan is between the two of you," she says. "You have your own relationship, totally separate from my relationships with you both."

"What, so now you and Allan have a relationship?" I scoff. "I thought you never spoke."

"We don't," she says, sounding exhausted. "We barely do."

"Well I don't have a relationship with him either," I tell her. "I don't want anything to do with him ever."

"What happened?" she asks.

"I don't want to talk to you," I say. "I can't trust you. You betrayed me."

My mom stands up.

"I'm going," she says. "I'm here when you want to talk. But I'm not going to force you to share anything with me. You're seventeen. You're practically an adult."

"So what?" I say. "So I can't get upset because I'm seventeen?"

"Sure you can," she says. "You can act like a baby forever if you want to. But you're old enough to choose who you want to be."

"Just go," I mutter.

She opens the door and then she pauses and turns to look at me. There's something hurt and tired in her eyes that makes me suddenly want to retract all the mean things I just said.

"I know you're angry with me," she says. "And I understand. I'm sorry if I made you feel betrayed. But I want you to know, it's okay to be mad at him, too."

After she leaves, I turn off the lamp and lie in the semi-dark. It's a dusky, dirty twilight, making everything look grainy. I close my eyes and dissolve into sleep.

I wake up when it's dark out. I look at the time. Nine fifteen p.m. I have four missed calls from Sam. I'm about to call him back when he starts ringing again.

"Hey, I was just about to call you," I say.

"Are you okay?" Sam asks. "I've been freaking out. I came downtown. I'm outside your house."

"Why? What are you talking about?" I ask.

"Those voice mails, and that text, and then you just disappeared," he says. "What happened to you today?"

I groan, remembering that I called Sam twice before the armory. After that, I didn't check my phone for hours.

"I'm fine," I tell him. "Today was just a huge disaster."

"Oh no," he says. "I'm here. Want to take a walk and tell me about it?"

I really don't want to see Sam right now. Won't he see my shameful day written across my face? But he came all the way downtown to see me. And it's Sam. He makes things better. So I say, "Okay. Let me see if I can convince my mom."

My mom is sitting in the living room reading a magazine when I emerge from my room. She doesn't see me at first, and I hover in the doorway and watch her. I'm dreading what I have to do. I almost change my mind. But then I'd have to tell Sam that I can't meet him, and I can't stand the idea that he is only a hundred feet away and I wouldn't get to see him.

"Hi," I announce awkwardly. "My friend Sam is here. Can I go get a frozen yogurt with him?"

My mom slams her magazine down on the couch next to her. It seems like she wanted it to make a dramatic noise, but it lands with a whisper. "Absolutely not. You must be out of your mind."

"But . . ." I start. "I just really need to see him. It's an emergency."

"An emergency?" she repeats. "Sadie, you're not leaving this apartment. You came home drunk today," she says. "Did you forget? Did you think I was going to forget?"

I ignore her because I know her well enough to figure out what to do. I make a sad puppy-dog face and plead. "We'll just sit on the stoop across the street. You can watch us the whole time. And I'll be back inside in half an hour."

She sighs. "Twenty minutes. And I'll be watching from the kitchen."

I'm so grateful, I almost want to hug her. But then I remember how mad at her I am and my heart turns back into ice.

"We have to stay here," I tell Sam, pointing to the stoop. It's the place we sat that night a few weeks ago. "I'm in big trouble with my mom, and she said she's going to sit by the window and make sure I don't leave."

"So your mom is watching us right now? Kinda creepy," Sam says.

"Honestly, I can't believe she even let me walk out the door after today," I say, sitting down.

"So what happened?" Sam asks.

"So bad. So so bad," I say.

And then I start talking. I tell him about Allan and our fight.

"Wow," Sam says. "That's rough. What are you gonna do now?"

"I don't know," I say.

"So why is your mom mad at you?" he asks.

"Oh right," I groan. "So then, I went to Phaedra's party and—"

"You went to the party after all of that?" Sam asks. "Why?"

"I thought I had to," I say. "But I shouldn't have. There was free champagne and they were giving it to us, and I ended up getting really drunk with this guy Noah, and then when I got home my mom was home and I puked on the rug in front of her, and she like had to hold my hair back while I puked more in my bathroom, and it's just, literally, the worst day of my life."

"Noah?" Sam repeats. "Isn't that the guy you were talking about yesterday? The one . . ."

"Yeah," I say, looking down at my feet.

"Hmmm," Sam says.

I look at him and he's not smiling.

"Did anything happen? With him?" he asks.

I'm stunned. How did he know?

"Well . . ." I start. "I was more drunk than I've ever been in my whole life. Everything was so messy. And then . . ."

"So you did?" Sam asks, squinting at me like he's staring into a too bright light.

"We kissed for like two seconds on the street," I say, feeling trapped. "It was nothing."

Sam nods like he understands, but he won't look at me. "Huh."

"Are you mad?" I ask.

"No," he says, but he's lying.

"What? It was nothing," I say.

"It's just this whole story," he says. "Getting drunk and . . . being with that guy who sounds like a loser. It's just not you. Or I thought it wasn't you."

"It's not me," I protest. And then, feeling judged, I say, "And why do you care? You're the one who keeps insisting we're just friends."

Sam bites his lip, fighting back something that I can tell he wants to say. I wish he would just say it. But then he says, "You're right. We are just friends. I don't care."

Even though I put those words in his mouth, they sting.

"Don't do that," I say.

"Don't do what?" he asks.

"Don't say something other than what you mean," I say.

"I didn't," he says.

"Yes you did. And you do it all the time. Why can't you ever just say what you really mean?" I ask.

Sam looks at me and the camera lenses in his eyes open for longer than I've ever seen them. I feel like I can see straight into everything inside of him that's hurting. Then he looks away from me and rests his head in his hands. He takes a deep breath. When he looks back at me he says, "Yesterday was a mistake."

His words rip something out of my heart. The only good thing left in my life felt like that kiss.

"I don't think so," I say, my voice a whisper. "The truth is, when Noah kissed me, which is what I've thought I wanted for forever, I kept thinking about you."

Sam looks at me but his eyes are unreadable.

"No," he says. "We're making this complicated. We should just be friends. I just got out of a relationship that was always like this. I can't start this cycle all over again."

"We're not in a relationship. You're the one who keeps saying we're just friends," I protest. "And I was drunk, I was having an awful day. It was a mistake. Can't you see that?"

Sam won't look at me.

"Sam?" I say after a minute, putting my hand on his knee. He stands up.

"I'm not mad at you," he says. "But I think I'm going to go home."

# Chapter 32

The next morning, my mom is working at our table when I wake up. If you can even call it "waking up" when what I did last night was not sleep. What I did was lie in the dark with my eyes open and spiral, but whatever.

When my mom sees me, she says, "Good morning."

It strikes me as oddly formal. I say, "Hi."

She's staring at me and I can tell there is something she wants to say.

I turn away, slump past her to the kitchen to make tea. I can feel her eyes on me the whole time.

"Sadie?" she says tentatively.

I turn and grumble, "What? What do you want to say?"

It catches her off guard and her expression flips from scared to hurt. She looks at her hands and says, "I just wanted to know if you want breakfast."

"I'm not hungry."

She takes a deep Yoga breath and then says, with false patience, "Whenever you're ready to talk about what happened, I'm here."

I want to scream *why now? Why didn't you talk to me be-*

*fore I made a fool of myself in front of Allan and went and screwed up my whole life?* But all I say is, "Fine. Okay. I know."

I want to get away from her as quickly as possible, so I skip the sugar, and rush back into my bedroom with my bitter, weak tea.

Today I have to sort through my photos from the summer and decide which ones I want to make finished prints of so I can hand them in for the final project. The final in Benji's class counts as fifty percent of our grade, just like a real college class would be. The assignment is to hand in ten final prints. They can be pictures of anything, printed at any size, and from any point in the summer. The only requirement is that the theme is clear.

I open up the folder where I keep my photographs, sprawl them across my floor, and sit cross-legged in the sea of pictures. On the wall in front of me, my postcards are lined up in a neat, orderly grid. There's such a big gap between all the pictures I've taken of the real world, and the perfect world that the postcards depict. I can feel the space between what I want and what I have widening, and it feels like I'm going to fall right through it into nothing.

I pick up the photograph I took of the little boy on the subway and Allan's words from yesterday slam at me. *He's right*, I think. *There is no point in being a photographer. The last thing this world needs is more stupid pictures.*

My phone rings. I look around but don't see it because it's buried somewhere beneath one of these pictures. I lurch onto my knees and begin frantically pushing aside photos, crawling around on all fours not caring if I do damage to the prints. *Please please please be Sam.*

Finally I see the screen glowing beneath a stack of pictures and I grab it. My heart sinks. It's not Sam. It's a New York number I don't recognize.

In the quiet, as I wait to see if the person will leave a message, my conversation with Sam plays over and over in my head. He was jealous. And maybe, I tell myself, that's a good thing. That means he likes me for real. But what if it doesn't matter anymore? What if I've ruined everything?

When the voice mail button lights up, I listen to the message.

"Hi, Sadie. It's Noah Bearman," the message begins.

My jaw falls open in disbelief. Noah, *the* Noah, the guy who ignored me for half a school year and never once asked to see how I was, has tracked down my phone number and called me. Not even a text but a freaking voice mail.

I restart the message from the beginning.

"Hi, Sadie. It's Noah Bearman. So. . . . Yeah. I owe you an apology. Yesterday got pretty messed up. It was fun for sure. Not saying it wasn't fun. But you know. Call me back, okay? I owe you one. Okay. That's all. Be good."

*Be good.* Those two words take me back to Warszawa. Those are the words that broke my heart. He has no idea about anything.

I delete the message. The universe is playing tricks on me. All I've ever wanted was for Noah to call me, and now just hearing his voice makes me feel dirty and ashamed.

Why won't Sam call me instead? Why can't yesterday

have just not happened? How is it possible with all the technological advances in the world—airplanes and Internet and astronauts in outer space sending text messages to Earth—that I still can't do something as simple as rewind the clock twenty-four hours and undo one stupid mistake?

*Chapter 33*

This is the last week of class before finals are due. We are supposed to be working on our final prints in the darkroom, while Benji talks to each of us one-on-one in his office.

While Izzy has her private meeting with Benji, I sit on a stool at the table in the photo lab and watch the second hands tick by on the old analog clock on the wall. Everyone else is in a finals frenzy, circling in and out of the darkroom and adjusting the dark and light and focus until their photographs are perfect. If I had any chance of getting this project done on time, I would need to be working, too, but I can't bring myself to move.

I wonder if I'll ever enjoy photography again after all the cutting things Allan said. How *no one should go to art school,* and *you can't do what's already been done.* Maybe nobody loves what they do. They just do what they're good at and what they think will take them the closest to the person they want to be.

Alexis places two test prints in front of me. They are photos of her cat sleeping. They aren't terrible, but they aren't great, either. In both, one of the cat's hind legs is tucked awkwardly underneath her so she looks sort of limbless, like an oval.

Even though her pictures are pretty blah, I envy Alexis right then. She has a normal, happy, not-intense relationship to photography. I wish I could feel that uncomplicated.

"Which print is better?" Alexis asks.

"I don't know." I sigh.

"Since when do you not care about photo? You're like the best in the class," Alexis says.

"I'm sick," I say.

Alexis shrugs. "Feel better."

She grabs her prints and pivots, heading back to the dark-room.

"The one on the right is better," I call out.

She stops and looks at me. "It's not too dark?"

"Lighten the top. Outside the window. You'll be good," I say.

"Thanks," she says. And then she says, "And if you do stop caring, can I have one of your prints? I love that picture of the kid on the subway that you took at the beginning. I'd totally frame it if you gave it to me."

"It's yours."

The door to Benji's office opens, and Izzy saunters out. Slips into the seat beside me.

"Benji is such a dork," she says. "Do you think his mom sat on his head when he was a baby? That would explain a lot of things. I mean, a lot."

Alexis pretends she didn't hear, and for the first time I feel embarrassed to be the target of Izzy's attention.

"Sadie. Are you ready?" Benji asks, poking his head out from the office door.

I sit down in the student chair in Benji's office, and he sits in the big swiveling teacher chair behind the desk. He looks even more gangly and teenager-like in that big chair than normal. He leans back.

"Let's talk about your final project," he says.

"Like what I am going to do?" I ask, shifting in my chair.

"Yes."

The window above the air conditioner is cloudy with condensation. I can't see outside at all. Still, the outdoors beckon to me. The darkroom and Benji and this office, it's become a prison.

"I don't know yet," I say.

"What do you think was your strongest work from the summer?" Benji asks.

I shrug.

"What did you enjoy the most?" he asks.

"I don't know," I say. "It was all the same."

Benji gives me a sideways glance, smiles. "That doesn't seem true. You really excelled at a lot of assignments. But I think we can agree that the pictures you take when you're out and about—the landscape and the boy on the subway—those are the best."

"I guess," I say.

"You're the kind of photographer who really shines when you look outward," he says. "You're not taking pictures of yourself or your body or using a macro lens and getting super close up on things. You show us the world outside of yourself."

I try to be seduced by Benji's words, but I just replay the things Allan said: *Every sixteen-year-old girl goes through a black-and-white photography phase.*

I think Benji is waiting for me to speak, but I just tap my heels on the linoleum floor and wait for the meeting to be over.

"What's wrong?" he asks.

"You're acting like I'm doing something so important, but it's been done already," I say. "There are a million people out there who are taking black-and-white pictures of the city. It's been done a thousand times."

"Sure, in a way," Benji agrees. "But not the world through your eyes. No one else sees exactly what you see."

"You know what I mean," I say. "It's a cliché."

"I hear what you're saying," Benji says. "But in a way, the beauty of being part of your generation of artists, and mine, too, is that everything has been done. It's not our job to do something new. Or it's not the only job."

"Art isn't a job," I reply, thinking about what Allan said.

"What do you mean?" Benji asks.

"My dad says the fact that art has become a profession, the professionalization of artists, makes it meaningless."

"That's the second time in the last couple of weeks that you've quoted something to me that I don't think really comes from you," he says.

"Obviously it doesn't come from me," I reply, getting in-furiated by Benji's patient manner. "I just told you my dad said it."

Benji looks like he might yell, but instead he just stands up. He walks over to the window. Pushes a few buttons on the air conditioner, trying to turn the temperature down, but nothing happens.

Then, he crosses to the shelf where he keeps all of his art books and starts searching for books. He pulls down three books, all big hardcovers, and drops them on the desk between us. They land with a thud.

"Take these home," he says. "These are all contemporary photographers who are doing things that I think are similar to what you're doing, but also different."

"I can take these home?" I ask.

"I don't usually let people take them home because they're expensive, and they're my personal collection, not the school's," he says. "But it seems like you need someone other than me to tell you that it's all right to be a quote-unquote traditional street photographer. Okay?"

"Benji is letting you take those home?" Izzy asks as we walk out of class together later, nodding toward the brick of books I'm lugging. "That's so crazy. He probably, wouldn't even let me touch those books."

"I'm sure that's not true," I say.

"It's so true," she says. "And he probably won't even be mad if you don't return them. He loves you no matter what."

"What does that mean?" I ask.

"Nothing," she says. Then she stops walking. "Listen, Sadie. I need to talk to you."

"About what?" I ask.

"I think you owe Phaedra an apology," she says. "She felt really sad that you didn't bring your dad to her party."

"Sad?" I repeat, because what Izzy is saying makes zero sense. "But I told you, we had a fight. We went out to lunch and—"

"Artists are difficult," she interrupts. "That's not the point. The point is, you promised her you'd bring him, and then you didn't, and you didn't even seem sorry."

"Of course I'm sorry," I say. "I was upset."

"Just call her. Phaedra is really amazing and I know she seems so confident, like you'd think she could never get her feelings hurt, but she's actually really sensitive," Izzy continues. "And she kind of holds grudges. So you should try and make up with her."

"Okay." I swallow. "I'll text her."

"I think you should call her," Izzy says. "It's nicer."

"Okay. I will." Suddenly, I just want the conversation to be over so I can get away from her.

And then Izzy gives me a hug. "And don't worry. Everything will work out with your dad. He's family. You can fight, but you're always going to end up together."

For a second, I glimpse how truly naive Izzy is. In her world, that's true. In mine, and maybe in Sam's, and probably in a lot of people's, parents can leave for good.

I want to tell Izzy that she's wrong about family. That as sophisticated as she wants to be, she might be more sheltered than I am.

But all I say is, "I know. Thanks for understanding."

When I get home, I call Phaedra from my room.

We've never talked on the phone before. Talking on the

phone feels like an intimacy reserved for real friends. More intimate even than talking in person.

"Hello?" she answers.

"Hi, Phaedra, it's Sadie," I say.

She doesn't reply.

"Can you talk for a minute?" I ask.

"Okay," she says softly.

"I'm really sorry I didn't bring my father to your party," I tell her. "I didn't realize it was such a big deal."

"Didn't realize?" she repeats. "We talked about it, like, all day every day for weeks."

*Did we?* I think. But all I say is, "I know. It's just that Allan—I mean my father—and I had this epic fight over lunch."

"It's just so unfair that you put yourself before the party," Phaedra continues.

"Honestly, I wasn't trying to do that," I say, growing frustrated. "But my dad is kind of like one of those people who only hears what he wants to hear. I can't explain it."

"You keep making excuses, and it's like fine, whatever, I get it. But the party was important. Don't you see this isn't about you?" she asks. "It was a nonprofit. It's for a really important cause. It's like, bigger than us. Do you know what I mean?"

"I'm really sorry, Phaedra," I say, even though the words are sticking in my throat. "I'm so sorry."

Phaedra is quiet for a minute and then she says. "My mom was really mad at me. She's super intense about certain things. And this is one of them. She acted like it was my fault that he didn't come because I didn't make it clear to you that it was important or something. She gave me a whole lecture about responsibility."

"I'm sorry your mom got mad at you," I say, feeling confused about what I'm apologizing for.

"It's okay now." Phaedra sighs. "She told me she wasn't that surprised. She said until we became friends, she didn't even know Allan Bell had a daughter. And then, when she asked around, she learned the whole story."

"What whole story?" I ask. My voice comes out an octave higher than normal.

"That he abandoned you and your mom when you were born," she replies simply.

All the air gets sucked out of my room. I try to gasp, but I'm in a vacuum and my chest pulls in on itself. *Abandoned?*

"Sadie? Are you there?" Phaedra asks innocently.

Finally, I manage to inhale. "I'm here."

"Anyway, I just wish you told me. I'm trying to be your friend, but I feel like you aren't being honest with me," she continues.

I'm not sure if Phaedra is oblivious to the pain she's caused, or if she is trying to inflict it. Either way, I need this phone call to be over.

"I'm sorry," I stammer again.

"Thank you," she says. "Thank you for apologizing. I was really mad at first but I'm not mad anymore. Everyone makes mistakes."

After we hang up, silence fills my room. And then, Phaedra's words come hurling at me out of nowhere like a meteor headed for earth. I squeeze my eyes shut. I don't see anything. All I hear is Phaedra saying *"He abandoned you."* And even louder than the words that she actually said are the implied words that lie beneath them: *"You're the kind of girl who gets left behind. And everyone knows it except you."*

## Chapter 34

There's only one person in the whole world I can think of who could possibly make me feel better right now. I'm just not sure if she wants to see me. And I'm not sure if I'm ready to see her.

The doorman lets me in to Willa's building and as I ride up to her floor, I wonder if she's still mad. It's been ten days since our fight but these ten days felt more like a zillion. It smells like sunscreen in the elevator, like some family with kids all lathered up and ready for the beach just rode in it. It's July. It's beautiful outside. I should be happy like everyone else.

From the hallway outside Willa's apartment, I hear voices and laughter, and suddenly I don't know if I should be here.

I'm standing there frozen when the door opens and Gene greets me.

"Hey, Sadie. The doorman just buzzed up and said you were here," he says.

"Umm, right," I mumble.

"They're in the living room," he says, turning away from me and padding down the hall.

*They*? I think. But I just say, "Thanks."

Miles is sitting on the couch next to Willa. Not on the couch opposite. Not in the armchair. On the couch *with* Willa and she seems totally happy about that, sitting there all cross-legged with her hair down and brushed. She's not wearing her glasses, and from where I'm standing, I can't be sure, but I think she might have blush on.

Willa sees me and she stops smiling. Then she says, "Oh."

I look from her to Miles and then back to her.

"Oh," I say.

For a minute, we are silent, reading each other's minds like books. Then, she gets up off the couch and walks over to me.

"Excuse us for a second," she says to Miles. She turns to me like I'm a little kid being dragged to the principal's office and points down the hall. "Go."

Willa closes the door behind us in her room. "What are you doing here?"

"I want to make up," I say. Because it's the only thing I can think of that's true. "I'm so sorry for what I said."

Willa rolls her eyes. "Why? Izzy and Phaedra didn't invite you to a party? Or, wait, lemme guess, it turns out Sam isn't the greatest guy in the world, after all?" she taunts.

"Leave Sam out of this," I say.

"Oh, is he your boyfriend now?" she asks, challenging me.

"No," I say. "It's all messed up but it's not his fault. It's mine. It's a long story."

Willa purses her lips and squeezes her eyes closed like she's trying not to scream. Finally she says, "I don't want to hear it, okay? I don't care about your adventures in social climbing."

Social climbing? Her words strike a match inside my heart, and a vivid, sharp rage ignites in my chest.

"Fuck you, Willa," I say.

Willa's eyes grow huge, but I don't stop.

"I'm sick of you judging me all the time," I say. "Just because I don't have everything figured out like you do doesn't mean I'm a bad person. Just because I want to make new friends doesn't mean I'm social climbing."

"Fuck me?" Willa almost shouts, stepping closer to me. "You're the one who accused me of being jealous of my sister. You're the one who lets people walk all over you and then you just expect me to pick up the pieces. Fuck *you*."

I've never said "fuck you" to anyone before. No one has ever said it to me. And suddenly, it seems like the silliest thing in the world and I begin to laugh. Not just a little chuckle, but a real, uncontrollable, belly laugh.

"I'm sorry," I say, covering my mouth with my hands. "I'm sorry. It's not funny. I know it's not funny."

Willa watches, horrified. "Why are you laughing?"

"It's just, I've never said, fuck you, before," I say. I'm laughing like a maniac, so hard I can barely speak. "And it's really funny."

Willa's face softens. We look at each other and suddenly

we're both laughing. It's the kind of contagious laughing fit that feels like it will never end.

"You looked really scary when you said it," Willa says, and she has to wipe away tears.

"It felt *crazy*," I say. "I felt like a crazy person saying it."

"Was it convincing when I said it?" she asks.

"Yeah, it was really scary," I say. "I mean, you looked tough."

"I felt like a big dork trying to act tough," she says.

Slowly, we begin to calm down.

"What is happening right now?" I finally manage, breathing deeply. "Are we still fighting?"

"I don't know," Willa says. "I don't know anything anymore."

"Me neither," I say. "Nothing makes any sense."

"That was really, really mean what you said about me and Danielle," she says, sobering up. "And it's not true. I don't know if you think deep down I'm jealous of my sister. But I swear on my life I'm not."

"I wouldn't judge you if it were, though," I say. "It's normal."

"But I'm not," Willa groans. "Everyone thinks I'm jealous of her and it's so annoying. Really, I just feel bad for her most of the time."

I nod. I know it's true. That's the kind of person Willa is.

"And I feel really bad that I didn't go with you to your dad's thing," she continues.

"You should feel bad," I declare. "It really messed with my head. I needed you there."

"I know," she says. "That was really selfish of me. Just because I didn't want to deal with those girls. I shouldn't let them get to me. You can be friends with whoever you want, and I'm not gonna be a baby about it. I can share you."

"Well, that's a whole other story," I say. "Those friendships are kind of messed up. But don't worry, I won't make you listen to my—what did you call it—'adventures in social climbing?'"

"Yeah." Willa giggles. "I memorized that line. I've been dying to say it to your face."

"Willa, you have no idea how much I love you," I say.

"Yeah yeah yeah," Willa says, doing that deflecting thing she always does when things get mushy.

"Stop it. I'm serious," I say. "You're my best friend. I love you. You're family to me."

Willa nods slowly. "You're my best friend, too. You always will be. Even after high school and everything."

"Not Miles?" I tease.

Willa looks at her feet, her cheeks growing red. She is wearing mascara, I think. And eyeliner.

"Omigod. You *like* him," I say. "Wow. Why didn't you tell me?"

"When? In between your stories about all the new stuff you're doing and your amazing photo teacher and your mysterious boyfriend from New Hampshire?" she asks. "I know you think Miles is a huge nerd."

"But I'm your friend," I say. "I don't care if he's a dork. All that matters is that you like him."

Willa looks up at me and when she speaks, her voice is

so tender it bends my heart. "Good. 'Cause I think I might."

"Besides," I say, putting a hand on her shoulder and speaking in a gentle voice, "you're a nerd, too. So it makes sense."

Willa swats my hand away. "Fuck you."

And then we start laughing all over again.

I sit in the armchair in the living room and Miles and Willa sit on the couch together. There's a foot of space between them so they aren't touching, but that space looks deliberate, like they're afraid if they touched, they'd explode.

"Don't ask Sadie any hard questions," Willa tells Miles, when we've settled in. "She's having a bad day."

"No hard questions. Done," Miles says.

"Thank you," Willa says.

"You're welcome," he says. And then he picks up a kernel of popcorn from the bowl on the table and throws it at Willa. "I'll save all my hard questions for you."

Willa laughs. She looks at Miles and her smile brightens. Then, she drops her gaze and reaches for the remote, blushing hard. It's a short moment, but it's an infinity, too, The same way falling off a tall building would be three seconds that lasted forever.

I wonder if that's how I looked at Sam, before I ruined everything.

## Chapter 35

On the way home from class the next day, Sam finally calls.

I practically drop my backpack in the middle of the sidewalk, I'm in such a rush to answer it.

"I'm so glad you called," I exclaim, instead of saying *hi*.

"Hey," he says.

"I'm so sorry. I am such an idiot and I haven't stopped thinking about all of it," I blurt.

"Wait," he says.

"No, I just have to say this. I really messed up."

"I have to talk to you in person," he says. He sounds sad. "Can I come over?"

An hour later, I buzz Sam in.

"Welcome," I say awkwardly when I answer the door. "My mom is still at work so it's just us."

"Nice," he says, shoving his hands in his pockets. He looks tired.

"Want something to drink?" I ask. "We have juice."

"Sadie," Sam says, and his voice is slow and broken. He sinks down onto the couch. I'm still standing.

"What's wrong?" I ask. "You're starting to scare me."

He folds forward, resting his elbows on his knees and his head in his hands. He presses his hands over his eyes. He lets out a ragged, exasperated breath and then relaxes, leaning back again.

I sit down next to him. He's so tense, I'm afraid to touch him, but I decide to anyway. I reach up and gently place my hand on his shoulder. He doesn't pull away.

"My mom and her boyfriend went away for the weekend, last weekend, you know?" he says.

"Okay," I say. "I remember."

"They broke up," he says, staring at the floor.

"Oh." That doesn't seem so bad to me, so I say, "That sucks."

He is still for a moment and then he turns toward me, catching my gaze with hard, burning eyes.

"We're moving back to New Hampshire," he says. "Next week."

A weight drops in my stomach. "But," I start, and then I have no idea what to say. "You can't just leave. You *live* here."

"Not anymore," he says.

"Can't you stay here without her?" I ask. "Just stay."

"And do what? That's crazy," he says.

Understanding hits me: Sam is leaving. There will be no me and Sam. No more walking around with nowhere in particular to go. No kissing and fighting and making up.

"I'm going to get stuck there," he says. "I know it. I'm going to end up just like him."

He doesn't have to say who, because I know.

"I don't know your dad," I say carefully. "But from everything you've said, I don't think you're anything like him."

Sam is resting his elbows on his knees, fidgeting with his hands. He hangs his head forward. I reach out and touch his hand. He looks at me and then I take it and hold it in both of mine. He's staring at me, but I can't look at him so I stare at our hands. My hands are small and pale from a summer spent in a darkroom.

"I'm so sorry about Noah," I say. "It didn't mean anything. I hate that that's the last thing that happened and now you're leaving. It's so unfair."

"Hey," he says. "It's okay."

I let myself look up at him, and he smiles a little bit. Maybe the saddest smile I've ever seen. His eyes moving carefully over my face.

And then he leans in and kisses me. It's slow at first. I can feel the shape of his bottom lip in between mine. And then he gently parts my lips with his tongue and I lean into him, my mouth melting into his as we pull each other closer. We pull each other so close that I have to climb up onto the couch so I'm sitting on his lap. I wrap my arms around his neck and his hands are on my hips and then holding my rib cage, his thumbs grazing the bottom of my breasts just the tiniest bit. I run my hands down his arms, wanting to feel all of him, feeling the hard belt buckle of his jeans against me. Something stirs deep inside me, and I can tell from the way he's holding me, guiding me toward him, that he feels it, too.

He pulls his face away from mine but he doesn't let go.

"I'm sorry, too," he says. "I shouldn't have made you feel so bad. I just can't stand thinking about some other guy . . ."

"I know," I say, cutting him off. "I know."

He reaches up and pushes the hair out of my eyes, the skin on his fingers is the perfect amount of rough.

Then he says, "I lied to you."

"What? About what?" I ask.

"I don't want to be your friend. I never wanted to be your friend," he says.

He lifts me up and rolls me onto my back so he's lying on top of me. His thigh is pressing in between my legs. The afternoon light illuminates the super-soft skin on his nose where the sunburn has peeled off, and I touch it gently with my finger. I look at the place where his skin disappears into his clothing, and I remember how he looked with his shirt off at the beach. I want to see all of him. I hook my finger into the collar of his shirt so that the tips of my fingers graze the top of his chest. And then we're kissing again, his arms are wrapping all the way underneath me and around me. We draw breaths in between our kisses, which are growing more and more heated.

"This is a bad idea," he says.

"I know," I say. "But I want to be with you now. While we still can."

"I'm going to be gone in a few days," he says. "I'm leaving. For good."

"You can always come visit," I say. "And maybe you can go to college in the city and—" my words trail off because he's smiling a little now. "Why are you smiling?"

"'Cause you're sweet," he says. "But I can't do this. I can't do something that could hurt you. When all I want to do is . . . *not* hurt you."

I finger a loose thread along the collar of his shirt. I can't look into his eyes. "Please don't go."

And then he says, "Sadie." And he says it in that way he does, like it's two fragile words barely held together.

And I know what he means. This is the end.

# Chapter 36

The next morning, Willa arrives at eight a.m. to take me to breakfast before class. I called her crying last night and she said she'd come over first thing, even if it makes her late for bio.

We share a stack of pancakes at the diner on First Avenue, and I tell Willa everything that happened with Sam, from beginning to end. As if I go over it enough, the outcome will change. But it always ends the same way: he leaves.

"Why can't you guys be together anyway?" Willa suggests. "I mean, during the school year everyone is busy. It's not like if he lived here you'd see him that much."

"But I'd see him *sometimes*," I protest. "Now, I'm gonna see him *never*."

"I think you're being a little fatalistic," Willa says. She's looking prettier, but not in any way that I can pin down, as if it's coming from the inside out.

"I don't know," I say, stabbing a piece of pancake and dragging it through a river of syrup. "How's Miles? Have you beat him in Dungeons and Dragons yet?"

"Shut up." Willa laughs. But then she looks down at her

plate and smiles to herself like she has a good kind of secret.

Willa takes a big bite of pancake, blushing and giggling to herself at the thought of Miles. I look down at my pancakes, not hungry. The cold vacuum that Sam left in my heart sucks everything good down into it, even my appetite.

The rest of the day unfolds the same as any other day this summer. I walk to class and listen to Benji lecture. I drink an orange soda from the vending machine by the janitor's closet. I laugh at Izzy's not-funny jokes. I get overheated on the walk home from school and buy an iced coffee. Then, I watch the ice cubes melt faster than I can drink it, and I throw it away when it becomes a watery mess. At home, I crank up the old air conditioner and listen to it wheeze and whine as it starts to thin the air in my room.

But all day, as my body goes through my regular routine, my thoughts are a million miles away. Or not a million miles away. It's more like my thoughts are buried so deep inside myself, in the darkest, quietest, most hopeless space in my heart, that I can barely taste or smell or even see the world around me.

I'm lying on my bed with my sneakers on because I'm too lazy to take them off when my phone rings. I peer at the screen where it's resting next to me on the pillow.

Sam is calling. I push ignore. I don't want to talk to him. What's the point? He's gone.

A minute later, it rings again. Again, it's Sam. Again, I push ignore.

Some people leave because they're selfish and only care

about themselves, like Allan. Some people leave because their lives are bigger and better somewhere else, like Noah. Some people leave because their families move to small towns, like Sam. The reason doesn't matter. Gone is gone. Left behind is left behind. And left behind is something I'm sick of being.

My phone rings a third time. I will myself to be strong. *Don't pick it up. Let him go. Gone is gone. Gone is gone.*

But then images of Sam flood my mind. I can hear him saying my name, see him sleeping on my bedroom floor in his dirty jeans. I lose my will. I squeeze my eyes shut and answer the phone.

"Hello?" I say.

"There she is," says the voice on the other end of the line.

My eyes snap open.

"Who is this?" I ask. Even though I think I might already know.

"It's Noah," he says. "I called you the other day. Not sure if you got my message."

I close my eyes. I try to picture Noah the way I used to see him when I liked him. But all I can see is Sam.

"You still there?" Noah asks.

"I'm here."

"I'm glad you answered. You're a hard girl to reach. You know that?" he says.

"No, I'm not."

He laughs. And then, when he speaks his voice is gentler, coaxing. "I want to see you."

I don't say anything and then he says, "Sadie, can I see you?"

It's so sad it's almost funny that it's this easy to make Noah pay attention to me. It's like he can sense that for the first time I honestly don't care about him.

I gaze at the constellation of cracks in my ceiling. Outside, sounds of the late afternoon traffic seep into my room. Things fall apart in exactly the way they're meant to. What's the point of trying to make anything different than how it wants to be? Sam is gone but Noah is here. And maybe, right now, just being the one who came back is enough.

*August*

# Chapter 37

It's weird to be getting ready for a first date with someone I've already done everything with. Maybe my order and Noah's is just moving backward, a movie playing in reverse.

When I'm dressed and my hair is done and my makeup is on how I like it, I stare at my reflection in the mirror. My lipstick is the right amount of dark. I imagine Noah looking at me. Leaning in to kiss me. I try not to think about Sam.

All week, I've tried not to wonder if he's back in New Hampshire yet. Or if he and Amanda will get back together. I've tried to press the image of his sad eyes out of my mind. Tried not to dream about the bright shimmering kisses we shared that felt like stepping into the sun.

Noah meets me on the corner of Sixth Street and Avenue A.

"Good evening," he says, smiling.

"Good evening . . . to you," I repeat awkwardly.

"You look really nice," he says.

"Thanks," I say. He looks nice, too.

We hug. We look like we belong together, in the stylish East Village on a warm summer night. So why do I feel so lonely?

Noah takes me to dinner at a sushi place near my street. "I like this place," he tells me. "It's been here forever. I can't stand all these places that keep opening up. I feel like every time I come home from school there's a new cupcake shop on my block."

I try to smile. "Yeah. What's the food like at school?"

"Bad. Fine. Whatever. I end up going out to dinner a lot," he says. "Do you know Mikey? He went to NYSA for tenth grade but then he dropped out and went to boarding school in Switzerland. He's awesome. He's a fool. I mean, he's nuts. But he's kind of a genius."

"I don't know him," I say.

"Oh, he's a character. For real," he says, laughing to himself about something he's reminded of. "His dad is like this high up diplomat. Mikey's like the opposite of a diplomat. People hate him, but also kind of love him."

Noah talks about Mikey the entire time we drink our green teas and wait for the server to take our orders. I try to stay focused on what he's saying, but I don't know who Mikey is and I don't care.

Finally, the waiter comes and I'm grateful that the Mikey monologue is over. But then, Noah launches in about another one of his friends named James who is also "a character."

When Noah segues from James into yet another friend, I stifle a yawn.

"What about you?" Noah says, as if realizing he's been going on and on. "Who are your best friends?"

"My best friend is Willa," I say, feeling proud.

"Don't know her," he says.

"You might recognize her if you saw her," I say. "She's in my grade and she has brown hair and glasses?"

"Nope," he says.

"You might know her sister, though," I say. "Danielle Davis-Spencer? She went to Eastside Prep but now she goes to Yale."

"Oh yeah, I know Danielle," Noah says. And he says "know" in that way that boys do when they're trying to imply they've hooked up with someone. "She's a crazy one."

"Yeah, she's kind of a party girl," I say uncomfortably.

"I have a buddy who goes to Yale and he and Danielle party together a lot. Trust me. There are stories."

And then, just like that, Noah is talking again. Telling me tales of all-night parties and middle of the night road trips to New Haven and I'm bored.

"What are you majoring in?" I ask, trying to get us on to something I can relate to.

"Probably semiotics," he says. "Like the philosophy of language or whatever. It's the best major at Brown."

"Sounds interesting," I say. "What's that like?"

"Hard to explain," he says conclusively.

It's funny. With Sam, it felt like every small topic opened up on to something bigger. Talking with Noah is the opposite, every conversation shrinking back to smaller things.

After dinner, Noah pulls out his phone and starts texting.

"There's a party at my friend Jack's apartment tonight," he says. "Wanna go? Come. I've been talking about myself all night. Let's keep hanging out. I want to know more about Sadie."

And then, he reaches under the table and grabs my knees. And I'm reminded of that other side of Noah. The side that knows exactly how to touch me to make the world disappear.

Noah's friend's apartment is enormous and fancy in a way that makes me afraid to touch anything. As soon as we get there, Noah goes to get us drinks and I stare out the movie-screen-sized windows that look down at the city by myself. We're up so high, I feel seasick looking down.

"Hey," Noah says.

I turn and he's holding out a beer to me, not smiling. His eyes are sparkling like I remember them.

I take a sip of beer and watch him. He steps toward the window and stares out at the view. This is the Noah who I liked: the one who was aloof and quiet and handsome. Someone I could project onto. Not the spoiled rich kid I just had dinner with. Would it be possible to date one Noah without dating the other?

Then, Izzy and Phaedra are there.

I haven't seen Phaedra since our fight. She gives me a hug. And then grabs onto both my shoulders and looks right into my eyes.

"We're fine, right?" she asks.

I nod limply.

"Good. 'Cause I love you," she says.

And then she turns to Noah and looks up at him with her heavy-lidded, blue-green eyes.

"Hi, Noah," she says, not smiling. "How are you?"

"Phaedra Bishop," he says, as if that's an answer.

"Do you guys want to smoke weed?" Izzy asks. "We were just going to do that in the bedroom."

"Sure." Noah shrugs. And then he looks at me. "Sadie? Do you smoke?"

"No," I say. "But I'll come."

"Atta girl," he says. And then he wraps his arm around my shoulders and walks with me like that down the hall, Izzy and Phaedra following behind.

The bedroom is lamp lit and cloudy, and thumping rap music is turned up so loud the whole room seems to pulse.

I sit in the desk chair and watch the others. Someone lights a joint and passes it around. Noah keeps changing the music on the speakers, and Izzy keeps taking group selfies. I feel as if I'm not even here. It's like I'm watching a play about a group of kids. I can see all of them, all of their fears and insecurities motivating each of their actions. There's Izzy: vying for Phaedra's approval; and Phaedra: the girl who is intent on making everything look so easy. But she's actually working really hard at it. I notice how she times her reactions to other people's jokes and never laughs too much, holding her approval close to her chest so that when she gives it out it means more. She tosses her hair at all the right times. Noah sits on the windowsill, trying to hang back but also aware that the girls keep twisting around to smile at him. He looks at me from across the room and half smiles. This is the dream I had for two years. Being accepted with these kids. Having Noah want me more than anyone else and having it not be a secret. I know I'm supposed to feel happy.

I wonder how long Noah's interest in me will last this time. Even though he's choosing me tonight, it's suddenly crystal clear to me that it's temporary. I can already see the other girls lining up to go next. Maybe Phaedra. Maybe Izzy. It doesn't matter. I don't care. That's how it works in these groups. People pass one another around. For whatever reason, I've popped up on Noah's rotation again. But it's not real.

I wonder if he knows that, too.

*Chapter 38*

The day after I lost my virginity to Noah was New Year's Day. It was a gorgeous, clear winter morning. The sky was an endless, unbroken blue that glowed over the city. The snow on the ground was the new kind, perfect blankets of unbroken white stretched across sidewalks like frosting.

I remember thinking: the only thing more beautiful than a beautiful winter day is a beautiful winter day when you just had sex with the hottest guy in your school.

My mom wasn't working that day, so we spent the morning walking around together. We walked through Washington Square Park, ducking under the bare black branches of trees that sagged under layers of sugary snow. Sharp icicles dripped from the old buildings circling the park like crystals. The air in my lungs was strong and bright and even my skin felt awake as we walked farther west and up toward Chelsea.

Even though it was freezing, we went up to the High Line and let the wind skirting across the Hudson slam against us. I remember looking at my mother when we were up there. The bright winter sun made her skin glow an almost blue white. Behind her, one of the brand-new glass luxury apartment buildings bounced sunlight back into my eyes, and I felt a jolt of happiness so strong it almost burned. My life was finally happening exactly the way it was meant to.

Later, I went over to Willa's. It was only three when I got there but at that time of year, the sun is already sinking. I told Willa everything that had happened with Noah the night before. When I was done, she looked at me hard. And then she said, "Are you okay? How do you feel today?"

That was the first crack in my happiness. That Willa seemed more worried for me than excited.

Later, I ate dinner with Willa's family as the world outside grew dim. The sun went down too quickly, and soon, it was night. And right about then, as we were clearing the table, something bad and aching and dark started to creep into the edges of my mind. I tried to push it away but I could feel its invisible pull, like gravity.

I hadn't expected Noah to call me. He didn't ask for my number or anything. But I guess I wasn't prepared for him to *not* reach out to me either. I started checking my e-mail and my phone compulsively. While Willa was brushing her teeth, I even logged into Snapchat and Yo and all these stupid apps just to see if Noah was online somewhere. But he was nowhere. The silence was deafening.

Then, just when we were getting into bed, my phone beeped.

I lurched for it, blood pumping hot in my ears.

I slid my fingers across the screen to see who it was. It was a text from a random girl in my English class reminding me about some school thing. My heart sank so fast that tears were coming by the time I was done reading her message. And by the time I went to put the phone down, I was crying too hard to breathe.

Willa was behind me on the other side of the bed. I think she thought I was laughing at first, because she giggled and said, "What's so funny?"

I wanted to say "Nothing." I tried to inhale but it sounded like an animal groan; it was this horrible wheezing sound.

Willa sprung across the bed and wrapped her arms around me.

"What's wrong?" she asked. "Are you okay?"

I couldn't speak. All I could feel was loss. Noah hadn't called me. He hadn't figured out a way to contact me. He wasn't thinking about me. It meant nothing. He had used me. He didn't like me. I had been easy. All these clichés, things I had always ignored because they had nothing to do with me, came back to me in a rush. There was a black hole in my chest and it was sucking hard at everything good.

I couldn't bring myself to look at Willa. Her world was still intact. Mine was shattered.

The next morning, though, I felt better. I was embarrassed that I had cried so much. I was just tired.

Over breakfast, I remember saying to Willa, "I'm fine now.

Noah probably just didn't call because it's a holiday and he was with his family or whatever. I'm sure we'll hang out again once school starts."

It's impossible to say now, looking back, if I really believed that.

# Chapter 39

Noah and I ride the elevator out of the building together. We lean against opposite walls of the elevator, and I can feel him staring at me the whole way down.

Outside, the night is still mild and warm. A little more quiet than usual because it's deep summer and people in this neighborhood are away.

"Where should we go now?" Noah asks as we wander down the street slowly.

"I don't know," I say. "I'm pretty tired."

Noah grabs my hand.

*He's so easy to manipulate,* I think. All I have to do is show indifference and he jumps into action.

Holding Noah's hand is strange. I remember holding his hand the night we had sex. I remember the way it felt like his thumb pressed all the way through my skin and into my palm. But now, it's just a hand. Just skin and bones and muscles contracting.

"Come back to my house with me," he says. "My parents are away. We can chill."

I stop walking and so does he.

A group of men in business suits spill out of a building.

The doorman whistles for a taxi, and the men pile in, drunk and rowdy.

When they're gone, it's quiet again.

Noah steps toward me and takes both of my hands in his. He squeezes them. The way he squeezed my foot that time.

I think about going home with Noah. I think about him picking me up and pressing me against the wall. Maybe the fact that I don't really think he's that nice or interesting wouldn't matter once we got back there. And then I think about how it would feel if I were going home with Sam right now. How I wouldn't have to talk myself into it. How everything about him—even the texture of his T-shirt, and the delicate skin on his ears—could make me melt.

"Why now?" I ask.

"Why now what?" Noah asks.

"Do you even remember that we hooked up?" I ask. "We had sex."

Noah's hands flinch nervously in mine. The amusement fades from his eyes.

"I know," he says.

"It was my first time," I tell him. "Did you know that?"

Noah drops my hands and takes a step back.

"For real?" he asks. "Fuck. I'm sorry. I had no idea. I'm so sorry. I wouldn't have. I didn't know."

I wait for him to go on but he doesn't.

"So why now?" I ask. "Why did you ignore me after that and now you're back? Out of nowhere?"

"It's not like that," he says.

"What's it like?" I ask.

"I don't know," he says, swallowing. "We're two people who have a connection. We went our separate ways, but it's still there. Don't you feel it, too?"

I look at Noah. He's as good-looking as ever. He hasn't changed. Maybe I'm the one who's changed.

"No." I shake my head. "I guess I don't. I'm going home."

"Wait," he says, stepping toward me again.

"No, seriously," I say, flinching away from him before he can touch me. "I'm not interested."

He nods like he understands, and then he turns away from me and heads back toward the building. I stand there, watching him go, and as he disappears into the lobby, I think, *Be good, Noah. Okay?*

And then I turn away from him, and as I walk down the street, I can't help but smile.

# Chapter 40

"I have to talk to you," Izzy says in class on Monday.

We are sitting in the two desks in the very back of the room. Izzy's expression is dead-serious.

"Is everything okay?" I ask.

"Eyes up here," Benji says, looking right at me.

It's Day One of the final critiques. Today, half the class presents. Tomorrow, the second half presents, including me. I'm one hundred percent not ready. Izzy is in the first half, but she doesn't seem to care at all.

"I know this is weird but I have to tell you before you find out some other way," she says. "Noah and Phaedra hooked up yesterday."

Even though I'm certain I don't like Noah anymore, my first thought is *ouch*. That was so fast. Too fast. It makes me feel dirty. The empowerment I felt when I walked away from him the other night is gone.

"Oh no. You look sad. Are you okay?" Izzy asks.

"I'm not upset," I say. "It's just really fast. How did that even happen?"

"I've upset you, I'm sorry," Izzy says, putting a hand on my thigh. "Phaedra doesn't want to do anything that's weird for you."

I look up at Izzy, and I can see a smile sizzle behind her mascaraed eyes.

"You didn't upset me; I don't care," I repeat. I don't want to give Izzy the satisfaction of knowing that there's even a little part of me that's still jealous. "Noah is absolutely nothing to me. I don't like him at all."

"Good," Izzy says. "Because Phaedra asked him about you and if it was gonna be weird or whatever, and he said no. He said you guys hooked up once when you were drunk but that it was never anything. And he told Phaedra he's liked her forever. Like since middle school. They stayed up all night talking. I feel like they're gonna be really serious."

"Okay, let's get back to work," Benji says, returning to the front of the room.

Noah told Phaedra there was never anything between us? It's like I'm being erased from history, or becoming invisible.

I glance at Izzy. She's grinning and hiding her cell phone under her desk and texting.

After class, I try to slip out of the room alone, but Izzy catches up with me.

"I am so glad this class is over," Izzy moans. "Benji has had it out for me since the beginning. He's the effing worst."

"I like him," I say lamely.

"Yeah, of course you like him," she scoffs. "He kisses your ass because of who your dad is."

Her words stun me. "Excuse me?" I ask.

"Whoa! Chill." Izzy laughs. "It's not a big deal. It's just the truth. Everyone was talking in the darkroom the other day when you were having your meeting with Benji."

I stop walking. "Everyone in the class thinks that?"

"It's not something everyone thinks," she replies, a little meanly. "It's a fact. Your dad is a huge artist, of course Benji is going to want to suck up to his daughter. Remember when you handed in a postcard for an assignment? He let you redo it. I mean, he would never in a million years let anyone else get away with that."

I want to speak, to tell Izzy she's wrong, but I can't find my voice. I want to tell her she's just jealous because she's bad at photo. I want to tell her that Benji doesn't like her because she's lazy and not talented and dumb.

But I know if I speak I'll start crying and that would be the most humiliating thing of all. So I turn and walk away. I can hear her calling out to me to stop, but I don't turn around. I keep walking, not slowing down or looking over my shoulder, until I'm back on my own block. Then, I slump down at the bus stop on my corner and rest my backpack on my lap.

Izzy's words chase me all the way home. *Everyone thinks that Benji only likes you because of who your dad is.* It can't be true, I tell myself. But didn't Benji go to Allan's opening? Didn't he tell me that Allan gave a lecture when he was at Yale and it was packed? Wasn't he shockingly easy on me about the postcard assignment? He could have failed me if he wanted. He could have done anything.

There's an ad for City College mounted on the inside wall

of the bus stop. It's been here for years. People have scribbled their names on it in Sharpie and scratched their tags into the plastic shell that's covering the picture. But the model in the ad still looks happy. She's sitting at a big desk table with a laptop screen in front of her. "Discover. Create. Become," read the words over her smiling face.

Follow your dreams. Everyone always says that. Everyone on the planet wants to find their passion and be good at it.

I wonder what's happened to the girl in the poster. I wonder if she was a model or a real student. I can tell the advertisers think that she's 'regular pretty' not 'supermodel pretty,' but she's still prettier and cleaner and happier than anyone in the real world really is. I wonder if she *discovered, created, became* or if she ended up selling cars in a lonely town, raising kids and hating her husband, or becoming a famous model and getting rich and living alone and wondering why her life didn't become what she hoped.

Eventually the world will flatten out my dreams just like it does everyone's.

Forget Benji. Forget photography. Forget Allan. What I need is to start from scratch. I need a good, clean do-over. It's time to accept the fact that this summer was a disaster and let go. And I know exactly how I'm going to do it.

# Chapter 41

Skipping class is easy. The hard part is deciding what to do with my day. First, I get an iced coffee and wander through SoHo. I have almost fifty dollars of allowance I've saved and I feel like spending it on something dumb. So I walk to all the trendy, polyester disposable clothing stores on Broadway. People scurry past me, striding down the street with briefcases, wearing suits, trying to fight the sweat that's breaking out all over their skin, smearing their makeup and making their aftershave evaporate off of them in pungent waves.

This part of the city is the worst. Crowded and packed with tourists year-round. Everywhere are screaming children and the flags of all the mega clothing stores wave from the sides of buildings like the sails of sad, commercial ships. I feel a shredding sense of nothingness, being stuck down here on a hot day, like if the city swallowed me up it might never spit me out.

I wonder what's happening in Benji's class right now. What will Benji do when he realizes I'm ditching? Will he fail me? If Izzy's right, he would never do that because I'm

Allan Bell's daughter. If he lets me get away with it, I'll know for sure that she was right.

It's not even eleven a.m. by the time I'm done window shopping and the day starts to drag. I try not to notice all the faces of the people walking past me on the street that I want to photograph. Photography is a thing of my past. It was just a phase I went through in high school. At least Allan would be glad to know I'm taking his advice.

As I walk, the morning drizzle turns into a heavy rain, and by noon, it has become a wild summer storm. Water seems to come at me from all directions. The sky is dark as night. You'd never know that behind the wall of clouds, the sun is still afternoon-high in the sky.

I duck into a deli and buy an umbrella. But back on the street, a gust of wind grabs the umbrella and suctions it so hard that the whole shell flips inside out. I tug at the stem and try to pull it back, but I feel one of its spidery legs snap from the pressure.

I toss the broken umbrella in a trash can on the corner and give up. I'm already drenched, anyway.

At home, I check my e-mail. Allan still hasn't e-mailed or called since our fight. It's funny in a depressing way that I'm not even surprised. He doesn't care about me at all. The realization is so huge, it makes me feel more numb than sad. Like thinking about climate change or overpopulation or the possibility of getting hit by a car. Some things about life are so hopeless, so impossible to control, they can only inspire apathy.

My phone rings, shaking me out of my daze. It's my mom. She's supposed to be teaching a class, but I don't answer. Then, a minute later, she sends me a text message asking where I am and if I'm okay. Then, before I can even write back, she calls again.

"Hello?" I say.

"Oh, thank God," she gasps.

"What's the matter?" I ask.

"Why aren't you in class? Your teacher called. He said you didn't come in today and it's the last day and—where are you?" she asks.

"Home," I say. "I just couldn't go to photo today. I'm fine. It's a long story."

"I'm leaving work early. I'm on my way home. You better be there," she says, and then hangs up.

My mom is soaked when she walks into the apartment twenty minutes later. Puddles pool at her feet. She doesn't bother taking off her shoes or her coat, she just collapses onto the couch next to me, getting everything all wet around us.

"What happened?" she demands. "Are you all right?"

"I'm fine," I grumble. "I told you. It's a long story."

"You love that class." She frowns. "I don't understand."

"I did love it," I say. "I thought I wanted to do an independent study in photo next year and go to art school and then Allan literally laughed at me when I told him."

My mom cocks her head, confused. "So?"

"So that's what happened," I say, because it's obvious.

**268**

"Allan ruined it. He's an artist and even he thinks being an artist is pointless."

She looks baffled. "Why do you care what he says? He doesn't know you at all. He's not interested in other people. It's not about you. It's about him."

"He's my father," I say. "And he's an artist. What do you mean why do I care what he thinks? He's the only person who gets it."

Her eyes are glued to mine and I can see her thinking. Then she sighs and sinks back down into the couch and closes her eyes, defeated. She reaches up and pushes her hair back off her face and it stays because it's still wet from the rain.

"What's wrong?" I ask.

"Allan," she says simply. "He's such a disappointing person. All I ever wanted was for you to not have to depend on him for anything. He lets people down."

For a moment I think she's going to cry, and my heart expands, threating to splinter inside my chest. I've never seen my mom cry. I'm not sure if I could handle it if she did.

But she doesn't cry. She just folds her hands carefully in her lap and nods her head, like she's thinking something through. Suddenly, I want to hug her for that. It's impossible to rock her. Someday, I want to be like that, too.

"Do you wish Allan was different?" I ask. "Do you wish he had been the kind of guy who wanted to marry you and be a father to me and everything?"

"Sadie." My mom drops her head forward in exasperation for a minute before looking at me. "What do you want me to say?"

"I don't know," I say, shifting around. "Anything. I want to know that you guys loved each other but circumstances pulled you apart. Or that you tried to make it work. I want to feel like I was born out of love. That I'm meant to be here."

Her expression shifts and I have the feeling, even before she speaks, that she's about to say something that she's never told me before.

"I was never in love with Allan," she says. "I was in love with someone else for ten years. Maybe more. And he was married. He moved away with his family a few months before I met Allan. I was just trying to move on."

"What?" I exclaim, shrinking away from her. Quiet settles as I try to picture what she just told me. An affair? *For ten years?* It's a billion times worse than anything that happened with me and Noah. It's worse than anything I could imagine.

"Maybe I shouldn't have told you," she says. "But you keep asking me about Allan and you're never satisfied with what I tell you. Allan only means one thing to me: he gave me you."

"Who was he?" I ask, my voice a whisper. "Who was this other guy?"

"He was a dancer. He was older. A principal when I was a student. He slept with everyone," she says, laughing to herself a little. "All my friends. And me."

"How come you never told me about him?" I ask.

"Because it's a terrible story to share," she says. "I acted horribly and I suffered so much. It's a really sad story. But it has a good ending."

"What's the ending?" I ask.

"You," she says, pulling me toward her. She's soaking wet, but I let her hug me. "You are the love of my life. Beyond anything I ever felt for anyone."

"But," I object, "I thought the love of your life was supposed to be a romantic thing."

"It can be whatever you want," she says, talking into my hair. "For me, it wasn't a man. Allan . . . I never loved him in that way. I mean, I love him because he's your father. And I respect him, in a way. But he never broke my heart. And I never wanted him to break yours."

She lets go of me and I sink into the couch.

"So, what? Allan's just a sperm donor?" I ask, brushing aside tears. I don't know when I started crying. I don't know why.

"You don't have to have a relationship with him if you don't want one," she says. "It's up to you."

"But I do. Or I think I do. He's just so frustrating. He gave me that camera. And I just felt like he knew I was gonna be an artist. I thought he wanted me to. And then . . . and then I was so wrong. He doesn't care at all. And it makes me feel so stupid for even trying."

My mom grabs my shoulders and stares right into my eyes.

"Listen to me. Allan can't make you stop being interested in art because he is not the person who made you love it in the first place," she says.

"He is though," I say.

"No, he's not," she declares, unblinking. "He might have given you that camera, but big deal! Do you know how many ballet shoes I bought you over the years? It didn't turn you into a dancer."

I laugh. "I wasn't very good at ballet, was I?"

"You didn't love it," she says. "You complained constantly. I couldn't make you a dancer. Allan can't make you an artist. It doesn't work that way. You aren't simply a combination of me and Allan. You are entirely one hundred percent your own person."

"But Allan is an artist. He's so powerful in that world. I can't do it without his support and he said—"

My mom cuts me off. "Don't dignify whatever stupid things he said by repeating them."

I stop talking.

"You loved this photography class," she says firmly. "You can't give up on it now. You can't give up on yourself."

I sink down into the couch and close my eyes. I know my mom is right. But what good is it now? After, ditching class, I ruined everything. "Benji's going to fail me. I'm such an idiot."

"He wants to meet with you," she said. "I called him after I talked to you and told him you were all right. He was worried, too. And then I said I'd bring you in tomorrow so you can talk."

# Chapter 42

Benji and I are alone in his office and it's awkward. My mom had a private meeting with Benji before mine. Now she's waiting for me outside.

"Are you going to fail me?" I ask.

Benji smiles, then frowns, then smiles. But the smile he lands on is not a happy smile. "I don't want to."

"Why not?" I ask.

"I've never failed anyone," he says. "And you don't deserve to fail, I don't think."

"Plus, I'm Allan Bell's daughter," I say. "So . . . there's that."

Benji shifts uncomfortably. "What does that mean to you?"

"What does it mean to you?" I counter.

Benji blinks. "It means you have a lot to overcome if you want to be an artist."

That makes me quiet. I've always seen it the other way, like having Allan for a father should make it easier for me to be one, too.

"That's not what I thought you were going to say," I admit.

"What did you think?" he asks.

"People in the class have been saying you only like me because my father is who he is," I say. "That I'm not talented."

Benji leans forward, but he doesn't look angry. "I know."

My eyes widen. "Wait. What? You know, too?"

"Another student talked to me about it," Benji says.

I sit bolt upright in my chair.

"When you didn't come to class yesterday, another student, whose name I will keep between myself and her," Benji continues, "talked to me. And she said that she might have upset you by implying that I play favorites with you because of your dad. She was concerned that she was responsible for your not coming to class."

"Izzy told you that?" I blurt.

"I don't want to name names," Benji says, but he says it in a way that means *yes.*

I'm shocked that Izzy confessed to Benji. I can't process what that means.

"You know that's not true, right?" Benji asks. "I don't play favorites."

"I don't know," I say.

I wait for Benji to go on, but he doesn't. He just looks at me, and I can see him contemplating whether or not he should keep talking. Then he says, "You know I just spoke to your mom."

I nod.

"She's great," Benji says. "You're very lucky to have a mother like that. She said you've had a rough time this summer. I hope this is okay, but she told me that your father hasn't been encouraging of you pursuing art."

**274**

I shrug. "Not really."

"I'm not a therapist or a counselor or whatever," he says. "But I'll just say this: you don't need your father's approval to be an artist. I'm not close with my family. I never have been. They don't understand what I do. They think I'm crazy for not living in the small town where we grew up and being an insurance salesman. I've always had to look outside my family for role models. And that can be disappointing. But it's also brought a lot of really great people into my life."

I look at Benji, and for the first time, I wonder about all kinds of things about him that I've never wondered—where he's from, and whether or not he's married, and what his parents look like. If he goes home for Christmas. If he was popular in high school or an outsider.

"Where are you from?" I ask.

"Indiana," he says. "But, that's not the point. We aren't talking about me. I have a serious question for you."

"Okay," I say, wincing a little. This is the longest and most personal conversation I've ever had with a teacher, and it's making me feel embarrassed for both of us.

"Tell me something," Benji says. "What's your favorite thing about photography? Your answer doesn't have to have anything to do with this class. I'm just curious."

I swallow. "I love taking pictures. I think I like taking pictures even better than printing them in the darkroom."

"Okay." Benji nods. "Good. What do you like about taking pictures?"

"I like how when I'm walking around with my camera on,

I notice things that I wouldn't normally notice. I know this sounds dumb, but it's almost like having the camera gives me a superpower and I can see invisible things."

Benji smiles slowly. "That's incredible."

"Not really," I say, sinking into my seat. "It's cheesy."

Benji shakes his head. "No. It's not. It's beautiful, really."

I take a deep breath. Then I blurt, "Am I gonna fail the class because I didn't show up for the final?"

"No," Benji says without hesitating. "If you do it. If you hand it in to me before grades are due next week."

"But I haven't even started," I confess. "I don't know what pictures I'm going to hand in for the final."

"You'll figure it out," he says. "You have a lot of great work to choose from. The only thing you need to do is ask yourself what you're trying to say."

"I'd need more time," I admit. "I haven't even started my final prints. So, I'd need . . . like . . . *days*."

"That's fine," he says. "You can use the darkroom this week. I'll be in my office grading, but you can print."

I don't know what to say to that. I'm trying to formulate the words when Benji stands up, ending the discussion.

He walks me to the door. "Thank you," I blurt. And then, right before I leave, I turn to him.

"Why are you giving me another chance?" I ask him.

"Because you're up against a lot," he says, "and I want you to win."

My mom and I walk home together after my meeting with Benji. All traces of the sweet, sparkling early summer have vanished. Now, the city sinks under the oppressive August heat.

I'm wearing sandals and the back straps are chafing at my ankles from sweat and friction. When I get home, I'll shower and then I'll be clean for five seconds before I start sweating again.

"Benji says you're really talented," my mom says as we cross First Avenue. "He said you're one of the best students he's ever worked with."

"It's so weird," I say. "This girl in my class, who I thought was my friend, told me that Benji only likes me because Allan is an artist."

"She's wrong," my mother says firmly. "I think you know that. And this person is clearly a jerk."

"But still," I say. "It's just so annoying. Even if I get into art school, everyone is always gonna think it's because of Allan. Even though it's the opposite and he's so discouraging."

My mom and I walk carefully around a pile of trash bags that are leaking a stream of brown fluid. The sour smell of garbage washes over us.

"I wish I could say you're wrong," my mom says. "But you're not. That used to happen with me all the time when I was a student. Because, you know, I had this . . . relationship with a principal dancer and he taught a lot of our classes. So whenever I got praise from him, everyone always thought it was because of our relationship."

I look at my mom. I can easily picture her being a young dancer. She was probably the prettiest girl in the class. No wonder her teacher singled her out.

"How did you know you wanted to be a dancer?" I ask her.

"I don't know, exactly," she says. "It started because I was good at it. That helped a lot. But also I enjoyed it. Even though it was hard. It was grueling at times. Bleeding feet and bunions and exhaustion and all of that. You know the stories."

"How did you enjoy something so hard?" I ask. "It sounds awful."

"Maybe enjoyment isn't the word," she says. "It was bigger than enjoyment. It's like, the world made sense to me when I was dancing in a way that it didn't anywhere else. I just, always understood what was happening in ballet class. I never felt . . . lost. Does that make sense?"

It does, because that's exactly how I feel about photography.

"And you think that's enough reason to do something with your life? Just 'cause you like it and you're good at it?" I ask.

"I think so," she says simply.

"Did it bother you that nobody really goes to see ballet anymore? I just feel like, why should I work so hard at photography when there's, like, nothing really earth-changing about doing it. That if I didn't do it, the world wouldn't be a worse place," I say.

"The world would be a worse place without your pictures," she counters. "You are bringing order and beauty into the world. And that's how I felt about ballet. And that's enough."

"What if that's not enough?"

My mom stops walking and looks at me.

"Sadie, I don't have all the answers," she declares.

That's not what I wanted to hear. But there's something comforting about hearing the truth, even when it's not perfect.

"You're gonna have to get your own answers," she continues. "But if there is one thing I want for you, it's for you to fight for the person you want to be and for the things that you love. Do you think it was easy being a dancer? Or being a mother? None of it has been easy. I fought for it and I still fight for it. And it's worth every single second because I love you. If you don't fight, you'll never find out what you're capable of."

Back in my room, I examine the picture of the boy on the subway I took earlier in the summer. It's good. Izzy was wrong that Benji is only nice to me because of Allan. She knows it. And deep down, I know it, too.

I look at the postcards on my wall. Their fake cheerfulness, which has always made me happy, seems so dark now. They taunt me by showing me this phony world that doesn't exist, where the sunset splinters into a zillion vivid colors and the city is made of glass. Why do I save these stupid things anyway? They erase everything and everyone I care about. In these pictures you can't see the way the city is constantly decaying and being repaired, or the heavy machinery and the rank tunnels. You can't see the way that grass sprouts up in the wrong places, or all the rusted fire escapes and the graffiti on the subway ads or any of the millions of people who live here. All that's left in these pictures are hollow buildings and empty streets.

I sink onto the floor with the photo books that Benji lent me and thumb through their pages. They are full of photographs of the way things actually are, the opposite of the postcards. Here is a lonely gas station on the side of a wide freeway. Here is a woman in a diner by herself, sadly sipping coffee that looks weak. Here are a group of sweaty teenagers at a concert. Their bodies are inked up with tattoos; their faces are red and pulsing with rage. This is the real world. The complicated, messy, invisible world that you don't see when all you're looking for is a prize.

Sad things are a part of life. Some sad things are big, like dads who don't care about their kids or moms who have you in high school and then have too many boyfriends and make you move around too much. Some are medium sized, like people who you think are your friends but who turn out to be strangers. And some are small, like grown-ups eating dessert alone. Like walking past my mom's bedroom at night and seeing the light on in her room, but not going in.

One of the pushpins that never stays put falls out of my board and onto the floor. The postcard drops, swinging crookedly from the one remaining tack. It's a postcard of the Brooklyn Bridge beneath a rainbow, with the words "I ♥ NY" stamped across the too-blue sky.

I stand up and take the postcard down off the wall. I remember when I bought it. My mom and I had just gone to see *The Nutcracker* and then we stopped for hot chocolate at a deli afterward where I bought this card.

I pick up my phone and text Sam. We haven't spoken

or texted since he left, but I write: what's your mailing address?

A minute later, he responds. No questions, no emojis, just the information. Still, it feels good to see his name on my phone again. I text back: thanx. He writes: it's really good to hear from you. I write back an emoticon of a person sticking out their tongue. He writes: is that all I get? I laugh. Then I write back: for now. Then, I sit down at my desk with the postcard and take a pen out of my drawer. And I write.

Hi, Sam,

I don't know why I'm sending you a postcard of New York because I know you know what the city looks like, plus if you didn't, this postcard wouldn't help since it's the fakest thing ever.

I've thought about you every day since you've been gone. I miss you. How is being back? Tell me everything.

Sadie

*Chapter 43*

Benji is giving me a second chance and I can't let him down. I have to make this the best Photo 2 final ever. This must be what my mom meant about fighting for things you want.

The idea came to me when I sent Sam the postcard with the Brooklyn Bridge on it. The next morning, I went to the big professional photo store on Eighth Avenue to see if they carried what I needed to make my project real, and they did.

I bought five packs of light-sensitive-postcard paper. Each piece of paper is regular postcard size, four by six inches, and the back is lined so that you can actually write in an address, put a stamp on it, and send it in the mail.

I arrive at the classroom ten minutes before Benji, because I want him to know that I'm all-in. On the first morning, Benji shows me how to mix the chemicals myself, which is a responsibility that's usually reserved for seniors. But Benji says he has too much grading to do, and if I want to use the darkroom, I have to set up and clean up myself.

For the next three days, I'm in the darkroom from seven thirty a.m. to four p.m. when Benji leaves. I only take breaks to eat and drink sodas from the vending machine on the empty quad. The days are getting shorter. It's crazy to think that in a few weeks, school will be packed.

I print seven postcards each day, laboring over the light settings so that these are the best prints of the summer. I print all my favorite pictures—ones I handed in for critiques, like the boy on the subway and the inside of my drawer, and also ones that I took for fun. Like the picture I took with the four by five of my mom in the kitchen and all of the lotions lined up in the bathroom. I even print a photograph I took one afternoon that just shows a cloud shaped like a hand. I want the collection of images to come together to make a tapestry of summer that is as much about the city and the sky as it is about my personal experience and all the things that happen behind closed doors.

I know Benji knows what I'm working on, because he sometimes walks through the lab and sees me hanging my test prints on the clothesline to dry, but he doesn't ask me about it. I think he can sense that I'm focused and he doesn't want to disrupt my flow.

After I'm done printing on the third day, I go to a stationery store and buy a pretty cardboard box, just the right size for my project. Later, I sit at my desk in my room and put stamps on the back of each of my postcards.

Part of my idea is that I want Benji to actually use the postcards. I want him to write notes to friends and family from other parts of the world and send them in the mail. I wish I could be there when someone who I've never met gets the postcard and sees my photograph. For that moment, the photograph will tie me together with this stranger, the way that all the books I've read and the movies I've seen and the photos that I love tie me to the people who made them. It's a mysterious bond, but a real one. I think, maybe, it's something worth fighting for.

I arrange the postcards neatly in the small box. On the outside, I write, *"Postcards from the Invisible City—Sadie Bell. Final Project. Photo 2."*

It feels like a lot of things are ending all of a sudden. When I hand in this project tomorrow, it will be the end of Photo 2. In a few weeks, school will start and it will be the end of the best and worst summer of my life. And in nine or ten months, it will be the end of high school all together.

I pick up my smooth box of postcards. It's heavy from all the paper inside. I run my fingers over its clean surface. Soon, my postcards will slowly be scattered into the world. It might take Benji years to get through all of them. It's nice to remember that not everything is ending. Some things have only just begun.

"Knock knock," I say out loud, because the door to Benji's office is open.

"Hi, Sadie," Benji says. "Can I help you?"

"I'm done," I say. I place the box of postcards on his desk. "I cleaned up the darkroom and dumped the developer into the chemical bins."

"Good, thank you," Benji says, but he's staring at the box.

He picks it up. Carefully opens the lid. Thumbs through the photographs.

"These are gorgeous," he says. "The print quality is beautiful. Look at the value of the sky there—wow. Nicely done."

After that, Benji asks me what I'm going to do with the rest of my summer, and he tells me that he is going to visit friends in upstate New York for a week before school starts.

"I should get back to grading," he says, after a few minutes. "This is my least favorite part of my job."

"Okay, I'll go," I say.

Before I leave, Benji says, "I'm impressed. Thank you for . . . I don't know. A great summer."

"Thank you," I say. "Thank you for everything. Seriously. I was about to quit."

He sticks out his hand.

I'm surprised. I've never touched, let alone shaken hands with a teacher. I take his hand and he shakes it firmly. He holds my gaze steadily as he does it. It feels like a real, adult handshake and while it makes me feel sort of embarrassed, it mainly makes me feel proud.

He knows what I know, I think. We might have had some hard times this summer, and we might never know each other outside the walls of this school, but we have a bond that is stronger than time. He wants me to be an artist like him, and he is going to show me how to do it. Or maybe it's not that he wants me to be like him. Maybe it's just that he believes in me. And I think that might be contagious, because right now, I do too.

*Chapter 44*

From: Sam M.

To: Sadie Bell

Subject: Re:

    I'm okay. Better now that I've heard from you.

    How are you?

    The postcard isn't all lies btw. The city *is* beautiful.

From: Sadie Bell

To: Sam M.

Subject: Re:

Dear Sam,

    Here's a scan of the picture I took of you on
the bridge to Randalls Island. That was such an
amazing day. I felt like the world went upside
down for a moment, in the right way, if that
makes sense.

    My father is coming over for dinner this weekend.
It's going to be so weird to see him after
everything. My mom is going to be there, too,
which is going to make it doubly weird. Or maybe

it will be good. Either way, I'm trying not to care
so much what he thinks.
I keep thinking about the time we spent together.
I know we only knew each other for a short period
of time but it felt longer. Am I wrong?

From: Sam M.
To: Sadie Bell
Subject: Re:
Dear Sadie,

Not wrong. It was crazy. Don't judge this like a
* real * photo because I'm sure it's not good
in that way. But this is me and my mom's old
boyfriend. The one with the tattoos who I thought
hated me. Guess what he doesn't. When I got
back I just swallowed my pride and called him. He
was really nice. He's helping me enroll in a NHCC
class this fall that's open to high school students.
Philosophy 101.

From: Sadie Bell
To: Sam M.
Subject: Re:
Dear Sam,

Your mom's old bf is cute. He has great tattoos. If
he was my professor, I'd probably think he was the
coolest. I actually like this photo even though it's
just a webcam picture. You guys look happy!

From: Sam M.

To: Sadie Bell

Subject: Re:

Dear Sadie,

   Send me a picture of you.

From: Sadie Bell

To: Sam M.

Subject: Re:

Dear Sam,

   How's this?

From: Sam M.

To: Sadie Bell

Subject: Re:

Dear Sadie,

   You were a cute ten-year-old. But I think you might be a better photographer than whoever was taking pictures for your elementary school yearbook. Send me one that you took.

From: Sadie Bell

To: Sam M.

Subject: Re:

Dear Sam,

   Here's a self-portrait I took for my final project. I didn't hand it in when it was due because I was too busy being a subversive conceptual artist.

From: Sam M.

To: Sadie Bell

Subject: Re:

Dear Sadie,

   I'm glad you didn't hand that picture in.


From: Sadie Bell

To: Sam M.

Subject: Re:

Dear Sam,

   Why?


From: Sam M.

To: Sadie Bell

Subject: Re:

Dear Sadie,

   I don't want anyone to see it besides me.

*Chapter 45*

The next day, I go for a walk with a new roll of film in my camera and start taking pictures. It feels liberating to have no assignments and to know these pictures are just for myself.

I point the camera up to the sky and take a picture of a helicopter that's looping the city.

Just then, my phone rings. It's a blocked number.

"Hello?"

"Sadie? It's Izzy."

I freeze.

"Don't hang up," she blurts. "I called you from my landline because I was afraid you wouldn't answer if you saw it was me."

"Okay," I reply tightly.

"I'm sorry," she says.

I tell Izzy I'll meet her at Tompkins Square Park and start walking there. I don't know what to expect or even what I want. I still don't know why Izzy told Benji about all that mean stuff she said to me. I still don't know why she said it in the first place. But between Sam leaving, and struggling to finish my final, and cobbling my love of photography back together after Allan trashed it, I haven't thought about Izzy very much.

I did notice, though, that she isn't taking Advanced Photo next year. Benji e-mailed the new class earlier today and I checked all the names. She wasn't on it. I can't help feeling a little relieved.

When I get to the park, it's packed. There are couples holding hands and clusters of people slung across the benches with straw hats. A group of old men linger around the fence, smoking cigars, yelling at one another in a foreign language. I photograph everyone I can. A girl in stiletto heels with too much makeup on, clutching her purse to her chest walks past me, and I photograph her from behind.

I spot Izzy sitting on a bench and she waves.

I sit down next to her.

"Hi. Thanks for meeting me," she says.

"Umm . . . you're welcome," I say.

Across from us, a gaggle of Goth kids are spread out on the grass. They're the real kind of Goth, the ones who sleep in subway stations and carry backpacks full of all their belongings. One of them is a pale-haired girl with an angelic face. Her black tank top is held together with a zillion safety pins. I snap her photo, wondering as I do it, if I'll be able to capture exactly what it is I'm seeing.

"I'm sorry," Izzy says.

I put down my camera and stare at her.

"When you didn't come to the final critique, I felt like it was my fault," she says. "I shouldn't have said that Benji only likes you because of who your dad is. It's not true. I told Benji what I said to you. I was so freaked out that you'd fail the class and that I ruined your life."

Her hair is in a ponytail and she runs her hands over it nervously. I've never seen her so worried.

"I know," I say. "He told me."

"He did?" she asks. "What did he say?"

"Nothing really," I say. "Why? What happened?"

"He just lectured me," she says, rolling her eyes. "But I don't care. I already knew I wasn't gonna get into advanced photo so whatever. I had nothing to lose."

I look at Izzy, and really contemplate her. Her blue eye shadow and her baggy sweater and her deliberately messed up hair. She puts so much energy into covering herself up, and it makes me wonder what she's afraid of underneath.

"I'm taking advanced photo next year," I say. "Benji let me hand in the final late."

"Omigod, phew," she says, placing a hand on her chest. "I really have been freaking out."

Izzy's remorse seems real, but I still feel guarded and uneasy.

"Why'd you say all that stuff to me anyway?" I ask.

She stares at her hands, looking super ashamed. She seems younger and more scared than usual. All of a sudden, I can picture little Izzy and it makes me feel a surprising wave of tenderness toward her.

Then she looks up. "I don't know. I guess I'm just pissed.

Because before this class, I was so sure I wanted to go to art school. And now I don't know where I want to go to college. I don't know what I want to be or what I want to study or, what part of the world I want to live in, even. I'm so confused. Benji's class really messed with my head. I struggled so hard."

"That sucks," I say. And I mean it. I've been so obsessed with my own worries that I never considered what Izzy was going through.

"You probably can't understand what that's like," Izzy says, forcing a laugh. "You're so good at photo. And you're just . . . you're special. Without even trying to be."

"What? No," I say, smiling. "Now you're going too far."

She laughs. "I'm serious. I try to be special, but I'm not. I don't know who I am right now. And Phaedra doesn't get it because her whole life is laid out for her. She can fuck up or not, it doesn't matter. The world basically revolves around her and she knows it."

"No it doesn't," I say.

"No what doesn't?" Izzy asks.

"The world doesn't revolve around anyone," I say. "And Phaedra knows that, too."

Izzy raises her eyebrows. "I don't know . . ."

"And besides," I say. "I don't *not-try* to be special. I try really, really hard."

Izzy looks at me and smiles. It's a real smile, the kind that smooths over the bumps between us. I smile back. And I realize: Izzy's not perfect. But neither am I.

Izzy's phone interrupts us with a text message.

"Hang on, it's Phaedra, I have to write back," Izzy says. When she's done typing she says, "Phaedra's freaking out because we were supposed to hang out later but I totally forgot my cousin is in town and I have to do a family thing tonight. She keeps bringing it up and trying to get me to change my plans but I literally can't. And it's so annoying because when she flakes on me, I'm not allowed to say anything to her about it."

I think about the way Phaedra twisted me around in our conversation about her party until I was apologizing for something that wasn't even my fault. I wonder how often she does that to Izzy. "Why do you put up with that?"

"What do you mean?" Izzy asks, looking at me like I'm crazy. "She's my best friend. I love her."

It's funny, because even though Izzy sounds insane, I know exactly how she feels. We can't choose who we love. Sometimes, we love people who are wrong for us.

I glance at the screen and see that it's almost five.

"I have to go," I say, standing up.

"Where are you going?" Izzy asks.

"Home," I say. "My father is coming over for dinner. He goes back to LA next week but he called last night and he wanted to see me and my mom once more before he takes off."

"That's great," she says.

"Maybe," I say. I'm sick of protecting Allan. "He's kind of a weirdo. I don't know if it'll be nice or just awkward."

She laughs a little. "We're going to our country house tomorrow for the last few weeks until school starts. So . . . I guess I'll see you at school?"

"Yeah," I say. "See you there."

"Thanks for talking," she says. "I am really sorry."

"It's okay," I say. "I'm okay." And I think, *you know what? I really am.*

My mom and I get Indian takeout the night that Allan is coming over for dinner. We line the windowsills with tea candles, and my mom puts her African-Celtic record on the record player in the living room.

"You know what I've been thinking?" my mom asks. She's up on a ladder, pulling down a bottle of the wine she keeps up high.

"What?" I ask.

She hands me the bottle.

"It would be really nice if you started coming to the Yoga Center this year," she says. "Just take one class a week. It doesn't have to be mine. You can go to Satya's or Eugene. Eugene is really gentle, you'll love him. But try it. For me."

It's funny, I've spent so much time trying to do what Allan does, and it never occurred to me that my mom wants me to see what she does. How blind can I be?

"I'll totally do that," I say.

My mom climbs down off the ladder and smiles. "Really?"

"Of course. Done," I say.

We set the table and for a second, it's like we are back in our old apartment. The smell of Indian food and hearing that record, watching my mom light candles, reminds me of our old life. Maybe the thing that makes where you live home isn't the place, but the person in it. My mom is the only home I've ever known.

When the table is set my mom repins her hair using the small aluminum curve of the tea kettle as a mirror.

Outside, the sky is darkening even though it's only seven thirty. The days are growing shorter. Fall, the best season in New York, is around the corner. And once school starts, the dominos of all the seasons will begin to tumble down and the next thing I know it will be summer again. In almost exactly a year, I'll be leaving for college.

The buzzer rings and my mom and I look at each other.

"There he is," she says.

"The man of the hour," I deadpan. And for some reason, that makes us both laugh.

Allan is wearing his green Windbreaker and trendy sneakers. He got a haircut, too; his almost entirely white hair is tighter to his skull than usual.

Allan stares at my mom intensely when she opens the door, taking all of her in. Then, they hug lightly and my mom smiles at him for a split second before she backs away and offers him a glass of the wine he brought.

"This is a great little place," Allan says to her.

While my mom goes to the kitchen to open the bottle, Allan looks at me.

He looks like he's about to speak, he runs his hand over his face, and when he looks at me I see some shame or pity or something in his eyes. "Sadie, I . . . the other day didn't go like I hoped."

"Oh?" I say.

"Yeah, you know, I was really hoping we'd have a good time, and it didn't go well," he says.

"You didn't think it went well?" I repeat, dumbstruck. I stare at Allan. He has no idea what I've been through this past week. He doesn't know that I almost failed my photography class or that him not coming to the gala caused a fight between Phaedra and me. He has no idea that because of our fight, I went out and got blackout drunk, and my mom had to hold my hair back while I puked.

"I could have been more supportive of the art school thing," he says. "I'm just a bitter old man. Don't listen to me."

He says it in a light tone of voice, but his words land hard.

And then, I say the only thing I can think of that wouldn't feel like a total lie. I say, "You're a really important artist."

I don't even really know why I thought to say it right now. But all the other things I want to say to him, all the things I've come to believe about what kind of person he is and what kind of father he is, I'm not sure if he would understand. This, I knew he could understand.

But something weird happens. Allan's expression changes and he looks suddenly sad. Sad enough to cry.

"Nice wine!" my mom says cheerfully, handing a glass to Allan.

"Thank you." Allan takes the glass, looking disoriented.

"Sadie told me your show was a big success," my mom says.

"Who knows," Allan says.

During dinner, my mom and I barely talk. We just let Allan tell us about his new exhibit until he's run out of things to say. Canyons of silence, long and shapeless, open up during the meal but I don't mind. Before, I kept pumping Allan with questions, desperate to prove that I was interested in him, that I cared.

After dinner, my mom sits down on the couch and I sit down next to her and curl up under her arm, resting my head on her shoulder the way I would if we were alone. Allan sits awkwardly on one of the wooden dining room chairs, his feet and hands ticking nervously.

"Why don't you show Allan some of your photographs from the summer?" my mom asks. She turns to Allan, "They are so beautiful. I'm so proud."

Allan swallows and nods. "Right. Please. I'd love to see."

I go to my room and come back with my portfolio. I take three pictures out and line them up on the bookshelf so that they are propped up and we can all look at them together.

Allan walks up to them, looks closely.

From behind, I see that the skin on the back of his neck is wrinkled and that the cowlick on the top of his head is actually thinning, turning into a kind of bald spot. For a moment, I see him differently—an old man, trying to stay relevant, losing his hair, his skin growing saggy. You can be famous or larger than life or the most successful person in the world, but you're still just a human in a body. It makes me sad and also at the same time, less afraid.

"These are wonderful," Allan finally says. "Congratulations."

"Thank you," I say.

"I'll write down the name of a few artists whose work you should really look at," he says. "Your photos remind me of this German woman's work who shows at the same gallery as me in Switzerland. You'll like it."

After he's gone, my mom and I clean up with the music on.

"That wasn't bad," I say, drying a dish.

"You were so impressive," my mom says. "I know I can't take credit for who you are, but I wish I could. You blew his mind."

"You think?" I ask.

"I think he is intimidated by you," she says.

"No way," I say.

"Yes," she says. "I can tell."

And then I say, "You can take credit for me if you want."

And she laughs.

September

# Chapter 46

Sam and I are walking through the woods. We aren't on a trail so much as a narrow path of matted dirt. It looks like a person or maybe a deer has been here earlier, and we follow the places where the tall grass has been crushed. Overhead, trees canopy the forest, layers and layers of leaves denser than anything I've ever seen. Light slips to the ground in small, shimmering patches.

Sam keeps checking to see if I'm okay. He's walking a few steps in front of me, clearing the way. He pushes through a dense patch of brush and then he holds a small tree branch back and lets me pass, like opening a door. As I walk past him, my elbow grazes his stomach and his skin is warm.

The clearing comes without warning, a curtain being raised on the world. A pale, grassy field ringed with pine trees. Everything here is more beautiful than I have dreamed.

"This is it," he says. "My favorite place in the world."

I left New York at six this morning, and Sam picked me up at the bus station in New Hampshire seven hours later. First, we went to his house where I dropped off my things and met his mom, who it turns out looks exactly like Sam. I'll be sleeping in their guest room for the three nights that

I'm here. That's what our moms agreed on when they spoke on the phone last week to make the arrangements.

"This is beautiful," I say to Sam, gazing at the long field of soft green grass. I already love it here. I love the way the sky is blue all the way down to the place where it touches the tops of the trees. Not like in the city, where it always seems scorched around the edges. But I love the dirty city sky, too. It's okay, I think, to love both.

Sam lies down in the tall grass and I lie down beside him.

Mosquitoes hum and the grass is itchy on my skin. But I don't mind. Everything is messy and imperfect and exactly how it's supposed to be. That's the thing about falling in love: It's not about illusions, it's not about pretending everything is perfect. It's about seeing things for what they really are and wanting them anyway.

I roll onto my side so I can see Sam better.

"I've known you for two months exactly," I say. "Isn't that weird? It sounds like so little."

"It's not long," he agrees.

"But it feels long," I say. "Remember that day at the beach? What did you think of me then?"

Sam laughs. "You're kidding."

"No. Tell me." I giggle, flicking a loose chunk of dirt in his direction.

"I thought you were smart." He shrugs. "And cute."

"You did?"

"And I still think those things," he says. "I just think it even more now because I know it's true."

"You do?" I ask, blushing. I know it's stupid, and that I'm

fishing for compliments. Over the last week, Sam and I have talked on the phone every night and said things to each other I never thought I'd hear or say aloud.

"You are out of control right now," he says.

I laugh.

I remember the first time I looked into Sam's green eyes. I wonder if that one moment held within it all of the moments that would follow, the way that a seed, buried within the snow, holds inside it the tree it will become.

Or maybe that moment didn't contain anything that happened after. Maybe there is no inevitable sequence of events. Maybe you make things happen by fighting for them. That's why I didn't mess up my order by having sex with Noah. There is no order. There is just one day followed by another.

Sam's hand finds mine in the grass and our fingers weave together. "What do you want to do tonight?"

"I'll do whatever," I say. "What do you want to do?"

Sam doesn't answer, he just bites his lip. The way he's looking at me makes me flush all the way down to my toes.

I feel the sun and the sticky September air and I hear crickets and faraway birds. Maybe tonight, Sam will sneak out of his room and crawl under the covers on the foldout couch to be with me. Maybe during Thanksgiving break, he'll visit me in the city. There is no way to know what will happen.

Sam rolls onto his stomach. There's a patch of dirt behind us where the grass has died and disintegrated and Sam smooths out the dirt with his palms.

"What are you doing?" I ask.

Without answering me, Sam starts writing something, carving it into the dirt with his pointer finger.

He drags his finger like a snake and makes an *S*. Then, he writes an *A* and then a *D* and then an *I* and then an *E*.

I don't say anything, or even move. It's just my name. It's the most boring, familiar thing in the world. But now, written in the dirt in a place I've never been, each letter touched by Sam's hand, hovering in the air between us silently, it's like something I've never seen or heard before. Brand new.

"Sam," I say.

I reach for him at the same moment he reaches for me. He winds his fingers into mine and then we are kissing in the grass, and I don't know anymore whose breathing is whose. The earth and the sun and the bright afternoon light and the hot darkness that comes when I close my eyes, all mingle together into one picture. An arrangement of light and shadow all my own.

## Acknowledgments

Logan Garrison and Stacey Friedberg, once again, you are the most amazing. Thank you for all your care and work. This book would not exist or be what it is without your tireless reading, editing, insights, and ambition. Also, at Penguin: Namrata Tripathi for your notes, Theresa Evangelista and Samira Iravani for the cover, and Rosanne Lauer for the copyediting.

Special thanks to Manya Fox for the crash course in 4 x 5 photography. And to Lily Simonson for reading an entire draft in Antarctica.

And to my loved ones, you know who you are, thank you times infinity. Especially to my own father, John Romano. Thank you for building me an imaginary room to write in.